THE
BEST
POSSIBLE
ANGLE

A NOVEL

BY

LLOYD JOHNSON

PROLOGUE

Det. Blake VanDrunen was in no mood to see another cadaver. His head was not in it. In fact, he was sure he had left both it and his heart in Santorini, Greece. The vacation had been a last-ditch effort to save his marriage. However, during lunch one afternoon, after his second bite of the Spanakopita, his wife announced that she resented him and didn't want to be married anymore. It was the last sort of memory he wanted etched in his mind. Now, the only thing he had to show from the trip was a burned, leathery tan that made his green eyes stand out.

It was not the first time in all his years on the force that VanDrunen felt like being somewhere else, but it was the first time he wanted to be back on the island of Santorini, flinging himself into the Aegean Sea.

"Earth to Blake?" a female voice said, bringing the detective out of his despondency.

The voice belonged to his partner, Det. Leticia Ramirez. Thank goodness she was there to keep him focused. He took the shoe covers and latex gloves she handed him. Seeing that hers were already on, he quickly covered his own.

The responding officers, Finney and Wright, were inside the apartment, in a corner re-checking what they already wrote down.

"What do we got?" VanDrunen asked.

"Deceased black female. Late twenties-early thirties. We've secured and canvased the premises, and spoke to some of the other tenants," Wright said.

"Landlord's mother discovered the body," Finney said.

Both detectives moved further into the living room. Their eyes were filled with an exuberant curiosity that asked the location of the body.

"In the bedroom," Wright said, beckoning them in with a closed together index and middle fingers.

"How bad is it?" Ramirez asked.

"It's bad," Finney said.

"Let's do it," Ramirez said, taking the lead. She made it three paces into the bedroom before stopping dead in her tracks, causing VanDrunen to collide with her backside.

VanDrunen lurched forward as though he had been kicked in the gut. He could feel that morning's jelly donuts move in his stomach, bubbling upward. He closed his eyes and swallowed hard, thinking of anything to keep from throwing up.

Between the two detectives, they had twenty-five years in homicide (him fifteen years, and her ten). They were seasoned professionals, used to seeing the very worst mankind inflicts upon one another.

It took a few moments for them to push through their visceral disgust and get down to why they were there.

"Whoever did this had a real issue with the victim," Ramirez said, staring at the body that was lying on the bed.

"That's an understatement."

Both detectives noticed the message written in the victim's blood, an odd and sinister proclamation scrawled out on the wall. It underscored the spectacular mess found on the bed.

"The nigger wanted a cunt," the message began almost boastfully, "So I gave it one . . ."

ONE

October 11, 2013

Hollywood Hills-Los Angeles

The cast of the soon-to-be released movie, *It Is What It Is,* gathered poolside behind the Spanish-stucco mansion, home to Hollywood's answer for working African-American actors: publicist and leading agent, Brenda Vaughn.

Amy Winehouse played in the background as Brenda watched her revelers from the balcony. Being mildly drunk was nothing new, in fact, it was part of her charm. Everyone knew she was a lush with the Midas touch for turning a modicum of talent into stardom.

Brenda paid for her astounding success with hard work and two failed marriages. And for that, the people frolicking by the pool owed their relevance in the industry to her. None of them could judge her; many had vices of their own. At close glance, they were a beautiful, emotionally vapid bunch; chemical dependency fueled their neurotic, insecure egos.

Brenda's glazed focus settled upon her client, toothsome Kendrick Black, and his girlfriend Sabathany Morris. Kendrick was a six-two, sculpted hunk of chocolate brown, with mesmeric eyes and inviting full lips, framed by a razor-cut goatee.

Sabathany ran her fingers through sleek, ombre hair, luxuriating every strand of it. With dark, brown skinned-perfection and a long slender neck, she stood model ready at five-ten.

Brenda could not deny how good they looked together. With any luck, her company, Living Color Agency, would turn them into Hollywood royalty.

The couple was off by themselves, their fiery energy noticed by more than a few. As Kendrick spoke to Sabathany, his hands flailed angrily.

Brenda waddled her ample physique down to the pool. Armed with her eighth vodka sour in hand, she intended to douse the squabbling duo's flame, which threatened the celebratory vibe of her get-together.

"Do you mind if I have a few words with this fabulous man?" Brenda asked, approaching the couple.

Sabathany's heavily lashed eyes warmed to a twinkle. "Only if you promise to return him to me," she said, thankful to be saved from an argument she was not winning. With a wink to Brenda, she played along and kissed Kendrick on the cheek before flipping her hair over her shoulder and slinking away.

"She's cute. Everything all right with you two?" Brenda asked.

"We're fine. Just a little disagreement." Kendrick's voice was rich and deep—a movie star's voice.

"Are you ready for this press thing?"

"Not looking forward to the travel."

"I've spent a lot of money building you up. Whatever headspace you need to get into, I advise you to do so."

"You don't need to remind me." Kendrick wanted to say more, but stopped there.

"And?"

"I'm just wishing I could've spent the entire summer promoting this film. Now everything seems so thrown together and last minute."

"The public's attention span is like that," Brenda said, snapping her fingers. "It's better to promote closer to the premier date because it'll still be fresh on people's minds when the movie opens on Thanksgiving."

Kendrick sighed. He felt swept up into a vortex of mismanaged time.

"Where are you booked again?"

Kendrick scratched his head, wondering why she did not know. Brenda had told her staff she wanted to handle Kendrick's itinerary herself. "I think I'm in Chicago, Atlanta, Miami, New York and then wrapping up back here in L.A. To be honest, I have to look at it again."

"Doesn't sound too bad."

"Yeah, I guess I should be okay. But first I've got to get through an early Thanksgiving dinner with my family this Sunday."

"When are you heading back to Minnesota?"

"Tomorrow. Sabathany's pouting because I told her she can't go."

"You don't think meeting your family would make her happy?"

"We're not there yet," he responded, hearing the defensiveness in his own voice.

Brenda blinked at the sharpness of his tone, and took a step back.

"I'm sorry. That wasn't called for."

Brenda's smile brightened her flushed face. "No, no. I get it. Any improvement with your dad?"

Kendrick snickered. "He still blames me for Alvin's death. What do you think?"

Brenda thought for two beats. "You'll be fine."

Kendrick nodded his agreement. "I'm just grateful to have a career to take my mind off things. I owe you so much for taking a chance on me."

"Well, I've got a lot invested in you, and I know you have talent. I expect to see a huge return on my investment. You just wait, when that movie comes out, your comet is going to be on fire!"

Kendrick visualized his future.

"I know it's none of my business, but I hope you get all that drama straightened out between you and Sabathany. You don't need relationship woes clogging your mind when you're promoting a film."

"Yes, Brenda. We're fine," Kendrick said with a playful eye roll.

Brenda shrugged good naturedly, then held her hands up, palms out. "Okay, if you say so. But just in case things don't work out with that one, know there are millions of women lining up to take her place."

Kendrick averted his eyes, embarrassed by Brenda's stroke to his ego. Shifting from foot to foot, he said, "I doubt it."

Brenda squinted with glee. Kendrick did not even understand his own appeal. She liked that.

October 13, 2013,

Kendrick Black had been living in Los Angeles for the last five years. Unable to shake feeling like a stranger in a strange land, he lacked roots, but knew he did not want to plant them in Hollywood. Kendrick found L.A. relationships to be mostly transactional, and despite exquisite surfaces, the people in and around show business were not very deep.

However, there was always something pulling him back to Minnesota, something unashamedly authentic and non-threatening. There he was the big fish in the small pond. In L.A., he was one of many fishes fighting for the next gig or all important contact, but he remained unsure whether he had the stomach for it.

Of course, he could do without his family's dysfunction. There was no glamor in repressed emotions and passive-aggressiveness. The only reason he agreed to return home was because everyone reworked their schedules, and his mother insisted.

When Kendrick appeared at his parents' doorstep, he was already in a horrible mood. Brenda had worked in a last minute press opportunity with a local Minneapolis news station. She told him the entire segment would be devoted to how a hometown guy made it to Hollywood, and his upcoming movie. Instead, Kendrick took second billing to Becca Larson, a local nineteen-year-old YouTube makeup artist blogger who had amassed two million subscribers to her channel. Becca shrewdly ate into his allotted time, leaving his segment with five minutes. The newbie on-air personality, Natalie Watts, never bothered to take control of the interview. When Kendrick complained afterwards, she said, "Look, you've probably outgrown Minneapolis anyway. You've got a huge Hollywood machine behind you, so I'm sure there'll be more opportunities to talk about yourself. Let the underdog have a nibble."

Kendrick knocked on his parents' door with heavy hands. Dread settled at the bottom of his stomach.

"Well, look who's here," Wallace Black said, upon opening the door. "To what do we owe the pleasure?"

"Hello, Dad," Kendrick said, like a teenager too cool for his parent.

"Is this what they've been teaching you in California? How to be ashamed of your family." He eyed the brown paper bag in his son's hand.

Kendrick flashed his Hollywood smile, an attempt to hide his contempt. He extended the package toward his father, a peace offering of sorts—an ornate bottle of Remy Martin Louis XIII, the only gesture of class his father appreciated. Kendrick remembered his father only drank the brown liquor for his "nerves." Wallace accepted the package, his eyes hard like the calluses on his hands.

"Leave him be, Wallace," Kendrick's mother, Diane, said. She gently nudged Wallace from the door. "It's so good to see you!"

"It's good to see you guys, too."

"Is it really?" Wallace asked.

Kendrick tossed his father a dismissive glance. "Enjoy the cognac, Dad."

He looked at his mother again, noticing the weight gain since the last time he saw her. There were even a few more wrinkles on her face. Though she wore them regally, Wallace was probably the cause of each one. Diane still went all out, dressing in her all-purpose black dress with the tiny pink and yellow flowers. She was not an attractive woman. Rather, she was sturdy and jolly. Though Diane did acquiesce to her wifely duty, the couple had only "made love" a total of five times during their marriage, each time resulting in the conception of their five children. Diane was wearing the perfume Kendrick sent her from one of those expensive boutiques on Rodeo Drive. Just a dab was enough to rev Wallace into a two to five-minute search for sexual gratification.

All that remained of Wallace's youth could be found in his glimmering eyes. His graying beard looked like thick soot smeared about his face. He had grown from a thin rail of a man into a husky-framed one whose belly shook when he spoke. This special occasion to welcome home his son for the pre-holiday was not enough to inspire any effort on his part to dress up; rather, he had settled into denim overalls and a tan shirt.

The house used to feel big when Kendrick was a child, now it was cramped. The old Zenith box TV set sat dejected in a corner, having been replaced by a new flat screen that appeared out of place amongst all the mahogany and antiquity.

In the den, Kendrick's sister Arlene breastfed her newborn. She looked up, smiling broadly. She wanted to stand, but caught herself before dropping the baby.

"Hey, sis!"

"When did your flight get in?" Arlene repositioned the blanket to ensure her breast was covered.

"Last night."

"Was it good?"

"A little bumpy for no good reason. Other than that, yeah, it was good."

"You look well."

"So do you. What is this, kid number three?"

"Yep."

"How do you feel?"

"I love it. Carl said he wants a dozen more. I told him only if he has them himself."

Kendrick and his sister laughed. Then, his face became serious. Kendrick's voice fell to a whisper. "Have you talked to Paris?"

"I just saw her the other day. She came over with some gifts for the baby."

"Is she doing okay?"

"You know she's not. Having to sneak around Daddy's back just to make time with the rest of us. You should call her."

"I was planning to. She's got the same number as before?"

Arlene nodded.

"Looking sharp there," Alex, another of Kendrick's brothers said, coming from behind and offering a hand shake.

Kendrick accepted the shake, noting how clammy Alex's hand felt, which was fitting considering that Kendrick always thought there was something slimy about him. Though he loved his brother, he did not like him, and suspected the feeling was mutual. "What's going on, man?"

"You in and out this time?" Alex asked.

"Yeah. My publicist has me scheduled to do some last minute promotion for *It Is What It Is*."

"When does that come out?" Arlene chimed in.

"Thanksgiving."

Pam, Alex's wife, appeared suddenly. "Why, hello there, Mr. Hollywood," she said with a singing joy. They fell into a warm embrace.

"How are you doing, Pam?" Kendrick asked, while simultaneously thinking she was too good for Alex.

"I'm too blessed to be stressed." Pam turned her attention toward Arlene's two boys, rough-housing on the floor.

Kendrick observed a fading black eye, and the heavy plum-colored eyeshadow Pam applied to hide it. He disliked his father, but could at least say he never saw him lay a hand on his mother. Kendrick had no idea where Alex learned to beat women. Every female who got involved with his brother left with a story of abuse as a parting gift. Although the two had no children, Kendrick was not sure Pam would ever leave.

"Okay, dinner's ready," Diane announced.

Suddenly, the dining room filled with adults and children. Kendrick remembered the family eating through numerous holidays and special occasions in this room. There was a time when the room felt majestic, with his father sitting proudly at its helm. Now, Wallace marked his territory with bitterness, like a cat spraying piss.

"Kendrick, would you say grace?" Diane requested.

Kendrick waited until every set of eyes were closed and all heads were bowed. "Dear Lord, we stand in the light of gratitude. We're so thankful to have this chance to fellowship as a family. I ask that You bless this food we're about to receive, that it will serve as nourishment for our bodies. I ask that You be with those who are without, and that You'll open our hearts to help them. In Christ's name I pray. Amen." Kendrick opened his eyes to find his father staring at him.

Wallace watched as the food was passed around the table. Once everyone filled their plate he asked, "Say, Kenny, you've been out in California for what, about five years now?"

"That's right," Kendrick said, noting the belligerence in his father's' eyes.

"And you mean to tell me that after five whole years, people *still* don't know who you are?"

"Wallace, please," Diane said through clenched teeth.

"I'm just saying. Most of the boy's roles have been low-budget, straight to DVD movies. And we all know those DVDs will collect dust before anybody watches them."

"Perhaps you ought to check my IMDb page. I've got way more film credits than you think. And don't forget the sitcoms I co-starred in."

Wallace cackled. "Yeah, but all those shows got cancelled."

Kendrick took a deep breath. "This time is going to be different," he said, fighting to stay calm.

Wallace continued to stare at his son. He grabbed a piece of white bread and spread a dollop of margarine over it. "It had better be, or else you're gonna wind up on your knees sucking off some film executive for your next great role."

"That won't happen. And you know what? I get that my line of work doesn't mean a hill of beans to you, but I'm proud of what I've accomplished. Just wait until my movie comes out, then you'll see."

Wallace's eyes glowed with delight. "Oh, I see. So now you're Mister Important because you've got your lil' flick coming out. Guess that means we all need to be kissing your ass, right?"

"You know that's not what I meant."

"Ain't it? All right then, let me ask you this. What's it like to inconvenience your entire family by making us celebrate Thanksgiving a whole month early? It must be nice getting everybody to rearrange their lives just to accommodate you."

"Wallace." Diane's eyes plead with her husband.

"No, Mom, it's okay. I think Dad has something he'd like to get off his chest." Kendrick turned his full attention toward his father. "For your information, I don't have to be here. I could be somewhere promoting my film, but I thought I owed it to the family to be here. Mom practically begged me."

"Like I said, you must be expecting us to kiss your ass or something."

"Wallace, I asked him to come early. This was the only time he had available to be with family. Now, if you're going to be mad with someone, be mad at me."

The unfazed children continued to eat as the adults squirmed uncomfortably. Wallace pounded the table with his fists, startling everyone. Kernels of food flew about; dribbles of red punch stained the table cloth.

"You say your little prayer like nothing's changed. What do I have to be thankful for, huh? I got one dead son because of you, and another child that may as well be dead! Then here you come, like some hot shot because you moved off to La La Land! What does any of that even matter? You ruined this family when you screwed your brother Alvin out of his chance to get into the NFL!"

"You still want to blame me for Alvin's choices? Go ahead, but his downward spiral isn't my fault, Dad. I can't believe that you'll stand behind the child who became a junkie and threw his life away, but won't speak to Paris because you think she's a disappointment."

"First off, don't utter that name in this house! Secondly, you're the one who told on Alvin. You told those folks that he raped that girl!"

"Because he did!"

"You don't know that! And even if he did, who are you to sell your brother up the river? And now he's gone—took his own life because he didn't know how to live without football. You took his dream from him, and I'll never forgive you for it."

This was the confrontation Kendrick needed, one long overdue. With the revelation of his father's true feelings, Kendrick was free to abandon the pretense of a mere dislike existing between them. He harbored a deep-seated loathing in his gut. Kendrick eyed the carving fork and knife protruding from the ham, deciding both were suitable for puncturing the perfect size hole into his father's throat. He imagined a deep red gushing forth, spraying his family as they applauded the deed. A malevolent smile crept across Kendrick's face, and for the first time he was unashamed of wanting his father's worthless life to bleed out.

Kendrick's glee was partnered with a tingling in his face, followed by a flowing heat that spread broadly across his skin. He had reached his limit. Time to leave before a fantasy of murder turned into reality. With nothing else to say, Kendrick left the dining room.

"Where do you think you're going?" Wallace's voice followed Kendrick out of the room.

"Sweetheart, come on back and sit down with your family," Diane urged her son, pulling at his arm. "I was up late last night cooking all your favorites. Barely got any sleep."

"Mama, I refuse to sit at the table of a man who doesn't respect me."

"Let Mr. Uppity go, Diane!" There was an unsettling delight in Wallace's words.

"Shut up, Wallace!" She turned to her son, who to her was the exemplar of perfection. She had no idea that his inner monologue ran so dark where his father was concerned. "Honey, you know we haven't seen you in Lord knows how long. You can't go now. You just got here."

"I didn't force the drugs into Alvin's veins. Dad can't keep blaming me for what ain't even my fault!"

"I know, honey. I know." Her words had a sing-song appeasement to them. She managed to get him back into the dining room. Everyone waited in silence; some had lost their appetites, though Wallace ate spiritedly, unbothered by the tension clouding the room. Diane pulled a seat out for Kendrick. "That's right, sit down right here."

Kendrick did not sit, instead he reached across the table for the bottle of Remy Martin, which glistened like citrine on the candlelit table. However, the theme song to *The A-team* interrupted his movement.

"I have to take this. It's better if I go outside." Kendrick left the expensive cognac, grabbed his coat from the back of the chair, and walked away before his mother protested.

"Remind me to plant a great big kiss on you when I get back to L.A," he said into the phone. Now that he was away from his family, he chuckled openly.

"I take it I called at a good time," Brenda said.

"Yeah, you just don't know." The cold air filling his lungs felt good. "What's up?"

"Got some good news. The people at *Live! With Kelly and Michael* want you to co-host with Kelly Rippa. Michael Strahan is out sick."

"You're kidding!"

"I'm serious. Got the call a few minutes ago."

"Whoa, this is big."

"Are you kidding me? It's huge!"

"But, what if they don't like me? Michael already has an established fan base."

"You're not out to steal his gig. You're just warming his chair for a day or two. Think of all the publicity we can get for *It Is What It Is*. The universe threw this one into your lap. America is about to fall in love with Kendrick Black."

Kendrick's dimples chilled when he smiled. "Wow! That would be an honor. I frickin' love Michael Strahan!"

"If you nail it, think of the doors this'll open."

"Yeah, but I'm not sure I can sit and be Mr. Charming for an entire hour. What if I suck?"

"Oh please! You're about the most charming man I know. Imagine all of the soaked panties in the audience," Brenda said.

Kendrick moved down the porch and across the stoned path which led to the metal gate. He threw back the latch with a gloved finger and walked through the gate, closing it behind him. He deactivated the car alarm, unlocking the door. He was sure his family got the hint that he was not coming back. He would call his mother later. Kendrick climbed into the 2013 black Escalade and started the ignition with the phone tucked between his ear and shoulder.

Kendrick sped off down the block, thrilled that he was going to be swapping jokes with Kelly Rippa Monday morning. Unfortunately, in his excitement, he did not see the young girl dressed in cotton candy pink cut between two parked cars, though he did hear the heavy thump of the impact.

"Oh, no! God, no!" Kendrick Black screamed, breaking at the red light. Panic entered his body with the same potency of snake venom entering the bloodstream. With closed fists, he pounded the dashboard and steering wheel, accidently hitting the horn, causing it to toot like an unintended breaking of wind.

"What's going on?" Brenda asked.

Kendrick tried to gather his wits. "Some asshole just tried to cut me off. I really need to pay attention to the road. I'll call you back." Kendrick ended the call and glanced through the rearview mirror. "I should just turn around and go back," he said to himself.

The light turned green. In a frantic, swift movement, Kendrick checked to see if anyone had witnessed the accident, but saw no one.

"Just go back," he whispered. He gripped the steering wheel as his foot squeezed the gas pedal. The Escalade eased forward. Through the rearview window the little girl shrank into the distance. His eyes teared, his heart thumped loudly in his chest. Thoughts raced, overlapping in a way that made no sense.

After an hour of aimless driving, he pulled into an alley which led to an abandoned warehouse. Kendrick parked behind three dumpsters.

Alone and out of view, Kendrick closed his eyes, visualizing the girl's rolling body coming to a contorted stop. He saw her lying there, twisted with a snapped neck. Crushed, dried leaves were matted into her side ponytail, and blood turned her once pink jogging suit crimson. Worst of the mental images, he pictured her eyes open, arrested of their innocence, staring out at nothing. He knew she was someone's child. He imagined the parents losing their minds when notified.

"That's somebody's baby," Kendrick repeated to himself as though it was an affirmation. An overwhelming impulse to cry came upon him. As he sobbed, tears spurt from his eyes like blood from a wound. His dry tongue stuck to the roof of his mouth.

"I'm not a monster. I should just turn myself in," he said into the dark interior of the vehicle. He took out his cell phone and speed-dialed a number.

"Hey, it's me. I think I'm going to hell for what I just did."

TWO

It was dark when a silver 2010 Audi pulled up beside the black Escalade. Lenox Hunter got out, dressed from head to toe in black, wearing mirrored aviator sunglasses despite the takeover of night. He looked like a chic, urban superhero; anyone else happening upon the scene looking as he did would have looked ridiculously contrived. There was a coolness in the way Lenox approached the vehicle, and rapped his knuckles against its tinted window.

The window rolled down immediately.

"You could've told me you'd have me out here waiting forever and a goddamn day! What took so long?"

"Ashley and I were messing around. The only reason I answered my phone at all is because I saw it was you."

"It took you that long to finish?"

"You know how she is. If I don't put in the work, I get the third-degree."

Kendrick anxiously got out of the vehicle for the first time since the accident to get a better sense of the forlorn surroundings.

"Try to calm down and tell me what happened," Lenox said.

A flickering street lamp cast shadows upon and around the building. Taken by paranoia, Kendrick inspected the areas closest to the vehicles. For all he knew there were derelicts roaming about, listening to his conversation.

"I don't know. It all happened so fast," Kendrick said, satisfied the two men were alone.

Lenox put a hand on Kendrick's shoulder. "Listen to me. If you want me to help you then you need to tell me everything that happened no matter how bad it is, you dig?"

Kendrick smiled despite his stress. Only Lenox could say, "you dig" with any current day hip believability.

Kendrick took a breath, trying hard to recall what happened. His head felt like someone took a sledgehammer to it. "I was on my cellphone talking to Brenda. There was no one on the road, and then suddenly I heard a banging noise, and I when I looked up there was cracking glass and the color pink going over the windshield. I got to the light, looked back and saw that I'd hit the little girl."

"Anyone see you?"

"I don't know."

Lenox intensified his grip, causing Kendrick to flinch. "You gotta be sure."

Kendrick pondered for a moment. "Honestly, I don't know. All I remember is telling myself to go back. Instead, I found myself moving forward, and the next time I glanced back into my rearview mirror, the girl got smaller in the distance. After driving around for a while, I turned into this alley and called you."

"Did you call anybody else? Sabathany? PR people?" Lenox asked, taking out his phone.

"No."

"Good. Don't." Lenox dialed.

"I guess I called you because I needed someone to talk to before I went to the police."

"Yeah, 911? I wanna report a stolen vehicle," Lenox said, nodding at Kendrick to indicate he heard what was said.

"What are you doing?" Kendrick whispered, reaching for Lenox's phone.

Lenox swatted Kendrick's hand, and waved him away.

Kendrick obediently stepped back, never losing the confused look on his face. After Lenox got off the phone, Kendrick approached again. "What did you just do?"

"Gimme the key to the Escalade." Lenox held his palm out and shook it urgently.

"Dude, I can't let you do this. This is so wrong."

Lenox tilted his head down, peering sternly over his glasses. "Do you wanna go to prison?"

Afraid of the prospect, Kendrick looked away. "No."

"Then gimme the goddamn key."

Kendrick glared despite his appreciation. Lenox seemed to have forgotten who was working for whom. He reluctantly passed over the key.

Lenox caught the warning in Kendrick's eyes, realizing how foul his tone sounded. He brought down the level of bossiness. "Okay. We need to junk it."

"You're crazy!"

"Uh, I don't think you appreciate the magnitude of what we're dealing with here. Someone's kid died because of you."

"I know," Kendrick said. Shame pulsed through his fingers.

"You ran. Plus, you're a celebrity on top of it. You already know they won't be very nice when they get a hold of you."

The shame moved past Kendrick's fingers, up his arms, and through his chest. His mouth was still dry. "But, you know me, man. You know I didn't mean to do this."

"Do you want me to help you or not?"

Kendrick wondered if the little girl's family had been notified, and again pictured them bawling in despair. He thought of a tattered pink jogging suit, the girl's angelic smile while the sun burned behind her. He gave Lenox a nod.

"All right. I'm gonna need about ten grand."

"For what?"

"We need to junk the Escalade."

"Yeah, you said that already, and I told you that your ass is crazy."

"Everything points back to you. Do you actually want the cops to find it? At least if it's so-called missing you can say you don't know what the hell happened."

"The junkyard is supposed to give *you* money for junking it."

"Yeah, but by law they're supposed to report vehicles. This way, they won't ask any questions, and there's money to take care of any penalty they would get if it ever got found out. But for ten grand they won't let it get that far."

Kendrick lived a very comfortable lifestyle, but was not A-list rich. He was fortunate to have been responsible with the money he made over the years, wisely investing most of it. He kept a nice chunk of it in a safe in his Minneapolis home because living in California made it unlikely that he would blow through it.

"We're going to have to swing by my place first."

"Whatever you need to do. Now, you take the keys to the Audi and once you get the cash, you can follow me to the junkyard. You'll wait for me outside."

"Okay." Kendrick's tone and look were solemn. "Why are you going through all this trouble?"

Lenox's facial expression, which had once been cold and matter-of-fact, softened toward his friend. "Because of you, I'm not sitting on a mountain of debt from when Ashley was sick. She may not know what you did for her, but I do. And I won't forget it," Lenox said. "This is the least I can do."

Eyeing Lenox's hand, Kendrick said, "Give me the key."

Lenox handed it over. "Let's do this."

Kendrick followed in the Audi. During the drive, he wondered how long it took the police to swarm the accident site, or the news outlets to begin reporting about the little girl. He wondered if there was still time to turn himself in; however, by the time he returned to his Loring Park penthouse and disappeared inside, those haunting thoughts ceased.

"Okay, after we do this thing I think maybe you need to get lost. Like tonight," Lenox suggests when Kendrick reappears with a thick manila envelope.

The logic of what Lenox said churned slowly. "I guess I could," Kendrick said semi-absently.

"You can and you will. Once you're in New York you should be all good."

Kendrick handed the envelope to Lenox, then backed against the car door. "You think this'll work?"

"For sure."

There was still panic in Kendrick's stare. He glanced down at his ringing phone and noticed Brenda calling. He chose to ignore the call.

"Seriously, you have nothing to worry about. You just gotta commit to it. Think of it as committing to a character. You can't go around acting like you're guilty of something. Go on your talk shows and do your thing. Talk about your movie. Smile at those people like you don't have a care in the world."

Kendrick nodded. "You always got my back."

"You're my best friend."

"Can you do me one more favor?" Kendrick asked as the phone rang. Again, he checked the phone. This time it was Sabathany calling.

Lenox sighed deeply, careful to trim off any exasperation. "What?"

"See if you can find out anything about the little girl's family."

"Man, I don't think that's a good idea, Kenny."

"Just do it, please," Kendrick said, powering off his phone.

"Fine. Consider it done."

THREE

"Hey babe, it's me. Call me when you get a chance," Sabathany said to Kendrick's voicemail before dropping the phone into her purse.

She parked her champagne-colored 2012 Lexus across the street from a run-down, white bungalow, located in Inglewood, California. The front yard of the house was overwhelmed by burnt grass and weeds. It was littered with a dirty mattress, a couple of beat-up tires and a rusty tricycle.

Sabathany had been sitting there for over an hour, having watched at least seven men come and go from the house. This confirmed what she suspected—her mother, Lola, was using again.

Sabathany blamed Kendrick for this. Once upon a time she begged him to buy her mother a place in a nicer neighborhood. She figured if Lola had a better place to live, void of the drug pushers and riffraff, she might be more careful of the company she kept. Maybe she would have a spec of pride in herself to stay on the right track.

Sabathany got out of the car, clicking the car alarm. Her white blouse flapped in the lazy breeze as the silver necklace she wore glistered in the waning sun. Sabathany's high-heeled feet carried her purposefully across the street.

After a series of impatient knocks, Lola finally came to the door. She stared at her daughter as though she were a stranger.

"Hello, Lola," Sabathany said.

"Did you bring it?" Lola asked, stepping aside to allow Sabathany entrance.

"You stink."

"Well, excuse me, Ms. Thing. I'll be sure to wash my ass the next time. Did you bring it?"

Sabathany went inside the house, glancing one last time at her car before closing the front door. There was a vague, putrid stench settled in the living room. It was familiar only because Sabathany smelled it the last time her mother was strung out. The last of the day's sunlight died in the fabric of drawn curtains. What little light flickered in the dark living room came from the television.

The two women were almost mirror images of each other. Lola used to be beautiful like her daughter. But that faded beauty was marred by scabs on her face, chest and arms from where she scratched away imaginary crawling bugs.

"If I'd known you were coming right this minute I would've cleaned up a bit," Lola said, sitting on the sofa and sneakily placed newspaper over a crack pipe.

"Why try to hide it?"

"Hide what?" Lola asked innocently.

"Cut the shit, will you? I already know you're using again," Sabathany snapped.

Lola paused, unsure of whether to even bother conjuring up another story—another lie. She looked up at her daughter with glassy, defiant eyes. "So?"

"We had a deal. I told you I would help you as long as you stayed clean. Doesn't look to me like you've tried very hard."

Sabathany grimaced at the squalor of the room. Dirty clothes everywhere. A dingy bed sheet draped over the sofa. Empty soda cans and take-out containers filled with congealed grease and cigarette butts were piled on the coffee table. Chicken bones lay atop newspaper. There was even a used condom on the floor near Lola's foot.

"Is that from today?" Sabathany asked, eyeing the condom.

Lola picked it up and tossed it into one of the take-out plates. She giggled.

"Oh, I guess this is one big joke to you!"

"Listen; don't come in here with that. I don't wanna hear anything you got to say. I know you're ashamed to be here. I can tell by the way you're standing."

"This place is filthy."

"Girl, please. You think you're Ms. high 'n' mighty, with that knock-off outfit you probably got from down at the swap meet. You got the nerve to act like you're better than me? I was doin' just fine back in Detroit. You the one come calling, talking about how much you needed your mama!"

"Is it so horrible to want to have a relationship with my mother?" Sabathany asked, surprised by the quaking emotion in her own voice.

"Did you ever stop to think there was a reason I gave your ass away? Did you think that maybe I don't want a relationship with you?"

"I thought maybe time might've changed that."

Lola laughed. "Let me tell you something, little girl. You and me both made our choices, okay? You told me things would be good when I got out here, remember? Instead, you went off to live the good life and left me in the dust. Chose your man over me. But that's all right. You keep on doing what you have to do and I'm gonna do me."

"That's just it, you're always doing *you*. Couldn't care less about me or anyone else. And don't sit there and act like I haven't tried to help you. I begged Kenny to let you live with us, but you had just gotten out of rehab, and we didn't know if the treatment would stick. Clearly it didn't."

"Well, I got news for you. Paying my rent is the least you can damn do for me giving birth to your ungrateful ass! I'm just glad you're finally putting that hole of yours to good use. 'Bout time you started using it for something constructive." Lola burst into a maniacal fit of laughter. "I remember when you were giving it away to every Tom, Dick and Harry. Gave it to that NBA player too, and he *still* dropped your ass. So, don't get preachy with me about a used condom when you're basically doing the same thing, bitch!" Lola fished the condom from the take-out plate and threw it at her daughter.

Sabathany stepped away in time for the condom to sail past her and hit the floor; the contents oozed from it.

Sabathany held up what she knew Lola was looking for. "Fine. I'm done. Since you don't want my help, you won't be needing this."

Some of the spite came down from Lola's voice. "God should knock me dead for talking to my child like that. Baby, I'm sorry. You know I don't mean what I say half the time. It's them drugs." She stood up from the sofa and ran dirty hands down her t-shirt. Her eyes remained fixed on the money.

Sabathany handed Lola the cash, who snatched it from her daughter in the same way she snatched money from a trick. She gave Sabathany a cold, obligatory hug, which lasted half a second, then counted the money, never noticing the smile spread across her daughter's face.

"Two-hundred? What am I supposed to with this?"

"Well, since I already paid your rent, use it to live. And don't smoke it up."

"I asked you for five." Lola flimsily held up what she perceived to be a piddly sum.

"I know, but all I'm giving you is two."

"Listen, sweetie, baby, I *need* more money. I already told you that I got this cat who's gonna be coming back around looking for his money."

"You mean to tell me you smoked up five-hundred worth of crack? What kind of dealer lets you smoke that much on credit?"

Lola shifted uncomfortably. "Because we've had certain arrangements in the past and he trusts me, see? But I need more money."

"I won't bother asking you what kind of arrangements you're talking about."

"What do you care?"

Sabathany removed keys from her purse and turned to leave. "Goodbye, Lola."

"Wait a minute . . . Sabathany, come on! You gotta help me out . . . I'm scared!"

"You must think I'm a fool. You need to either take what I gave you, or give it back."

A look of alarm claimed Lola's face. Unhappy with the choices presented to her, she said, "Then, I guess I'll have to make do with what you gave me."

"Good answer."

On the way home Sabathany's phone rang.

"Hello?"

"Baby, please don't hang up. I know I was wrong for how I spoke to you, but you have to help me! You don't understand, he'll kill me if I don't get the money."

"If you needed my help then why did you talk so disrespectfully earlier?"

"I was embarrassed. But I'm sorry." Lola waited for a response. When none came she continued, "What do I gotta do? Tell you that I'm worthless? All right, fine, I ain't shit! Are you happy now?"

Lola's hysterics drew a smile from Sabathany. "When's he coming?"

"He told me ten o'clock tonight. Daughter, please! How many times do I gotta say it? I'm sorry!"

"Yeah, I know you are. I've got to swing by an ATM. Another three-hundred should do it, right?"

"Yes, please," Lola sniffled.

"Okay. I'll see you in a little bit."

"Thank you! You're a good daughter . . . a *merciful* daughter . . . and I love you."

"Yeah right," Sabathany muttered before ending the call.

Sabathany luxuriated in a bubble bath with a glass of champagne. Justin Timberlake's "Suit and Tie" caressed the atmosphere, but neglected to block out the incessant ringing of her phone. She put down her glass and counted the twelve missed calls. The phone rang again at 9:45PM. Turning down the music, she picked up.

"Hey, I'm on my way," Sabathany said, then clicked off before her mother could speak. At 10:05PM she answered the phone and was greeted by a commotion coming through the line.

"What I say I was gonna do, bitch?" said a booming male voice in the background.

"My daughter said she's coming with the rest! She should be here any minute! Sabathany, girl, where are you?"

"I ain't got time to be playin' with yo' ass! Now, where's my money?"

"Here, you can talk to her yourself. Sabathany, please tell him you're on your way!"

Sabathany chuckles. "Lola, I'm not talking to one of your imaginary friends. I already gave you money, now tough it out."

There was a brief pause before Lola replied, "All right, then. Whatever happens is on your head."

"Bye, Lola! Do me a favor and lose my number!" Sabathany ended the call, holding the phone to her glistening chest.

When Sabathany finished her bath, she dried herself off and found her favorite terry cloth robe. After refilling her glass, she gazed out the floor-to-ceiling window. The Los Angeles night sky glowed with twinkling lights that extended a far distance. Bringing the glass to her supple lips, she felt a tear fall, brought forth because of Lola's earlier mention of her first love, Michael Wray, who played shooting guard for the Los Angeles Knights.

When they were a couple, life was finally beginning to resemble the vision board she had kept since her teen years. She envisioned herself with a dream man who would give her the lifestyle she ached for, but Michael left her, surrendering to his proclivity for transsexuals. Michael gave Sabathany a nice piece of change to keep his secret, but soon after, one of the working "girls" he picked up on Santa Monica Boulevard shot off her mouth to the wrong person and got them both shot to death in his yellow Maserati.

Sabathany raised her glass, hardened by the memory. "To Lola and Michael . . . may they both go straight to hell!"

FOUR

11AM the next morning, Sabathany received a call from the police informing her of what she already knew. She did her best grief-over-the-phone impression, hoping it would be enough to keep them away. However, not only did the multiple in-coming calls on her cell phone not go unnoticed by the cops, they inspired further questions.

They could've called me last night with this mess, she thought to herself in the shower. She had expected to be awakened in the middle of the night. At least then she would still be in the moment, capable of giving the police the performance they wanted. She had managed to keep hints that anything was wrong from Kendrick when they spoke just before she went to bed. But that morning she was off her mark, worried she would be asked questions intended to trip her up.

Sabathany was ready to leave, giving herself a last-minute check to make sure she looked appropriately mournful. Her wet, hanging hair supported the illusion that she was too distraught to bother with it.

Sabathany arrived at the precinct, announced herself to the first officer she saw, then took a seat. The police station was quiet. She expected a bustling place, filled with petty criminals being booked and prostitutes being led away, walking on broken high-heels as they popped gum and gave their skirts a tug for modesty. Sabathany expected ringing phones and officers scribbling down anonymous tips.

She guessed that the officer sitting at the front desk was content in his boredom, and would probably be annoyed should he be called into some major action.

"I must watch too many cop shows," she muttered.

Soon, a broad-shouldered man with dreadlocks appeared. He wore a fitted, white collared, button-down shirt with the sleeves rolled. He introduced himself as Det. Daryl Trueblood, the person she spoke to on the phone.

Sabathany was escorted into an office where another detective waited. Det. Trueblood sat behind his desk, while the other sat on the desk's edge, snapping a rubber band. Sabathany recognized him immediately.

"Ms. Morris, this is my partner, Det. Matthew Howards."

Sabathany offered a slight nod to Howards, whose eyes glowed with animus.

"Yes, I know Matthew," she said.

"Well, here his name is Det. Howards," Trueblood admonished.

Sabathany fought the smirk she felt forming on her lips. "Got it."

"There's nothing funny about why you're here, Ms. Morris. Unless you want us to get the wrong impression, I'd advise you to wipe that smirk off your face," Howards snapped.

"Again, I'd like to offer my condolence for your loss," Trueblood said.

"Thank you." Sabathany allowed her eyes to fall mournfully to the Kleenex she walked in holding. Toying with it, she shrugged helplessly.

"Would you like us to give you a moment?"

"No, I'm okay."

Her eyes met Howards' cold stare, but not because she expected sympathy. He was a familiar, albeit hostile face. *I can't believe he's still pissed,* Sabathany thought to herself just as her memory took her back . . .

It was March 2011 when she and Matthew met, just two months after Michael Wray passed away. They were both in attendance at a wedding reception of mutual friends in Simi Valley. It was getting late, and Sabathany's ride left her to score sex. She was on the lookout for a man who could give her a ride not only to her house, but possibly in the bedroom. Sabathany had already been dancing with Matthew Howards. His body was doughy, hardly the body-conscious-type she usually went for. But his five o'clock shadow contoured his face nicely, and his eyes held an intensity she found alluring. As the night progressed, tipsy from the tequila shots and wine, Matthew became her catch for the evening.

Later at her apartment, their sex romp was aborted when his penile dysfunction kicked in. Without saying anything, Sabathany angrily got up and hopped into the shower, signaling the end of the evening. If he was smart, he would be gone by the time she finished her shower. She didn't want to have to embarrass him any further about his "little problem" than he probably already was. As the hot water rinsed away her disgust, he appeared in the bathroom doorway.

"I guess I should be going," Matthew announced.

"Yep. See ya."

"You think maybe we could . . ."

She began to clear her throat, her way of warning him not to continue.

"Well, anyway. You take care of yourself."

"Yep. See ya!" she repeated.

"Listen, I didn't mean for any of that to happen, so you don't gotta act like that!"

"And you really didn't have to waste my time. Someone should let unsuspecting ladies know about you."

"Whatever! Find your own way home next time!"

"Won't be a next time," she said, watching his silhouette through the frosted shower curtain disappear from the doorway. She listened for the closing of her apartment door, and was satisfied when she heard it.

"Ms. Morris?" Trueblood said, snapping his fingers which transported Sabathany back into the present moment.

"I'm sorry, what did you ask me?"

"When is the last time you saw your mother?"

"Yesterday. She said she needed money."

"How much did you give her?" Howards asked.

"She told me she'd just paid the rent and didn't have anything left to buy groceries, so I gave her fifty bucks."

"Did you know that your mother used drugs?"

"Yes. In fact, as soon as I walked into the house I could smell it. That's all she did back in Detroit. If I would've known it was going to be more of the same, I would've left her there."

"You moved her out here?" Trueblood asked.

"Yes."

"How long had she been in California?"

"Just over a year. The agreement was that she would get treatment out here. If she stayed clean for at least a year we'd talk about her moving in with Kendrick and me."

"Who's Kendrick?" Howards asked.

"Kendrick Black. He's my boyfriend. Surely you know of him," she dripped in a sugary sweet tone.

Howards shrugged. "Should I know who that is?"

"He's an actor," Trueblood replied.

"Oh. Is he any good?"

"He's not bad. I let my wife drag me to a couple of his movies." Trueblood admitted. "The ladies like him a lot."

Sabathany rolled with Trueblood's light-heartedness. Bedding one of Hollywood's sexiest, up-and-coming actors was a big deal, especially if it made a cop with erectile problems like Matthew Howards jealous. She had her fun. Time to get back to the issue at hand, and make the detectives think she had every intention of getting to the bottom of who killed Lola.

"She gave me up when I was a baby, so I was hoping this would be a second chance for us, you know?"

"Then you weren't close?" Trueblood asked.

"Never had the chance to be. In the end, all I was good for was giving her an allowance. I feel like such a fool."

"I don't know. Maybe if I felt like someone made a fool of me, I'd want them dead," Howards said.

Sabathany glared at him. "Fortunately, my mind doesn't operate that way."

"So you say."

"Yeah, I do say. Look, instead of wasting my time, why don't you go out there and find who did this?"

"What time did you leave her house?"

Sabathany took a calming breath. "Between 7:15 and 7:30. I don't think I was there ten minutes. Her place was filthy and I just couldn't take anymore of her lies."

"What lies?" Trueblood asked.

"She claimed she needed fifty bucks, but once I got there, she started begging for more money. She figured because I'm with Kendrick that I'd be good for it. And she didn't say it quite that nicely. When I left, she called me again and tried to change her tune. She was insistent that I give her more money, saying she owed some guy. I didn't believe her, though. I figured it was a ploy to get me to give her more allowance because she's always acted so entitled. After that, I stopped answering her calls because I knew it would be more of the same. In the past I found the best way to deal with her was just to ignore her. Eventually she got the hint."

"Yeah, but you answered at 9:45PM and 10:05PM," Howards said.

"That's true. The first time I asked if she could take a hint, then I hung up. The second time I told her to lose my number."

"And that's all you said?"

"No, I told her that I hoped she enjoyed what little she managed to scam out of me because the gravy train had come to an end. She called me a bitch and I told her I always knew the real Lola would show herself eventually. And that was the last time I spoke to her."

"Are you sorry she's gone?"

Sabathany looked at no one in particular. "Right now, I can't get over falling for her lies again. I mean, she had no intention of getting herself together. But yeah, I'm sorry she's dead. At least I can make my peace with God because I tried to help her. But I refuse to waste anymore tears on a woman who told me she didn't want anything from me except the rent. I truly hope you find the son of a bitch who did this, but in a way, and I hate to say this, she brought this on herself."

After thirty more minutes of questioning, the detectives saw Sabathany Morris as a young woman desperate for a mother's love, but disappointed that she was unable to resuscitate their relationship. And she seemed both saddened and angry that Lola had not kicked her drug habit.

"Say, where was all of that tension between you two coming from earlier?" Trueblood asked after Sabathany left.

"Just a woman scorned. We slept together one night and she got pissed because I didn't call her afterward. To get even, she started spreading some untruths about me to her lady friends," Howards answered.

"You don't think we made a mistake letting her go, do you?"

"Naw. But remind me never to get on that bitch's bad side ever again. She clearly has abandonment issues."

"Sounds to me like you dodged a bullet with that one," Trueblood said with a dry chuckle.

Howards sighed wearily. "You could say that."

An immensely relieved Sabathany was thrilled to be let go. She walked victoriously to her car, excited that both detectives were satisfied enough to remove her from their persons of interest list in the murder of Lola Morris, and that she had gotten away with it.

FIVE

October 16, 2013

The plane began its descent, slipping through clouds which caused a mild turbulent shake of the aircraft. Kendrick stared out the window, recalling how beautiful and welcoming the California sunlight was the first time he came to Los Angeles. It had been five years since he arrived by bus, a hopeful twenty-five-year-old with a thousand dollars and a duffel bag filled with clothes and dreams. In less than thirty minutes, Kendrick would be back in the land where his dreams had come true.

Now, Kendrick sat in business class, besieged by captivated flight attendants going above and beyond to be close to him. Yes, things had changed.

By the time the plane landed and arrived at the gate, a small crowd of airport employees gathered, all with delighted anticipation on their faces. Some already had their cellphone cameras out at just the right angle for when the actor walked through the gate door.

A black woman with long, swinging braids was the first to approach Kendrick the moment she lay eyes on him.

"Can I get a selfie with you?" she asked.

"You sure can." Kendrick put his arm around the woman. "What's your name?"

"Kim. I ain't gonna lie, Michael Strahan is my dream husband, but you and Kelly had great chemistry!"

"Thank you for watching. I'm glad you enjoyed me on the show. Kelly was great to work with, but I'm glad Michael's feeling better and back where he belongs."

After Kendrick heard the soft click of the camera, he faced the young woman, making sure his gaze penetrated her senses. Kim giggled, then cupped a hand over her mouth.

"Damn, you're sexy," she said.

"Aw, shucks. Thank you so much."

As the crowd grew, Kendrick found his attention pulled in all directions by those wanting to take pictures, or offer words of flattery. He noticed passersby slow their pace, curious about the commotion he is stirred.

"Can I have my picture with you, Morris?" another woman screamed, elbowing her way through the group of fans.

"Who?"

"Aren't you Morris Chestnut?"

"Uh, no, ma'am."

"Oh, well, can I get a picture anyway?"

"Sure, just as soon as you call me by the correct name." A warm smile thawed the chill from his words.

"Oh, you won't tell me who you are?"

"Folks, thank you. That's it. I gotta go. You all take care, those of you who know my name."

Kendrick headed off to find Brenda Vaughn awaiting him at Arrivals. Brenda warned him of the occasional mistaken identity. He was not yet an A-lister like Will Smith, Kevin Hart or Denzel Washington. He still belonged to an obscure group of actors who people somewhat recognized, whose names lingered on the tip of the tongue as they snapped their fingers trying to remember the name. Unfortunately, many belonged to this ever-growing pool of interchangeably talented actors. Brenda told Kendrick it would be his responsibility to carve out an identity for himself so that people knew who he was by face and name.

Kendrick followed the Arrivals sign outside. He spotted Brenda's blue, 2012 Porsche with its top down after she beeped the horn at him.

"Uh, Mr. Black, you need to get a move on it. The airport cops already made me loop around twice."

"The fans wouldn't let me out of there. Sorry."

"Oh, well, in that case I forgive you."

"One lady thought I was Morris Chestnut."

"Well, I told you it's to be expected."

"It still sucks."

"Well, you do look like him. Either way, you're both nice looking men who won't have any problems getting the opposite sex to like you, or the same sex for that matter."

"Not the kind of reassurance I was hoping for . . . and for the record, he looks like me."

"Oh, excuse me, I stand corrected. And don't be so quick to throw your nose up at the gays. They make up a nice, healthy chunk of the demographic who watch your films, too. Just thank the boys in WeHo, Chelsea and the ATL."

Kendrick buckled himself in. "I already know all that. I got no beef with the LGBT community. Anyway, thanks for picking me up."

Brenda drove off. "No problem. By the way, my phone's been ringing off the hook since your appearance with Kelly Rippa."

"Really?"

"Oh yeah. Jimmy wants you . . . Kimmel *and* Fallon. I got a call from the folks at Letterman. Even *The View* wants you to stop by to promote the film!"

"Stop it!"

"Kendrick Black, I bullshit you not."

"That's great news!"

"I'm telling you, you're on fire. So, how was the flight?"

"Hands down that had to be the best flight. They treated me like a god in business class. And then, when I got off the plane, there was a gang of airport employees who recognized me. And not just to say, 'hey, ain't you what's his name?' People knew my name. Well, *most* people."

"Sweetie, when I'm done with you, *everyone* is going know your name."

Kendrick smiled broadly. His body tingled at the possibilities. He already enjoyed and counted on recognition from the late-teenagers and twenty-somethings; they were the primary demographic watching his films. But what Brenda promised to do would make him a household name in every house.

"Now, all I need to do is get home and smooth things over with Sabathany."

"She's still angry about you not letting her go?"

"Yeah. She's been really short with me over the phone."

"Tell her to get over it."

"Brenda!"

"No, I'm serious, Kenny. This would all be a lot easier if I could sell you as the sexy bachelor looking for love. That would seal your status as a sex symbol for sure. You want everyone to think they've got a shot with you. Relationships kill the fantasy."

"Sabathany loves me."

"What's your point?"

"Wow, that's cold."

Brenda shrugged. "No, really, what's your point?"

"My point is I can't deny she exists. Wouldn't be right."

"Look, Sabathany is a beautiful woman. She's giving me Tika Sumpter look-alike all day long. But she's going to have to go along to get along. She needs to get with the program."

"What program?"

"You know exactly what I'm saying," she said, glancing into the blank expression on her star client's face. "I'm saying there are plenty of women who want this life, and will make the necessary sacrifices to be with the latest it-boy. Hell, I can think of a few ladies off the top of my head who wouldn't have an issue sharing you."

"Sabathany doesn't share anything."

"You're missing my point," Brenda sighed, tapping into her backup of patience. "I'm just saying that there are a lot of women out there who want a slice of the good life, who are willing to put up with practically anything to have it. You can do whatever you damn well please and they won't be standing at the front door to nag you about it. So, if Sabathany wants to benefit from your success, then she needs to let you be the star you're meant to be without hassling you."

"Okay, now I get it."

"And believe me, I know I'm the last one who should be offering relationship advice. Just be careful."

"Any more nuggets of wisdom?"

"Yeah. I really hope you know what you're in for, because it's going to be like buzzards sniffing out the dead. People know when you hit it big, and they'll start coming out of the woodwork with their palms out, saying they knew you when. You better learn how to handle them. Now more than ever, you need to know the people you surround yourself with."

"I hear you."

As they talked, most of their words became lost in the passing breeze. Kendrick rested his eyes and fell asleep to the wafting smell of eucalyptus.

"We're here. Wake up," Brenda said with an amply hostile nudge when they arrived in front of his house.

"Thanks again for picking me up."

"You're welcome. Glad I could play chauffer while you sleep. Give some thought to what we discussed."

"I heard what you were trying to say. And don't worry, I know how to handle Sabathany," he insisted with a wink.

Brenda was not convinced.

Later, Kendrick and Sabathany enjoyed reuniting bliss. He lay on his back, gazing up at her, wrapping the whole of himself around her.

"I love having you inside me, baby." Sabathany leaned forward to whisper in his ear. Her breath was sensuously warm and light.

He nodded, adding an upward thrust. "And I love being inside you."

Sabathany leaned away from him, holding her hair up so it would not become mussed. Kendrick relished shattering her resistance. Her vanity and anger fled the room as her normally beautiful face contorted into something ugly when he brought her down onto himself. He could tell by her rapturous whimpers and crazy sex face that it was just a matter of time before she surrendered to the pleasure he intended to give her.

The low rising platform bed, adorned with rose pedals and musk—an invitation to a lovers' oasis—was now a rumpled, stained mess. Neither of them cared. Kendrick pulled out, staring at the part of himself gleaming wet in the soft, late-afternoon light. Sabathany flipped on to her back, and held her legs until her knees aligned with her shoulders. Kendrick plunged deeply, the sensation as rich as the first entry. Sabathany held firm to his biceps; her now scraggly hair covered her eyes.

I'm about to . . ." he began, his words faltering on his tongue.

Sabathany smiled, convinced of the power she wielded.

"Aw shit!" Kendrick moved to pull out.

Sabathany drew him close, vice-gripping his waist with her legs. He struggled like caught prey. Then, the fullness of his climax rushed through him. When they finally parted, Kendrick was unable to read the meaning behind her beaming smile. He rolled away to the edge of the bed, like a one-night stand who had gotten his sexual fill and had now lost interest. Without saying a word, he went to the bathroom.

After both showered and dressed, Sabathany grilled dinner out on the massive wrap-around patio. She held a set of tongs in one hand, and a glass of blush in the other. Kendrick nursed a beer while he watched from the dining room. Despite succulent aromas of steak and baked potatoes, he had no appetite.

When dinner was served, Sabathany enjoyed the meal while Kendrick raked a fork over his potato.

"Are you just gonna sit there?" Sabathany asked.

"Why'd you do that?"

Sabathany put down her utensils. "Do what?"

"Now, you're going to sit there and act brand new, like you have no idea what I'm talking about?"

Sabathany shrugged. "I really don't know what you're talking about."

"Grabbing hold of me when you knew I was trying to pull out? This some kind of con you're running to get me to marry you?"

"You think I'm one of these desperate females who has to give birth in order to keep a man? You've got a lot of nerve!"

"Looks that way to me."

"Did you ever stop and think that we haven't made love in who knows how long, and I was in the moment, enjoying being close to you?"

"Yeah, right!"

"Fine, don't believe me." Sabathany bolted from the table.

Kendrick paused for a moment, deciding to rein back his own anger. "Look, all I'm saying is that I'm not ready to get married, and I'm definitely not ready to be a dad."

"We talked about this already. And it was agreed that you should concentrate on your career. I want you to be successful. I'd be a fool not to. But, I'm also a woman who wants to get married one day. I don't want to reach a certain age only to find that the option is pulled off the table. And no one is saying we must get married today or tomorrow. I just want to know it's something we're moving towards."

Kendrick eased behind her, placing his hands on her shoulders. "That's all you had to say."

"Well, I thought I already said it . . . two months ago. You're not the only one who's been inside their own head."

"You still act as if you expect me to get up and walk out on you."

"Sometimes it feels that way. I find myself wondering if you're secretly ashamed to be with me. You don't' want us photographed together, I hardly know any of your friends, and you got upset when I asked to meet your parents. We're coming up on a year and a half; I don't think it's unreasonable to share in more parts of your life."

Kendrick turned Sabathany around to face her. "Babe, the reason why I don't want us photographed is because Brenda told me that in order to build a fan base, I should pretend I'm single. People want to feel they have a chance with me. Frankly, I don't care if it's a million women who pay to watch me on the movie screen or a million dudes."

"Dudes?"

"You know what I mean. Yeah, I'm a good-looking guy. I ain't afraid to say it. And I'm not too uptight to be anyone's fantasy who wants to put me in their dreams at night. Now, that's just me. Secondly, besides Brenda, I don't have any friends here in L.A. You know how I feel about the culture out here. I work here, but I don't want to live here. I really want to move back to Minneapolis, so I can stay centered. As far as my family, yes, I want you to meet them. But, I knew there was going to be a lot of drama and you didn't need to see that."

"I can really meet them?" She beamed.

"Yes, really."

"When?"

"I want to head back there before I really take off on this press stuff. Why don't we use this time to get out of L.A.? You can even come with me on the press junket."

Sabathany squealed with delight, rewarding Kendrick with a thankful kiss and a hug.

I got her right where I need her to be, he thought victoriously to himself.

SIX

"I hope you don't mind, Mr. Black, but I took the liberty of bringing you more shrimp cocktail," the spiky-haired male flight attendant said, offering a flirtatious smile.

"Thanks, man," Kendrick replied.

The flight attendant began to walk away when Sabathany jumped in. "Um, excuse me!"

"Yeah?"

Both Sabathany and Kendrick were taken aback by his tone.

The flight attendant fumbled to correct himself. "I mean, yes?"

"*I'd* like more shrimp cocktail, too, if you don't mind."

"We ran out. Just now. Sorry 'bout it." He turned on his heels, and walked away.

Sabathany tossed her napkin down. "Now see, if I called him out his name he'd think I did him wrong,"

"Babe, don't even let that bother you."

"And you're no help. You're encouraging him."

"No, I'm not."

"If I didn't know any better, you seem to like it."

"You don't get it, do you? This is all about playing the game. If I'm nice to that dude, he's going to pay to watch my movies. And maybe, he'll bring his boyfriend, or a whole gang of friends."

"You mean to tell me that you don't mind a fan base of a bunch of . . ." Sabathany stopped herself.

"Like I said, a fan is a fan no matter who it is. I don't have a problem with what that dude likes. I'm secure in my sexuality."

"I get all of that, but he's still been rude to me the entire time. I may as well not even be here."

"Just remember this . . . who do I make love to? You or him?" Kendrick whispered in her ear.

Sabathany's body tingled from remembering his mastery in the bedroom and their shared ecstasy. "Say no more."

"Yeah, so, don't even let any of that bother you, because you're the one going to the premier. You're the one who's going to be living the life. Only thing that dude can do for you is fetch the champagne when you call for it, and maybe cook your food." Kendrick winked, offering up a giant prawn.

Lenox Hunter was parked outside when Kendrick and Sabathany emerged from the airport like Hollywood's "It" couple.

Kendrick signed an autograph for a fan before taking his tenth fan selfie of the day, still enjoying the newness of it all. Thanks to mentions on *Entertainment Tonight* and *E!* praising his two-day appearance with Kelly Rippa, people were beginning to know who he was, and the movie had not come out yet. Sabathany grabbed the roll-on luggage from him, giving Kendrick the opportunity to do his thing with the medium-sized bunch of people. Lenox flung the cigarette he had been smoking to the ground, and rushed over to help her. This was his first-time meeting Sabathany in the flesh. He instantly saw the resemblance to Tika Sumpter Kendrick spoke of.

"Let me help you with these," Lenox said, taking both roll-ons from Sabathany.

"Thank you. And you must be Lenox."

"Last I checked."

Lenox dragged the roll-ons to the open car trunk, all the while keeping his eyes on Kenny—his longtime friend, as he used a west coast, laid-back swagger to charm his fans. It was a change that had not gone unnoticed. This Brenda Vaughn creation named Kendrick, swarmed by fans vying for his attention, walked and talked differently each time he returned to the Twin Cities—each time a little less recognizable than the last time. Yet, Lenox was still mesmerized enough to stare into the Kendrick Black shine. Without lifting his eyes to Sabathany, Lenox said, "It must be rough, being on your way somewhere and having to stop to deal with all that."

"No, he's adjusting to it, actually. Just wait until the movie comes out. It's going to be nuts!"

"I bet," Lenox said, unaware of how wistful he sounded. Lifted from a trance of admiration, he shuddered, then resumed fitting the luggage into the trunk of the car. "So, how long are you guys here for?"

"Didn't he tell you?"

"Yeah, but you know, things can change."

"We're here for a couple of days. I'm going to meet his family. Then, we're off to do press."

Lenox opened the passenger door for her. "You're going to meet his parents? That ought to be interesting."

The two locked eyes. Sabathany was unsure of what he meant, but did not like the tone. Standing eye to eye with Lenox, she maintained a neutral face.

"I'm sorry, and how do you know Kenny?"

"Been knowing Kenny since high school. We're like family, he and I," Lenox said. It sounded like both a proud announcement and revelation of power.

"We should get along fine, then. After all, we share his best interest." Sabathany extended her hand.

Lenox eyed it as though it were infected, but shook it anyway.

Put off by Lenox's reservation, Sabathany climbed into the back seat of the town car.

As long as you recognize that he knew me first, and I'll always have his back, yeah, we should get along just fine, Lenox thought to himself as he closed the door.

"You guys are the best!" Kendrick yelled, backing away from the dispersing group.

Lenox moved to the front passenger seat and held the door open for Kendrick. He appeared uncomfortable doing the task.

Kendrick dove into the seat, and Lenox closed the door.

"They love you, baby!" Sabathany tapped his shoulder from the backseat.

"The crowds are getting bigger and bigger." Kendrick touched her hand.

Lenox got in and started the engine. As soon as he drove from the curb, Kendrick lowered his voice. "Say, man, did you take care of that thing like I asked you to?"

Lenox caught Sabathany's reflection through the rearview mirror. Their eyes met again. She sat back in her seat. He turned the radio on, flipping through random channels until he reached the oldies but goodies station. The Four Tops sang "Bernadette." Lenox used the Motown Sound for cover. Raising the volume, he said, "Yeah, I took care of it."

"You should've called to let me know." Kendrick spoke like an authority reprimanding a subordinate.

"It took more time than I expected," Lenox replied, careful to carry his voice just beneath the hard driving treble and base.

"Man, if I'm going to do this press stuff, I've got to know that you're handling things."

"What are you guys talking about?" Sabathany yelled over the music.

The volume came down to normal level. "Kenny left me in charge of some finishing touches for a surprise for his mother."

"Oh," Sabathany said, disappointed with Lenox's revelation.

"Yeah, I owe her for running out like I did the last time I was here," Kendrick chimed in.

Sabathany tapped his shoulder again. "I don't remember you telling me you ran out. Why run out?"

"I was having issues with my wife and needed someone to talk to. Since things had gone so wrong with his dad, we met up a lot sooner than expected," Lenox said.

Sabathany noticed the crafty smiles shared between the two men.

"Aw, best buds to the end. That's sweet. I wish I had girlfriends who'd do that for me." Then, she reclined back in her seat. She knew they were lying.

SEVEN

"It's a pleasure to finally meet you, Mrs. Black." Sabathany played this scene out many times in her head and never had she imagined this. A perfectly sincere sentiment followed by awkward silence. Not knowing what else to do, she gave Kendrick's mother a hug, taking in Diane's scent—a hint of gardenia and a tease of spice.

She felt just as Sabathany imagined she would—like unconditional love would feel if it were tangible.

"Oh well, all right then," Diane said, flustered by the gesture. "Aren't you precious?" She broke from Sabathany's grasp, laughing cheerily while straightening her dress. "My goodness, Kenny, what a pretty girl."

Kendrick smiled a smile that warmed his mother's heart. Maybe if she were happy, her English springer spaniel-like keen senses would pick up good vibes from Sabathany. He decided to keep his fingers crossed.

"So tell me, Sabathany, what do you make of Minneapolis?" Diane asked.

"I'm not sure I could ever get used to this chill."

Diane laughed. "You think this is bad? Wait till February."

"I'll take your word for it."

"This is sort of freak weather. It's not usually this cold yet," Kendrick added as they followed Diane into the dining room. While Sabathany passed through, Kendrick paused in the doorway, taking note of the four table settings.

"Please tell me dad isn't joining us," Kendrick said.

"Your father's working."

"Then who's the extra setting for?"

"When's the last time you saw Paris?"

"Been awhile."

"Mmm, hmm, that's what I thought. She'll be along here after while"

"I guess you're going to meet my sister," Kendrick said, taking a seat next to Sabathany.

Suddenly, as if on cue, a smoky feminine voice called from the kitchen, "Yoo-hoo! Hello?" followed by the closing of the backdoor.

Sabathany did a double take when Paris entered the dining room, wearing vintage beauty with the same ease she wore her maxi-length, brown sable coat and matching fur hat. Her face was applied with the best makeup. Her beauty stretched across the ages. Sabathany, a stunner herself, was momentarily stunned, and then intimidated. She extended her hand. "It's nice to meet you, Paris."

"Nice to meet you too. I swear, I could smell the grilled cheese the moment I walked in," Paris said, tossing the coat and hat onto a chair next to her. "So simple, yet so tasty. And I know you made tomato soup to go with it, right?"

Diane pointed to the ceramic tan and red striped pot resting on the pot holder in the middle of the table. "Of course. What do you think that is? Oh, and before you get comfortable, could you bring out the sweet tea?"

"I can get that, Mrs. Black. I just love sweet tea." Sabathany headed toward the kitchen before Diane or anyone else could object.

"Are you a southern girl?" Diane asked when Sabathany returned, holding a pitcher of tea.

"Me? No, I was born in Detroit and raised in L.A."

Diane laughed, taking the filled glass of tea Sabathany poured for her. "Then what do you know about sweet tea?"

"My grandparents were from Macon, Georgia. Sure, they moved to L.A, but they never forgot where they came from, never forgot those southern comforts."

"My goodness! I'm from Savannah!"

"Wow," Sabathany gushed, "Small world."

As soon as everyone had tea, Sabathany ladled soup into four small bowls. Kendrick was pleasantly surprised with how well things seemed to be going.

"Thank you so very much," Paris said when she received her soup. "So, how did you and my brother meet?"

"A friend of mine brought me to this party to meet an agent he thought might represent me, but once Kenny and I laid eyes on one another, I can barely remember anything else that happened that night. We've been together ever since. A beautiful year and a half."

"So, you're an actress?" Paris asked.

"I had aspirations. Now, I write mostly."

"You write books?" Diane asked.

"No, screenwriting."

"Has anything you've written ever been made into a movie?" Paris blew on her spoonful of soup.

"I've done my share of pitches to the studios, but no, nothing made yet."

Kendrick was amazed at how easily the lies dribbled from Sabathany's lips. He tried to mask his disbelief.

"It all sounds very exciting," Diane said.

"It is, ma'am." Then in a pivot, Sabathany asked, "And what do you do, Paris?"

"I counsel at-risk youth."

Sabathany looked perplexed. She imagined Paris doing something that centered around beauty. "Sounds challenging."

"Paris has always been a great listener," Kendrick said.

"Yeah, I bet that trait comes in handy," Sabathany replied.

Paris tore the grilled cheese down its middle, the gooiest cheese stretched between the halves. "Actually, today at work I spoke with young people who identify as part of the LGBT community. Their parents tossed them out like garbage. Suicide rates among the LGBT youth community are higher than in the general population."

Sabathany pulled her sandwich apart as well. "Hmm, interesting," she said, taking her first bite of the sandwich. "Oh my goodness, Mrs. Black, I don't think I've ever tasted a grilled cheese this good before. But there's something else I taste. What do you do differently?"

"I spread a thin layer of mayonnaise on the inside of the slices of bread before I put on the cheese," Diane revealed.

"That's genius." Sabathany savored another bite. She watched Diane reach over and pull a string of cheese from Kendrick's chin.

"Can you believe it? He's thirty years old and I'm still babying him," Diane confessed.

"I'm jealous. I wish my mother and I had this kind of relationship." Without looking at Paris, Sabathany said, "I sort of know what you mean when you talked about parents throwing their kids away."

"Is that what happened to you?" Paris asked.

A faraway look entered Sabathany's eyes. She crossed her arms and nodded. "Yeah, she let my grandparents raise me. Then they gave me away because they started having health problems. That's when I became part of the system."

Kendrick placed a supportive hand on her leg.

"Did you ever find your mother?" Diane asked.

"Oh yeah."

"We moved her out to L.A. from Detroit," Kendrick said.

Diane's face brightened. "Well, then, see? It may take a little time, but it's not too late."

"No, it is. She's dead," Sabathany said flatly.

It was the first time Kendrick heard it. He found the emotionless, matter-of-fact way she spoke unsettling. Sabathany took Kendrick's hand from her leg and squeezed it hard. He did his best not to wince from discomfort.

"Oh, honey, I'm so sorry to hear that," Diane said.

"Thank you." Sabathany's eyes were downcast. She continued squeezing Kendrick's hand until the confusion left his face.

"If you don't mind my asking, how did she pass?" Paris wanted to know.

"My mother was an addict. Can't say I'm surprised it was the drugs that got her into trouble." She looked at Diane, then to Paris, expecting judgmental stares, but none came. "Anyway, it just happened and I'm not sure that I'm ready to talk about it."

"We understand."

Paris reached across to touch Sabathany's hand, an overture of support. Sabathany opened herself to be touched.

After lunch, Sabathany learned more about the Black family than she intended to. She watched old sports trophies receive a good dusting off, while team wins were explained in depth. Family photo albums were flipped through page by page. Memories were jogged. And while Kendrick and Paris grew bored from the rehashed minor details, Sabathany considered it time well invested in bringing her closer to the family.

"I think we should get going," Kendrick said, unable to withstand the boredom. "Paris, we were thinking about going out later, did you want to join us?"

"Yeah, we'd love it if you would," Sabathany cooed.

"Sounds like fun."

"Great. Paris, where are we picking you up from?" Kendrick asked, helping Sabathany into her coat.

"I'll text you my address."

"Good idea." Kendrick put on his own coat. "Babe, are you ready?

"I was born ready." She noticed Kendrick staring at her. It was an uncomfortable kind of stare. She expected an interrogation on the way back to the apartment. "Mrs. Black, thank you so much for the afternoon. I had fun."

"Well, I'm glad you enjoyed it."

"Say, Ma, did they ever find the person that killed the little girl in the hit and run?" Paris asked.

Diane shook her head. She extended her hands towards Heaven. "My word, that poor little girl. No, they haven't found the lowlife!"

Kendrick hugged his mother. "I love you."

"Love you, too. Got a minute?"

"Of course. Sabathany, why don't you warm up the car? Mom needs a minute."

"Sure," Sabathany said, going in for a second hug from Diane. "It was really a pleasure meeting you."

"Likewise, dear." Diane beamed.

"I'll walk out with you," Paris said. "Kenny, I'll see you later."

"Okay."

Sabathany smiled at them before following Paris out the door. Once the door closed, Kendrick turned to face his mother. She was no longer smiling.

"That's the best you could bring home?" Diane asked, her expression turning serious all of a sudden.

"What do you mean?"

"Sabathany."

Hurt compounded the surprise on his face. "What's wrong with her?"

"Seems phony to me, like she knew all the right things to say."

"You hound me that I deserve to have someone in my life, and when I get someone who makes me happy, she's not good enough?"

"Not for you. I'm sure there are plenty of eligible women out there in a state as big as California you can meet. Because I'm telling you, you're a fool if you hitch your wagon to that one."

"Sabathany is a great woman, Ma. You've known her for what, one afternoon? I've known her a year and a half."

"Time wasted if you ask me."

"What happened to you telling me that you would respect whatever decisions I made in my personal life because ultimately I'm the one who's got to be happy with the decision? In fact, I distinctly remember you telling me you wouldn't care who I brought home just as long as I didn't bring a . . ."

"Just because that's what I said I wanted doesn't mean that's what I wanted."

"Then why say it?"

Diane ignored the question. "Look, I'm not naïve. You're a little curious about these around-the-way, 'hood girls. I get it. I suppose you're going to have dalliances. Just do me a favor . . . remember that you screw women like that, you don't marry them."

"I didn't know it was any of your business."

Diane continued, "You two aren't getting married, are you?"

"We've talked about it."

Diane gritted her teeth. "Damn it, Kenny. What am I supposed to tell your father?"

"You don't have to tell him anything. And even if you do, so what? What's he going to do? Not speak to yet another one of his kids?"

"Just don't knock her up, or you'll never be rid of her."

"I'm going to try and pretend we didn't just have this conversation. I'll talk to you later."

Kendrick walked to the car. Sabathany had started the car and was talking to Paris from a lowered window. Sabathany took notice of Kendrick's angered face.

"Something wrong?" Sabathany asked.

"Everything's fine," he said.

"Any idea where you guys want to go tonight?" Paris asked.

"A new club is opening. Thought we could check it out."

"Okay. Are you sure everything's okay?" Paris asked, stroking her big brother's cheek.

"Fine." A slight twinkle returned to Kendrick's eyes.

"Okay. See you two tonight."

Kendrick got into the car and glared at Sabathany. "When were you going to tell *me* about your mother?"

"I just did."

"I mean, before you decided to use it to score points with my family."

"How dare you!"

"It's bad enough you tried to get over on my family; don't think you're going to get over on me, too!"

"Why, what did your mother say?"

"Nothing."

"Bullshit. I saw your face when you came outside. What did she say to you?"

Kendrick's thoughts raced. "She told me she thought I should reach out to my dad. I told her I thought it was a bad idea."

"It is," Sabathany agreed.

"Let me worry about my family. Why don't you try answering my question?

Sabathany sighed. She knew he wasn't going to let up until she gave him something. "All right. I didn't tell you because you were dealing with important career stuff. I didn't think you needed to be bothered with it."

"When did she die?"

"The day you had your family dinner."

"How did she die?"

"She OD'd. How do you think?"

"We talked every single night I was gone. And it never once dawned on you to tell me your mother was dead?"

"No. And to be honest, I'm surprised you even care. You weren't trying to help her when she was alive."

"I moved her out to California."

"Big whoop."

"And I paid for her rehab."

"Okay, so you moved her out to California and you paid for her rehab."

"And what's all this crap about you writing screenplays?"

"I was embarrassed. What did you expect me to say, 'Hi, I'm Sabathany, and I'm a gold digger?' I wanted to make it seem like we were on an even playing field."

"I'm going to tell you right now, there ain't gonna be too many more opportunities if all you're going to do is play games. If we're going to do this, then I'm going to need for you to be honest from the jump. No secrets"

"I bet you know all about secrets, don't you, Kendrick?"

"What are you talking about?"

"You've got your share of them, so don't get too high and mighty."

"Don't have the slightest clue what you're talking about."

"That's okay. You don't have to tell me if you don't want to. This just gives me an excuse to get a little creative."

"You sit around pouting because I'm not breaking my neck to marry you. Acting like this won't make it happen any quicker."

Sabathany realized she was getting ahead of herself. Why fight over trifles when a far bigger prize awaited?

"I don't know what the hell is wrong with me," she said, running her fingers through her hair.

"I don't either."

"I owe you an apology. You did reach out to my mother. You tried to help her. I'm the one carrying bad feelings about the way she abandoned me, and how the only reason she wanted me in her life was to use me. I figured since I was still angry about all of that, there wasn't any need for me to tell you she was dead."

"But what's with all the insinuations?"

Sabathany teared up. The air inside the car was getting too warm. She rolled her window down a crack. "Just me trying to deflect from the fact that you busted me out just now for not being honest with you about my mom. Baby, you're right. I'm not giving you any reason to trust me. I am so sorry."

"Okay, now, don't start crying. You know I hate it when you cry."

"I can't help it. I'm such a horrible person," she said, forcing a shake in her voice.

"No, you aren't. You're just stuck in survival mood. When are you going to learn that you don't have to do all of that? I've got your back."

Sabathany looked out the window. That way Kendrick couldn't see her struggle to keep from smiling. He said all of the words she needed to hear, which meant he was no longer angry. Mission accomplished.

EIGHT

The Blue Lounge was nothing more than a rented space with a rollaway white, rectangular block set up as a bar in the middle of the room. Dirty, worn-through blue carpet covered the entire floor. Cheap, white tables and chairs were placed in a seating area in front of a massive tinted window. A stream of blue Christmas lights adorned the walls, cascading like tacky neon waterfalls.

Kendrick didn't mind the bare-bones of the place, and for the $7000 appearance fee Lenox snagged on his behalf, he was more than thrilled to spend a half hour mingling with fans.

Kendrick filled himself with his favorite tequila, which besides the money was reason enough to ignite his festive mood. "Hey, you two, come on over here and do a shot with me," he instructed Paris and Sabathany.

Stone-faced and arms folded, Sabathany remained pressed against the wall, a deliberate indication of her discomfort. She visualized balmy evenings in L.A, being surrounded by some of the city's most beautiful people, all the while enjoying top shelf infused cosmos and exquisitely perfumed night air. She had no idea what this Blue Lounge place was beyond a bad joke.

Eventually, Sabathany joined both Kendrick and Paris to receive her tequila shot, surrounded by D-listers and outright failures watching her every move. "I'm not trying to be funny, but is this the best nightlife Minneapolis has to offer?" she asked.

"No. I brought us here as a favor to Lenox's buddy, Carlos. He's paying me, so please pretend to have a good time."

"Are you sure this Carlos guy is going to pay you?"

"Lenox is supposed to be handling it." Hearing it said out loud, Kendrick knew it sounded amateurish. "I'll be sure to ask him when I see him."

Lenox elbowed his way through the masses, wearing his red and black down-feathered parka and holding a clipboard. "Hey, glad you guys finally made it. I still got people waiting to get in."

"To this dump?" Sabathany muttered to Paris.

"So, how are we supposed to do this? Carlos came over, said hello, thanked us for coming and said the booze was on him. He said nothing about my money," Kendrick said, his expression becoming stern. He pushed tequila shots toward his sister and girlfriend.

"Hold up. I'll be right back." Lenox disappeared through the same mass of people. After about fifteen minutes, he returned with a check in hand.

"Took you long enough." Kendrick took it, giving it a long glance before folding it and placing it in his wallet.

"Carlos wanted me to thank you again for helping him fill the joint up. I mean look around!"

"Yeah, forget about that. The check better be good!"

"It is."

"It better be, because if it ain't then that's your ass."

Lenox looked stung by Kendrick's tone. "Wow. You're gonna play me like that?"

Kendrick threw back another shot then started on his newly ordered whiskey sour. "There's no such thing as friendship when it comes to business."

Some fans congregated around him. They held cell phones in hand as well as partially-wet cocktail napkins to be signed.

Without looking at him, Kendrick handed Lenox the empty glass. "Do me a favor, will you? Get me another drink."

Lenox snatched the glass, unamused by Kendrick's haughtiness, which came and went, but usually kicked in when he was around people he felt like impressing. Lenox was transported back to their high school years, playing the role of the dead weight loser friend willing to do anything just to stand in Kendrick's sunlight. Years later, he still hoped some of whatever it was that made Kendrick so special would rub off on him.

When Lenox made his way up to the bar, Sabathany gave him the once over. "Hello, Lenox."

"Hey."

"What do you drink?"

Lenox ignored her, then sized up Paris. He grimaced but said nothing.

"Can't you speak?" Paris snapped.

Lenox didn't bother with a reply.

"Did you have to bring Paris?" Lenox asked, returning with both his and Kendrick's drinks.

Kendrick turned sharply. "What kind of question is that? You two got some kind of beef I don't know about?"

Lenox shook his head, then walked away as Rick Ross's "3 Kings" bumped over the speakers, moving the diverse crowd into a slow swoon.

A beautiful redhead woman in a short, green, strapless dress boldly approached. Her eyes appeared sensuously locked on her target.

"Say, aren't you Kendrick Black?" she asked, already knowing the answer.

"Yes, I am." Kendrick was taken by her confidence and beauty.

"Damn, you're gorgeous."

"Thank you. So are you."

"I'm your biggest fan." Her stance was coquettish.

"Glad to hear it. I need all the fans I can get."

"I've been seeing commercials for that new movie of yours. I'll have to check it out."

"I would really appreciate that. Make sure you go with a whole group of your closest girlfriends." He gave her a look sure to make her shiver with dirty thoughts of what she wanted him to do to her.

The crashing movement of the crowd shoved her into the actor. "Sorry. Didn't mean for my tits to fall against you," the woman said, enjoying the intrusion of personal space. Her stare was as dazzling as his; her lips were moist and kissable. She read the look in Kendrick's eyes. It told her he wanted to screw her silly.

"The name is Whitney." Her eyes remained locked on his.

"It's *real* nice to meet you, Whitney." Kendrick imagined himself pulling her dress up around her waist and unashamedly having his way with her enticing fruit.

Taking advantage of their closeness, Whitney turned around, making sure the fullness of her ass nestled in the cradle of Kendrick's crotch.

"Ooooh, excuse me," she said before slinking away. She gave a parting look over the shoulder, while the lingering intoxication of her perfume worked its spell.

Whitney especially wanted Kendrick's woman to know it was done on purpose, and received a glare for it from Sabathany, who witnessed the entire thing. Unfazed, Whitney rolled her eyes and melted into the partying throng.

Paris witnessed the encounter as well. She shook her head at the brazen woman's audacity. "You know, these skanks kill me. They have no respect. She knew you were with my brother."

"Oh, I know. But, I'm not worried about it. It all goes with the territory of being with a celebrity."

"Still though, that was just plain disrespectful."

"I know, right?" The two women clinked their glasses. "Ready for another one?"

"Absolutely. This time I'll have what you're having."

Sabathany waved the attention of one of the bartenders. "Two Sex on the Beaches, please."

"Anything for you, beautiful," the attractive male bartender yelled over the music.

Sabathany smiled.

"Thank you," Paris said as her drink was passed to her.

"Of course. So tell me more about the teens you counsel."

"Most of the teens came in pretty banged-up from their folks beating the hell out of them. But, despite it all, they still want and need that love and acceptance from their parents."

"Did you tell them that sometimes they can wait until the cows come home, they'll never get it?" Sabathany asked.

"Uh, no. The idea is to help them see hope and possibility. But I do try to instill the importance of self-love and acceptance. It all starts there."

Sabathany's face became forlorn. "Yes, it does. I wish I had someone to teach me when I was little."

Paris picked up on Sabathany's sadness. She dug into her purse and pulled out a business card. "Look, I know it's none of my business, but if you ever want to talk about anything while you're in town, maybe we can meet for coffee or something."

Sabathany took the card. "Is this your cell number?"

"Both my cell and office numbers. Since I'm extending the invitation, you can call me whenever."

"Thank you. I really appreciate that." Sabathany dropped the card into her purse.

Paris offered a smile as she sipped her drink. She thought how proud her brother would be of his sister's and girlfriend's bonding. That is, if he ever brought his nose up from the rabble of bouncing breasts.

Sabathany noticed Kendrick's preoccupation, too. A mere flirtation she could tolerate, but she viewed these women as wanton sluts, shamelessly shaking their asses and pussies in Kendrick's face. In her book, it went beyond disrespect. Sabathany's initial indifference gave way to furor.

"Would you excuse me for a moment?" Sabathany bulldozed her way to the ladies' room before Paris responded.

Inside the bathroom, she paced back and forth, hoping the incessant movement burned off her impulse to hurt someone. Stories about celebrity men stepping out on their significant others were common place, especially in Hollywood. She knew Kendrick was a man who enjoyed the attention, and feared he could be lured by the allure of another woman. To Sabathany, most of the women present were out of their league, but stopped at nothing to get their cheaply manicured nails into a growing star like Kendrick Black. Sabathany was especially bothered by the woman in the green, strapless dress.

That whore deserves to be kicked in the throat, she thought, moving faster and faster. She imagined the bottom of her foot contacting with the meatiness of the woman's neck, and the subsequent cutting off of her air passage. Then she envisioned stomping her, leaving shoe imprints etched into her flesh. The vision made her want to laugh, but she bit her bottom lip, short of drawing its blood to kill the urge. The last thing she needed was the person occupying the stall to think she was crazy.

She stopped pacing, and stared into the eyes of her reflection. A light sweat glistened on her forehead.

"Get yourself together, girl," she whispered. "These bitches can only wish they're going home with your man. You've already got the prize."

The pep talk caused a smile to break through. Her heartbeat slowed. "Yeah, but if any one of them gets out of line, don't be afraid to get in that ass!"

Suddenly, a stall door latch clicked. Sabathany ran the faucet, pretending to wash her hands. The stall door opened. The woman in the green, strapless dress came through it. She met Sabathany's stare with provocative eyes of her own. She walked over to the sink and took a compact from her purse, her eyes never breaking their confrontational gaze.

Sabathany giggled and said, "You know, just because you're an ass, doesn't mean you can leave your stench on other people's clothes."

The woman turned completely to face Sabathany. "Say what?"

"Aren't you the bitch who thought it would be cute to rub her funky ass on another woman's man?"

"Yeah, that was me! And for the record, the name's Whitney, and my ass is far from funky."

"Kendrick Black is *my* man!"

"And? What's your point?" The woman moved in closer, standing eye to eye with Sabathany.

Sabathany grabbed a fistful of Whitney's tresses. In one swoop, she brought the woman's face down onto the sink. Hearing a soft snap, Sabathany looked to the sight of blood smudged along the outside counter of the basin, with a few speckles of blood on the counter. The woman's nose hung flimsily to the side. Blood trailed from Whitney's nose into her mouth. Shards of glass from her fallen compact spread across clumps of translucent pressed powder.

"Oh, my God, my nose! You broke my nose!"

Sabathany swung open the same stall door Whitney came through, managing a glimpse inside the toilet. "You were in here changing your tampon, bitch? This is why toilets get clogged-up, because of nasty whores like you!" Sabathany again grabbed Whitney by the hair. She gripped her hair tightly, feeling the fire-red extensions coming loose. She dunked

Whitney's head into the toilet, causing Whitney's loud gurgling to echo throughout the bathroom.

Whitney pulled herself from the toilet and gasped for air. She remained on the floor, curled into a fetal position, wailing in excruciating pain.

"You can cry blood for all I care! Now go rub your ass up against someone else's man, trash," Sabathany hissed as she kicked Whitney in the leg.

Sabathany backed away from the woman, and gave herself a final check in the mirror. Rogue strands of hair upset her otherwise perfect hairdo. After placing the strands, she left Whitney slumped on the floor.

With a newfound pep in her step, Sabathany breezed past the people—the nothings they all were. A woman wagged a breast at Kendrick in one hand, and held a lip liner for him to sign it with in the other. Sabathany whirled over with aggressive energy which warned the woman to get out of the way.

"How's my baby doing?" Sabathany whispered in his ear. After placing her arm around Kendrick, she planted a wet kiss on him, and then scowled at the woman.

"Cool it, baby. They're just fans," Kendrick said.

Lenox stepped in to address the now embarrassed fan. "Ma'am, do us all a favor and put that saggy tittie away."

Sabathany continued hugging her man for all in the bar to see. She broke their embrace in time to see Whitney rush past, cupping both hands over mouth and nose; her hair looked like a wet nest. Sabathany's smile turned victorious.

Paris came back to the group. She gave Sabathany a high-five.

Kendrick said to Lenox, "Carlos said a half hour, right?"

Lenox checked his watch and nodded.

"Yeah, so I think we've given him that and then some."

"We're cool to split."

Kendrick got up from the stool a fan relinquished to him. "You all ready?" Kendrick asked.

"Where are we going now?" Paris asked once they made their way outside.

"Back to my place. Why don't you ride with Lenox," Kendrick said.

Lenox's jaw tightened, followed by a soft groan. He didn't care whether or not Paris heard him. "Listen, man, thanks for helping Carlos pack 'em in tonight. But I really think I should be getting home. I'd like to have one evening when I'm not getting into it with Ashley."

"For the thousandth time, do you have the information I've been asking for?"

Lenox took out a small folded piece of paper from inside his wallet and handed it to Kendrick, who unfolded the paper and peered at it, looking satisfied with what he read.

"Been doing a lot of thinking, and I don't know how much longer I can go along with this. The shit's really messing with my head. I think I should just get it over with and go to the police."

Lenox's eyebrows raised. "For what?"

"Because this has gone on long enough, and it's the right thing to do."

"Look, I got rid of your car like you asked me to. You're good."

"Wait a sec', I never asked you to get rid of anything."

Lenox ran his fingers over the smoothness of his shaved head. "Yeah, well, you never said not to either. It's done. There's no going back on this."

"Still, it's the right thing to do."

"Okay, fine. Say you go to the cops. It'll come out that I helped you."

"I won't say anything. And I'll put that on everything I hold dear."

"Dude, these things always have a way of coming out, whether you want them to or not."

"You don't know that for sure."

"And you don't know that it won't. I've got a family to think about. What are they going to do if you decide to talk? Like I said before, it's taken care of."

Kendrick was quiet for a moment. "Maybe you're right. Listen, why don't you drop my sister at my place. I need to smooth things out with Sabathany. She's pissed, and thinks I was encouraging the ladies in there. After you drop Paris, then go on home to your family," Kendrick insisted. His tone was less arrogant and more appreciative.

Lenox nodded his understanding. He threw a glance at Paris from over Kendrick's shoulder. "Hey, Paris, I guess you're riding with me," Lenox called to her, not sounding too happy about it.

"I'm sure there are worse things," Paris said. "This isn't a delight for me, either."

"Good. You can suffer in silence. Now get your ass in the car!"

Once Kendrick and Sabathany buckled in, he started the rented car and drove up alongside Lenox's. Paris let her passenger window down.

"You two play nice," Kendrick playfully chided them. "Last one there is a rotten egg."

"What are we, in the fifth grade?" Paris asked.

"All right, see y'all in a few," Kendrick said before speeding off.

Paris rolled the window back up. "What were you guys talking about?"

"Don't worry about it."

"Do you have to act like you want to throw up every time you see me?" Paris asked, sounding hurt.

Lenox took her hand and kissed it. "Sorry, baby. Just don't want him figuring things out."

"Maybe he already suspects something. Why else make me ride with you?" Paris placed the kissed hand to her cheek as though she intended to cherish it forever.

"Trust me he doesn't know anything."

"How can you be so sure?"

"Just a vibe I get. Say, did you ask him for that loan yet?"

Paris sighed. "Not yet."

"Tick-tock, don't you think you ought to get that handled?"

"Don't you think you ought to tell your wife you're leaving her?"

Lenox faced the driver's side window. "That's not fair. I can't just walk in and tell her I'm leaving her. It requires some thought."

"Asking my brother for this loan requires some thought, too."

"We've been over this before. I'm not telling Ashley a damn thing until you take care of that situation. Period." Lenox started the car and drove away. Regretting the harshness in his voice, he held Paris's hand for the duration of the ride. By the time they arrived at Kendrick's apartment he snuck one last look at her as she unbuckled her seatbelt.

"I'm sorry about how I acted earlier. I'll try and dial it back a bit. But you know I didn't mean it."

"Why don't you come in for at least one drink?" Paris said.

"I gotta get home. We'll talk tomorrow, I promise."

Paris smiled at him, but said nothing. No words seemed necessary. The man she loved since high school understood how she felt. That's all she could ask from him. This time she kissed his hand, and placed it to her heart before releasing it.

NINE

Kayla stopped for a moment, maybe two, for which Kendrick was grateful. He took those precious moments to rest. But, before the dryness left his throat, she was off again, running up the hillside, towards the sun.

"Maybe Kayla isn't her name," Kendrick thought. He checked the folded paper from his wallet for reassurance that he wasn't calling the child by the wrong name. The paper said Kayla Jones, seven-year old daughter of Yvette and Antwon Jones. Maybe if he told her that he knew her parents she would let him catch up to her. But that would be some weird tactic employed by the most depraved child molesters, wouldn't it? Kendrick wasn't a child molester. He just wanted the chance to tell Kayla he was sorry.

"Jesus, Kayla, you're killing me! Will you please stop? I'm not going to hurt you. I promise."

This time Kayla giggled as she waved. The cotton candy pink of her outfit was so vibrant that it made him crave the confection. Suddenly a long plastic bag of pink, white and purple cotton candy materialized in his hand. He offered it up, hoping it would keep Kayla still. It did.

Kendrick's tread was wobbly. His heart wanted to explode inside his chest. Despite the hurt, he held the cotton candy high. All he needed was for Kayla to wait just a few more seconds. Then, she would see into his spirit; she would know that he meant no harm.

This was the closest he ever got to her when they played this game before. Usually she remained smiling. This time her smile

71

faded, and she backed away as though she knew danger lurked. Kayla ran up to the top of the hill, toward the dulling sun, then disappeared down the other side.

With the once raised bag of cotton candy now flapping at his side, he ignored the pain in his chest, eventually making it to the top. But there was no sun by the time he arrived. The other side of the hill led into a forest. Kendrick knew only bad things happened there. He wondered how many dead bodies had been given over to it.

"Kayla!" Kendrick cried out. He looked toward the sky as unusually large black birds passed overhead. The sound of their wings flapping drowned out his call. Twigs snapped beneath his feet, bringing his attention back to Kayla, who stood only a few paces away from him. The pink of her outfit turned the color of soaked blood. Her messy hair was covered in dried, crumbled leaves. Kendrick waited for her to smile again, but she collapsed to the ground, her bones smashing on contact.

Hyper flies swarmed the body as Kendrick delicately turned it over. Kayla's once angelic face disintegrated into a caving dust. As the disturbed maggots fed on her body, Kayla's jogging suit moved in ripples. More of Kayla's flesh broke open while the maggots taunted Kendrick by the sound of their munching . . .

The nightmares began the night of the accident. At first he dreamed of a giggling Kayla running through sunny pastures. He almost got the impression that things were good for her in the afterlife. Now his dreams became overrun with images of her mangled corpse transmogrified into nourishment for bugs.

Kendrick bolted awake, his entire side of the bed soaked from sweat. Sabathany was still asleep. He got out of bed and went to the kitchen. Kendrick swallowed hard and often, fighting the inclination to spew. He ran the remaining paces to the sink. Multiple whiskey sours, tequila, and partially digested grilled cheese sandwiches oozed from his mouth in a saffron, textured paste. Kendrick paused, bracing for a second rush from his still opened mouth.

Satisfied that he had gotten it all out, he wiped his mouth with the back of his hand, and sprayed the vomit away with the side sprayer. Emotion remained caught in his throat. He wept. Kendrick tried to quiet his bellow, placing the same vomit streaked hand over his mouth, but the tears continued, and the guilt sitting in the pit of his stomach since the day Kayla died in the street finally moved.

"Oh my goodness, Kenny, what's the matter?" Paris asked.

"I'm sorry, I didn't realize you were still up," Kendrick said, revealing a soggy face. "I was watching *Mrs. Doubtfire* when I heard you."

"I'll be fine. Go on back and watch your movie."

"You are *not* fine. A grown man doesn't cry out for no reason."

Of all his siblings, Kendrick felt closest to Paris who was two years his junior. To him, both she and their mother were the only family members genuinely happy for his growing success.

"Instead of standing here in the dark by yourself, why don't you come watch the movie? It might get your mind off whatever's bothering you."

A second wave of emotion attacked Kendrick at his core. He doubled over as though having been kicked in the gut. He shook his head; tears rained from his face.

"What is going on?"

"I did something really bad," Kendrick whispered.

Paris stroked his back. "What did you do?"

Kendrick shook his head again.

"You can tell me." Paris stood in a judgment-free zone like a beacon of understanding.

"I'm afraid you won't love me anymore if I tell you."

Paris became fearful, but tried to remain strong for the both of them. "You listen to me. There's nothing you could ever tell me that would make me love you any less. That's a lesson I learned from you. I will never stop loving you. Do you understand me?"

Kendrick's secret sat on the tip of his tongue. He imagined feeling lighter once he cast it out.

"You're scaring me, Kenny. Just tell me."

Kendrick sunk to the floor, putting his palms to his sweaty forehead. "I killed someone."

"Wait. What?" Paris tried yanking her brother up to eye level, but he wouldn't follow the tug. "Kenny, you look me in the eyes and tell me you didn't just say what I thought you said."

While Kendrick remained on bended knee, his face shadowed. Paris found it difficult to stand herself. She stooped back to Kendrick's level, waiting for him to raise his head.

"Okay. The Kenny I know wouldn't do something like that unless there was a reason. What did they do to you? Did they have dirt on you? Was it self-defense?"

Finally, Kendrick raised his head, looking less like a leading man and more like the brother Paris remembered from her youth. "That hit and run involving the little girl . . . I'm responsible."

"Kenny!" Paris dropped his hands and stood back up. The sudden yelling out startled Kendrick.

"Shhh! Sabathany's asleep. You can't say anything. Paris, please, you gotta keep this between us!"

"That's not fair, Kenny. I wasn't expecting you to tell me something like that!"

"Paris, please. Keep your voice down."

Paris backed away from her brother. "Did you talk to the police?"

"I thought about it."

"What do you mean, you thought about it?"

Kendrick couldn't explain what it meant. Quite possibly he didn't know himself. "Please don't say anything."

"You took away that little girl's chance at life."

"I know that. You asked about me going to the police. I did think about it, but I figured since Lenox got rid of the vehicle . . ."

"Wait a minute! You made him a part of this?"

"I didn't make him do anything! After the accident, I called him to talk. I dunno, I guess I wanted someone to talk to before I went to the cops. He was the one who came up with the idea. Before I knew it, he'd taken over. I was still in shock by what had happened, I just went along with it."

Paris bit her lip. She looked as though she wanted to say something else, but Kendrick couldn't bear another question.

"Look, don't think this has been easy for me. I've been sick about this, but, Lenox says getting rid of the car was for the best. I mean, things are going so well with my career right now. I'm about to blow up. You know I've been grinding for the past five years, and my hard work is finally paying off."

Paris didn't look at him, but she nodded silently.

"Don't worry, I'm going to make this right. I was thinking about setting up some trust fund for the family. I wasn't going to put my name on it, and they don't have to know it's from me."

"You think throwing money at this will make it better?"

Kendrick thought for two beats. "With time, maybe." He now stood perfectly on his own. "You won't say anything, will you?"

As Paris faced him, she felt a lump pass in her throat when she swallowed. There was remorse in her brother's eyes, and she took some comfort from that. The Kendrick she knew always apologized immediately after making her cry when they were children. *That* Kendrick was too sensitive of a person to deliberately kill a child, or anyone for that matter. However, he *had* killed someone. Paris hoped he would do what he said he was going to do. "I won't say anything," she said.

Kendrick's tears flowed again, this time from relief. "You won't?"

Paris shook her head.

"Thank you."

Paris watched her brother stir with gratitude. "Just make sure you do what you said you're going to do."

Kendrick nodded, then sighed relief before rolling his shoulders to break up their tension. "I'm going to fix this. I'll make it right. But do me a favor, don't let Lenox know I told you."

Paris sighed exasperatedly. She noticed desperation return to his face. "Fine, I won't say anything." As Kendrick's face relaxed again, Paris decided if she was going to ask for the money she needed to do it soon. "Listen, if you want me to keep all of this to myself, it's gonna cost you."

Kendrick's eyes narrowed. "What?"

"My silence comes at a price," Paris said.

"You're blackmailing me?"

"Not at all."

"Sounds that way to me."

"I look at it as one hand washing the other."

"All the fights in school I got into defending your ass, and this is how you repay me?"

"You can't look at it like that. Think of it as one favor repaying another. I've decided to take care of that situation we talked about a couple of months ago, but I need money to do it."

"I hope blackmailing me is worth it. How much do you need?"

"Don't call it that. Look, I was going to ask you for a loan. At least this way you can say we're even. Give me $35,000 and I'll take your secret to the grave."

"What if years down the road you have a change of heart?"

Paris looked directly into Kendrick's disappointed eyes. "I won't."

Kendrick reached beneath the kitchen island and grabbed the whiskey. He didn't know how his stomach would take it now; he just knew the situation called for whiskey.

"Want one?" Kendrick asked.

"No."

"This doesn't sound like you. What changed your mind?"

Paris looked away, partly from shame, and partly from knowing there was no going back. She knew she had to tell Kendrick the truth. "Actually, I think I will take that shot," she said, motioning toward the bottle.

After taking his swig directly from the bottle he passed it to her. As she downed the whiskey, she noticed Kendrick's body language become closed off.

"Lenox won't leave his wife until I take care of it. And, I'm willing to do it because he loves me."

Hearing Lenox's name was jarring. Was this the same Lenox who back in the day had special ordered posters of Pam Grier plastered on his walls, who owned bootleg copies of every Blaxploitation movie made, and whose own swag came from watching his favorite Blaxploitation actor, Richard Roundtree? Those movies had been Lenox's escape from his own family's dysfunction. As a kid, he had watched helplessly as his father left his mother to make a life with another woman.

"Wait, wait, wait! My best friend, Lenox?" Kendrick almost stammered.

Paris nodded.

"Did he put you up to this . . . asking for the money?"

"Of course not." Paris refused to meet his gaze. "I mean, not exactly."

Kendrick crossed his arms to keep from hitting something. "How long have you two been . . .?"

"Since high school."

"Way back then? And neither of you said a goddamn thing?"

"What were you expecting us to say?"

"So what, did he seduce you?"

Paris downed a second swig of whiskey. Thinking for two beats she said, "Remember all those times you used to leave Lenox downstairs in the TV room with me? You'd go flirt with the girls who came to the house looking for you. That's when it started. I used to give him Little Debbie snack cakes to sit and watch me do my impersonations of the group TLC. After a while, he stopped expecting food, and just started to enjoy watching me."

"This isn't right. None of this is right!" Kendrick pounded his fists against the counter-top.

"After what you just told me, *now* your moral compass kicks in?"

Sabathany appeared in the kitchen entryway. She was groggy from a deep sleep. "What are you two doing up?"

"I'm sorry, babe. Did we wake you?"

"No, I just wanted some water." She bumped her knee against the island. "Ouch!"

"You all right?" Paris asked.

"Yeah." Sabathany motioned to be let through. She reached for a glass from the cabinet. Paris and Kendrick exchanged quick glances between each other, watching as Sabathany drank her water.

"What are you two talking about?"

"How Kendrick thinks everything is about him, and how the fame is going to his head," Paris said quickly.

"Well, that's true." Sabathany giggled. "Honey, are you coming back to bed?"

"In a little bit, babe. We were just about to go finish up *Mrs. Doubtfire.*"

"All right. Goodnight."

"Goodnight," Paris said, putting a bag of microwaveable popcorn into the microwave.

Sabathany kissed Kendrick's cheek before leaving the room.

Paris turned back to do a quick study of Kendrick's face. "So, do we have a deal?"

"I'll cut you a check in the morning."

There was something in his tone that rubbed Paris the wrong way. "Seriously, Kenny, I'm not blackmailing you."

Kendrick began to leave the kitchen to go back to the living room. "If you say so."

"And you won't mention any of this to Lenox, right?"

Kendrick continued toward the sofa. "I won't if you won't."

"Then we're good?'

"You're getting your money. Don't push it."

TEN

The next morning, Sabathany sipped her latte, having just finished her breakfast of half a grapefruit and buttered rye toast. She found the news articles in that morning's *Star Tribune* especially riveting.

Kendrick crossed through from the sofa, his vision adjusting from the sunlight reflecting off the stainless steel appliances.

He loved the ultra-modern touches throughout the apartment, complete with angular, futuristic pieces of furniture, and psychedelic pop art paintings on the walls. The floor-to-ceiling windows offered views of Minneapolis just beyond the dandelion fountain in Loring Park.

"Good morning, sleepyhead," Sabathany said, glancing up from her reading.

Kendrick leaned in for a kiss.

Sabathany recoiled. "Morning breath, Honey. You know better."

Kendrick ran his tongue along the thickness on his teeth. Cupping his hand in front of his mouth, he both breathed in and grimaced from the smell of his own bad breath.

"I just had breakfast. I can make you something if you want."

"I'm good for now."

"How did you sleep?"

Kendrick paused as the memory of conversation with Paris came to mind. "Fine."

"Couldn't have been all that fine, you never came back to bed."

"Yeah, I just have a lot of stuff on my mind. I didn't want to wake you again, so I crashed on the couch."

Sabathany put the newspaper down. "Did it have anything to do with what you and Paris were talking about?"

"Not really."

Sabathany blinked at the fast response. "No?"

Kendrick made a point to look directly into her eyes. "No."

"Okay, then. Well, you know that I'm here in case you want to talk about it."

"Appreciate it."

Sabathany's face disappeared behind the newspaper again, leaving Kendrick happy with a dropped subject.

"You know what? I think I will have a bowl of cereal after all. Good morning, Paris."

Paris entered the room. "Good morning, you two."

Sabathany smiled dryly. "And how did you sleep?"

"Pretty good. I barely have a hangover."

"Want breakfast?" Sabathany asked.

"No, I need to get home."

"Is Lenox coming to pick you up?" Sabathany asked.

Both Paris and Kendrick looked at her.

"Uh, no."

"He was kinda rude to you last night. What was all that about?"

"We've never gotten along. He tolerates me because of my brother, otherwise there'd be no reason for us to even interact."

"That's all there is to it?"

"Is there something in particular you'd like to ask me?"

"No. I was just curious."

Kendrick spoke up. "Babe, she's right. Lenox can be an ass sometimes for no reason."

"Paris, I wasn't trying to get all in your business. I just noticed he was a tad chilly last night, and I wanted to ask you about it at the lounge, but we started talking about your counseling."

Paris's face relaxed. She pushed the elevator button. "Oh. Okay. Well, I'm leaving. I got a lot to do today."

"You don't want me to drive you?" Kendrick asked, hoping for a no.

Paris stepped through the elevator doors when they opened. "No, Kenny, I'm good. Thanks for a fun night last night. Sabathany, my offer still stands. Call if you need to." She waved to them as the doors closed.

"What do you want to talk to her for?"

"Oh, that's in case I needed someone to talk to about my mom."

"Cool. Was there anything special you wanted to do our last day in Minneapolis?" Kendrick fished a large bowl from the cupboard.

"Whatever you want to do is fine. By the way, I hope Paris didn't misinterpret my question."

"No, she's fine. "Kendrick looped around the island, grabbing the milk from the refrigerator. He placed the milk next to the bowl and brought the box of cereal close. Kendrick stared at the three items. *Spoon,* he thought, reaching into a drawer to get a spoon.

"She sure ran outta here quick enough," Sabathany said, facing where Paris once stood.

"Like I said, she's fine."

Sabathany continued reading the newspaper. "Not that I'm naïve, but I wouldn't think you all had serial killers here in Minnesota."

Kendrick watched the cereal rise from poured milk. "Where did that come from?"

"Says here that several murders may be the work of a serial killer. You're about to eat so I'll spare you the graphic details."

"The world is going to hell in a handbasket," Kendrick said, chewing the synthetic berry flavored flakes.

After breakfast and a quick shower, Sabathany rejoined Kendrick in the living room and talked him into what amounted to uninspired, lazy sex. There was none of their usual organic chemistry, mostly because she acted like she was directing a porn film.

"A little to the left . . . don't squeeze my titties so hard . . . plop up and down on me . . . let's try it standing up . . . let me ride you . . . doggy style . . . kiss more on my neck . . . eat me out some more . . . good . . . now stick it back in . . . yeah . . . go faster . . .I think I'm gonna . . . oh wait . . . never mind . . . kiss me . . . that's too rough . . . yeah, like that . . . let me lay on my back again . . ."

While Kendrick did as he was directed to do, taking whatever physical pleasure that wasn't stripped from the experience, a little red flashing light lodged between some books on the bookshelf went unnoticed.

ELEVEN

Lenox knew something was wrong when Kendrick ignored the open passenger door, opting to sit in back with Sabathany. His lack of eye contact drove the feeling further.

"You're not gonna sit up front with me?"

The way the pampered couple stared forward gave Lenox his answer. Their refusal to speak was an intended punishment. Had to be.

Lenox started the car and pulled off, tuning into the same oldies station from when he picked them up from the airport. Stevie Wonder's "Uptight (Everything's Alright)" attacked the awkward silence.

"Is it possible to listen to something else? From this century, maybe?" Kendrick asked.

Lenox changed the channel to a top forty station. Robin Thicke's "Blurred Lines" was finishing. Hoping to try again with some conversation, Lenox lowered the volume of the stereo.

"I didn't hear from you all day yesterday. What did you two wind up doing?"

Sabathany cleared her throat. "We went to the Mall of America."

"Oh. How did you like that?"

"We had a nice time. I was amazed how big it was. I had some items shipped to L.A."

"Hey, Kenny, you remember when we used to chase females on Friday nights out there?"

"Yep."

Sabathany patted Kendrick's leg and nuzzled to his ear. "I bet you boys were wild! Did Lenox keep up with you, Sweetie?"

Kendrick didn't even break a smile.

"I did okay with the ladies back in the day. But Ashley and the kids are the best things that ever happened to me."

"Wow. That's really beautiful. I wish this one would hurry up and follow your lead." Sabathany locked an arm with Kendrick's, and rested her head on his shoulder.

Kendrick turned outward as Minneapolis passed by on the ride to the airport. He wondered if it was difficult for Lenox to say the things he just said. Evidently Ashley and the kids weren't enough. In a morbid sort of way, he wanted to know how Paris factored into all of this. When he spoke to her, she seemed so sure of her storybook outcome that she should be the last woman standing. After all, she convinced her brother to give her money to put toward that end. Kendrick controlled his urge to knock Lenox in the back of the head with his fist. *At least she won't go blabbing about Kayla,* he thought. Then, needing to convince his Higher Power, "God, you know my heart. I'm trying to make this right. *I'm going to make this right.* I just don't know what right is at the moment."

The thought of going to the police came up again stronger than before. Anxiety bubbled in his stomach then rose like a belch. He wanted to free his conscience. He wanted the nightmares to end, and Kayla's soul to rest. And yet, a different tangent of thought snuffed out those before it . . .

I've got this amazing woman sitting next to me. Why can't I give her a ring? If it's worth it to her, she'll have to just wait, goddamn it! But we'd have great-looking babies, wouldn't we? But what if she takes the babies and runs? Wouldn't be the first time that happened in Hollywood. If she wants to be with me I need to test her. I want to sell the house in Laurel Canyon, and make Minneapolis my real home. Better place to raise kids, assuming we have any. Plus, my mom is getting older . . . I want to buy her a home closer to me. But that's much later down the road.

"Honey, you seem really deep in your head. What are you thinking about?" Sabathany asked.

"Trying to mentally prepare to do this publicity. I don't want to sound like some wound-up robot when I answer questions," he lied.

"Nothing wrong with talking points. Everyone uses them. It's all in how you deliver them that keeps them fresh."

"You sound just like my agent. Brenda better watch out," he joked.

At the airport, Kendrick was besieged with more requests to take pictures and sign autographs. Sabathany remained close by incase some overly enthusiastic female tried to invade her man's space. As Lenox busied himself taking luggage from the trunk, he watched Kendrick's bourgeoning fame with pride.

When the crowd thinned out, Sabathany proceeded inside with the luggage, leaving Kendrick to say goodbye to his friend.

"Are we cool, man?" Lenox asked after receiving what he perceived as a stiff hug from Kendrick.

"Yeah, we're cool. Why wouldn't we be?" Kendrick said, looking everywhere else but at his friend.

"I don't know. Just a feeling I'm getting."

Kendrick laughed. It sounded forced. "You were always so damn sensitive."

Lenox held his hands up, palms out. "Can't argue with it."

Kendrick checked his watch, then turned toward the automatic sliding door to see Sabathany waving her hand as if to say, "Wrap it up!"

"Chi-town next, right?" Lenox asked, noticing Sabathany's gesticulation.

"Yep. Anyway, you take care of yourself. I'll be in touch."

Lenox backed away, sensing some return of his friend's normal vibe. It was also nice to see Kendrick drop the Hollywood razzle dazzle and ease back into his guy next door charm.

"Okay. You two have a safe flight."

"We'll do our best. Oh, by the way, Paris left before I had a chance to give this to her. Could you make sure she gets it? I mean, if you happen to see her." Kendrick pulled a folded check out from his coat pocket.

Lenox's expression was quizzical at first, then he unfolded the check and gave it a peek. His expression became one of knowing and fright. He had to will himself the ability to speak. Finally, he managed a faint, "Sure."

"She'll know what it's for. And judging by the look on your face, you already do."

TWELVE

Paris had only been in her new place for a couple of months. She lived on the top fourth floor unit. The walls of the apartment were exposed brick, painted white. Her living room was decorated with a beige couch and loveseat, and an oak coffee table covered with *Us Weekly* and *People* magazines.

Yards of fabrics were draped about the living space, giving the room colorful depth. Some of the same fabrics and others were neatly folded and stored in the built-in shelves. On a small table tucked in a far corner was a sewing machine and several plastic canisters filled with sequins, rhinestones and bugle beads. There were also several dress mannequins adorned with garments she hoped to finish.

A loud pounding disrupted her relaxed state of mind.

It was Lenox, wearing a mixture of hurt and anger on his face. He wore the long, black leather coat she bought him, which reminded her of his hero, Richard Roundtree, in *Shaft*. Lenox looked dashing in it as he stormed past her, causing a breeze.

Paris was unaccustomed to Lenox showing up at her apartment during daylight.

"What possessed you to tell Kenny about us?" Lenox demanded to know. "And don't bother acting like you don't know what I'm talking about. He knows, Paris. Kenny knows everything, and I sure as hell ain't the one who told him!"

Paris flinched. "Calm down," she said, closing her apartment door. "What did he say to you?"

"Naw, what did *you* say to him?"

"Have a seat."

"I don't wanna sit down!"

Paris sat down on the sofa, leaving Lenox to tower over her. She was tempted to mention his involvement with Kendrick's problem. Maybe it would take some of the heat off of her. "I wish you'd sit down. You know I don't like people standing over me."

He complied. "I'm sitting. Talk!"

Paris rolled her head back and forth, while massaging her own neck. After a full exhale she said, "Okay. I wasn't planning on telling him, but I had no choice. There was a whole lot of stuff going on in the conversation. I had to come clean so that he'd understand why the money was so important. I told him that you wouldn't leave your wife unless I took care of everything."

"Who told you to tell him that?

"Was I lying?"

The veins at Lenox's temples were pronounced despite his almost midnight-blue skin. "You don't get it."

"I know my brother. He just needs some time."

"Naw, naw. You didn't see how he looked at me, like I was dog shit he wanted to wipe off his shoes."

"Welcome to the club. You know, Kenny asked me if I'd thought all of this through, but I think I should be asking you the same question!"

There was still traces of love in the way he looked at her, but the anger boiling was stronger. He leapt from the sofa and walked the floor, running his hands back and forth along the slickness of his bald head.

"I'm not sure you have thought this through. I won't continue to be your little secret. No more booty calls when the wife and kids are asleep. If we move forward, then we do it openly."

Lenox stopped walking around, but still buzzed with frantic energy. "You don't understand. Ashley won't let me see my kids. She's gonna turn the courts against me. I can't lose my kids, Paris. I can't."

"I don't want you to lose your kids. But I'm not going to sneak around with you, either."

"You've gotta be patient."

"Not this again."

Lenox went into his pocket and pulled out the check Kendrick instructed him to give to her. He held it out as if meaning to hand it to her, but when she reached for it, he let it go. Both watched it flit its way to the coffee table.

Lenox went to the door and opened it. With his back to her, his words drifted over his broad shoulder. "You know how I feel about you, but, if that ain't enough, then I don't know what else to tell you."

Lenox stepped through, closing the door behind him. And in the moments that followed, he realized what he felt for her would never be enough. He knew he needed to walk away. Without a doubt he loved his five-year-old twins, Keyshawn and Toya, more. They gave him focus and a whole lot more respectability than the complicated mess he left behind in Paris's apartment. He was certain Paris would wonder if this was goodbye. She would wonder if she pushed too hard, or expected too much. And he expected she would no doubt call him, demanding those answers. But Lenox also knew that Paris was a very smart cookie. If she took the time to look within herself, Lenox didn't need to explain anything. She would figure it out.

THIRTEEN

Det. VanDrunen was still at the precinct by 7:00PM. He promised his wife that he would be home at a decent hour, but it looked like the Kayla Jones case wasn't going to allow that to happen.

His eyes bounced from one crime scene photo to the next. Clockwise, and then counter, each photo received the precise scrutiny expected from a detective with his experience. All he could do was hold onto the possibility that each would piece together a story, or provide even the smallest clue as to what happened to the little girl. However, the longer he stared—especially at the pictures of Kayla's dead body—he was reminded of his own children, a son and daughter. They were older now, practically adults. His son, Caleb, was going to graduate from the University of Minnesota with a journalism degree, and his daughter, Emma, was busy finding herself in the artsy, bohemian part of town. Both called on Sundays to check in, send their love, and ask for money. It had become their predictable pattern, one that annoyed VanDrunen. However, looking at the close-up of Kayla's torso, which was covered with baby ants, he felt a sense of gratitude that he still had children left to annoy him at all.

His cell phone rang again. This was the fourth time his wife, Lacey, had called. This time he knew to answer. It was his own fault for telling her he would be home by 5:30.

"Hey."

"I won't bore you with the details of how much effort I've put into finding the correct recipe that you like for veal. I don't even like veal, and yet, here I am running around like a mad woman trying to make a meal you'd find worthy to actually show up on time for."

VanDrunen gave a long sigh. He knew he was in trouble. Despite the futility of it, he said, "Honey, I'm sorry. It's just this case is driving me crazy."

"Yeah, I know."

VanDrunen could almost envision his wife rolling her eyes through the phone. "We're at a dead end, and well, I'm really frustrated."

Lacey sucked her teeth. "It's always something, isn't it? Did you know that for years I used to tell myself at the start of every year that things would get better? That you'd eventually slow down?"

"For Christ's sake, Lacey, we're talking about a little girl here!"

Lacey was quiet, then sniffled as though she'd been crying. "You're right. I'm sorry."

VanDrunen took a breath. "No, I'm sorry. I shouldn't have yelled. I'll call when I'm on my way."

"Fine."

VanDrunen ended the call, looking at the phone as though he didn't know what it was. He peered up at the pictures again. This time directed to a photo of a smashed headlight laying in the street. VanDrunen thought for a moment. The only person who claimed to see anything was a man who was about to walk his dog. He saw a large black vehicle whiz by, though he didn't see the make of the car. His dog was still new to him, and was being especially difficult that day. The dog got lose and ran back into the house before the owner had the chance to close the door, thereby preventing him from having seen the hit and run take place.

"What if?" VanDrunen said, still staring at the picture of the broken headlight.

Just then, his partner, Det. Ramirez came into the room, holding two cups of coffee in her hands. She noticed a light go on in VanDrunen's eyes. She liked the sight of that.

"Tell me what's percolating in that big noggin of yours," she said, handing him a coffee.

"Well, I got an idea of how we could possibly find out the make of the car," VanDrunen said excitedly.

"Oh yeah?"

"Yeah. And I think you could be a big help."

"I aim to please."

"Glad to hear it. Any good with puzzles?"

Confusion flickered in Ramirez's eyes. "Isn't that what we do day in and day out?"

VanDrunen realized his attempt at word play had fallen to their feet. "I meant actual puzzles, as in jigsaw puzzles."

Ramirez's face brightened. "Oh sure. Back in high school. It was a picture of the Colosseum in Rome."

"I'm thinking we can get an idea of the kind of car the perp was driving if we piece together the shattered headlight."

The veil of confusion returned to Ramirez's face. "How do you propose we put it together?"

"Good ol' fashioned glue or tape, I guess."

"Now, by 'we' do you mean me?"

VanDrunen smiled sheepishly. "But don't worry, you can get started tomorrow."

"I'm so thrilled." Ramirez paused thoughtfully. "I guess I could take a stab at it."

"Good. Gotta get home to Lacey. She made veal for dinner, and I'm about an hour and a half late."

Ramirez grimaced. "I hate veal."

VanDrunen slipped into his overcoat. "So does she. Have a great rest of your night."

When VanDrunen took off towards home, he rang Lacey to let her know he was on his way. He hoped to hear an enthusiasm in her voice, but there was none. He knew there was no chance of Lacey greeting him at the door with a glass of wine from the boxed merlot, and piping hot veal awaiting him in the dining room. And there was even less chance of a little up and down in the bed afterward. It was his juvenile way of asking for sex, and it usually put a smile on Lacey's face. That night of all nights, he could have used some up and down in the bed, because the Kayla Jones case was like a vice grip on his brain.

As VanDrunen continued onward, he turned to the jazz station on the radio. Billie Holiday was singing "You've Changed." He laughed at the irony. He hadn't changed at all—not in any way that mattered to his wife.

FOURTEEN

Kendrick Black was riding high on his publicity tour for the film, *It Is What It Is.* The local TV and radio personalities in both Chicago and Atlanta were charmed by the actor. Kendrick was especially pleased with how well things had gone in Atlanta that he agreed to meet with a gay YouTube blogger that was not previously scheduled on the itinerary. A few of the blogger's questions related to the upcoming movie, but most pertained to how he was handling his sex symbol status amongst gay men.

Kendrick's smile was immediate and Mid-western humble. "It's a blessing, really. Hell, I'll take a compliment from wherever I can get it. But let me add that I'm thankful to my parents for giving me decent genes."

"So, it doesn't bother you to have thousands, if not millions, of gay men wishing they could take you home with them at night?"

Kendrick continued smiling. "Not at all. Look, it's 2013. The world is a much different place then it was even twenty years ago. I'm grateful that anyone is paying attention to me at all."

Sabathany perched in the far corner of the coffee shop. She wasn't the least bit personable. Her body language from the very beginning of the interview had been closed off, her face a seething pout. Kendrick did his best to remain light-hearted in an attempt to deflect her negative energy. The "Fabulous

Flamboyant" Ja'brell Hunty didn't pay Sabathany the slightest attention, which only unnerved her further.

At the end of the interview, Kendrick took a couple of pictures with Ja'brell Hunty and a few of his friends. Sabathany approached the group, giving Ja'brell Hunty a full once over. He wore a voluminous, teal blouse, white skinny jeans and shimmering high heels. One side of his head was shaved, while long Brazilian waves cascaded down the other side. His face was a makeup work of art.

"Your parents must be so proud," Sabathany said.

"They most certainly are! I make much coin being me! I sent them on an all-expense paid cruise for their twenty-eighth anniversary, darling. Now, catch that tea!" Ja'brell Hunty replied.

Kendrick came from behind Sabathany and steered her away by her shoulders. "Thanks guys! I had fun!"

Once they were out of earshot, approaching the waiting limo, Kendrick yanked her by the arm. "What was all that about?"

Sabathany pulled away. "You're hurting me."

Kendrick loosened his grip. "Why'd you say that to him?"

"He looks like a clown with all that crap on."

"What business is it of yours what he does?"

"Okay, I think you better get on the right team, Honey."

"No, maybe you should. Ja'brell Hunty is very influential in the ATL. Why'd you dig at him like that?"

Sabathany saved her response until after they were inside the car. "Uh, is there something we need to talk about?"

"Hell no! You already know that ain't my thing."

"Do I?"

"Don't clown on me. What I want to know is why you're so put off by them? They ain't done nothing to you."

"Because those people disgust me. Sorry, but I don't understand why they have to be everywhere throwing their buffoonery in my face."

"You sound just like Lenox. I get why he would want to . . ." Kendrick stopped himself.

"No. Finish your sentence."

"I get why dudes act like that. But females have always been more open-minded."

Sabathany looked out the window, chased by a memory.

"Okay, babe, whatever is going on inside your head right now is a lot bigger than some ATL personality. Are you going to tell me what's wrong?"

Sabathany could feel the corners of her eyes become damp. She tilted her head back in hopes of keeping those unwanted tears from spilling, but they were unrelenting.

Kendrick sensed more to the story, and that Sabathany's mind was taking her to a very dark place.

"I had a foster parent named Tyrone. He worked at some cabaret as a drag queen, and a lot of times he'd come home still dressed up. He'd bring this guy named Silk home. They would sit up half the night drinking, then sometimes they'd go in Tyrone's bedroom and close the door. They would turn on the stereo to cover all the noise they made."

Sabathany's voice moved from sadness to disgust as she recalled the past. "Sometimes Silk would see me when I'd still be up waiting for Tyrone to feed me because he kept the food locked up. And there were times when I caught him staring at me as I ate whatever scraps Tyrone gave me."

Sabathany leaned into Kendrick for comfort. The memory continued playing itself vividly behind her closed eyes.

"One night, Silk had come over and he and Tyrone had been drinking like usual. I'd gone to bed, but got up at some point to use the bathroom. When I looked in the living room, Tyrone was passed out on the sofa and Silk was still up watching TV. When I went back to my bedroom Silk was standing in my room. He said, 'Hey there! Why don't you show me around your room?' I told him to get out of my room. He said, 'you better get over here and sit your little ass down!' So I did. He took his shoes off and pushed me further onto my bed and started dry humping against me."

Sabathany's cry turned convulsive. She lurched forward into a steady rocking. Kendrick hugged her to bring down some of the shaking.

"At twelve years old I froze. I didn't know what to say or do. He kissed all over my body, and felt my privates. It didn't bother him at all that I didn't like it."

"What happened next?" Kendrick asked, fully engrossed in the story, and fearful of what she would tell him next.

"When I told him to stop," she whispered, "Silk's hand froze. I could hear his heartbeat thumping through all the gold chains hanging from his neck. He left and didn't return until two weeks later. Again, he waited until Tyrone passed out, and snuck into my bedroom. That time he made me go all the way with him. He kept on until I was fourteen. Tyrone never knew, and kept letting the son of a bitch come over because he thought he had Silk all to himself."

"Tyrone never found out?" Kendrick asked in disbelief.

"Eventually. Silk had warned me back when it all started that bitches who run their mouths get their throats slit. He said if I wanted to end up like them, all I needed to do was say something."

Kendrick squeezed her shoulders. "Goddamn him!"

"But Silk started to get scared I was going to tell, so one day out of the blue, he decided to lie to Tyrone and say that on a number of occasions I'd been waiting outside the bathroom, ready to expose myself to him after he finished using the toilet."

"What?"

Sabathany sat up straight. Rage swallowed sadness. "Yep, he sure did. And Tyrone said to me, 'I guess you're never too young to be a slut! Now I know why Silk be lettin' me drink my ass to sleep! Here I am tryin' to give you a place to stay and all the while you up here tryin' to take somebody's man!' He tore through my room, throwing every piece of clothes I had into a garbage bag. He grabbed a couple of Ding Dongs and a juice box and put them into a smaller paper bag and threw it all at me and said, 'Take your fast ass on somewhere! Go wave your little coochie in somebody else's face!'"

There was a break in Sabathany's anger. She began to melt back into vulnerability. "He didn't even bother to ask me if it was true or not," she said, weeping into Kendrick's chest.

Kendrick held fast to her, rocking her into an eventual calm. But Sabathany's confession cast a dark cloud on the ride to the airport. And what lie ahead in Miami did very little to make things any better.

FIFTEEN

October 25, 2013

The Fontainebleau Hotel

Kendrick Black walked into the conference room not expecting to see what he saw. The room was filled with media. TV cameras were set up everywhere. On an elevation located at the front of the room, there was a rectangular table with an elegant, burgundy fabric draping the front. Two bottles of water had been placed in front of each chair. Two easels with large movie posters of *It Is What It Is* were positioned, one on either end of the table.

Kendrick sat down. Only a few members of the media bothered taking pictures, a rather subdued response given the number of reporters. A hotel employee approached the actor and wanted to know if she could bring him something to drink.

"No, thank you. This bottled water is just fine," he said with a wink.

The employee blushed, touched her cheek as if it had been kissed, and walked away.

The double doors opened and Shannon Dwight, Kendrick's co-star, came through, surrounded by entourage. Every media person leapt to their feet, snapping pictures of the actress in her black vintage, A-line dress, a contrast against her milky white skin. She wore a string of pearls, and her hair was pulled back into a messy bun. Shannon's red lips popped the perfect color.

She seemed to float through, as though carried by her team. As she texted, she appeared oblivious to everyone there.

With four consecutively high-grossing films, Shannon Dwight carved out a spot as one of Hollywood's most bankable actresses. Although she had classic beauty and sophisticated sex appeal, she took her craft seriously, often being labeled as the young Meryl Streep.

Shannon was still texting by the time she sat next to Kendrick, who had been under the impression that he was going it alone on this press junket, and thought she was still on location shooting another film. She nodded a quick acknowledgment and muttered an even quicker, "Hey." Hair and makeup people emerged from her little mob and tended to last minute touch-ups.

Working with Shannon had been hell. Kendrick thought she was too young to take herself so seriously. But she was a brilliant actress, a true chameleon with great comedic timing. Kendrick was willing to put up with her sourness because he stood to benefit from her appeal and connection to the project. Bringing Shannon on this leg of the media blitz guaranteed more attention to the film, and to him, since she already enjoyed the mainstream celebrity Kendrick hungered for.

"I wasn't expecting to see you," Kendrick said, leaning into her as she clicked out her texts.

"Just go with it." Her tone was impatient, like someone chiding an amateur.

When Judith Martin, host of the local TV show *Today in Miami* arrived ready to field questions from the press, Shannon Dwight turned "on".

"Shannon, tell us what drew you to this project?"

"I wanted to do more romantic comedies. And I love that the obvious racial difference between the characters isn't harped on. Yeah, Margaret is white and David is African-American. So what? The couple is allowed to be in love, and experience that love without their races playing a huge role in any of it."

"Kendrick, same question . . ."

"Exactly what Shannon just said. Love is love, no matter what packaging it comes in. I see all kinds of interracial couples walking down the streets together. This film reflects the normalcy of it. That's what makes the script so great. I think people knew they couldn't hold up an entire movie on racial conflict. Not that it doesn't exist, but I think they recognize the overall trajectory society is moving in, and wanted to create a film that showed that."

"What was it like to work with one another?"

Shannon beamed as she placed a hand on Kendrick's chest. "Let me tell you something about this guy. This man is absolutely fabulous. He's incredibly giving. A true pleasure to work with. Not to mention that he's incredibly easy on the eyes."

Kendrick smiled, amazed with how fantastically insincere his co-star was. "Yeah, Shannon drives herself, man. She's the ultimate pro. And she's easy on the eyes, too."

The room turned warm. Kendrick swigged from his water. He relaxed and allowed Shannon to have her moment, figuring the media was mostly there to see her anyway. But he knew what to expect going forward. The next time they did press together he would handle her differently, going for his glory from the outset. No sudden slick conversational maneuvers, and no surprises.

While Shannon flung charm to the reporters, Kendrick scanned the room to see if Sabathany had changed her mind and come down to show her support. She had not spoken since her revelation, opting to sequester herself in the large penthouse suite. Last he saw her, she was lying in fetal position with sheets pulled over herself. He did not want to pry any further, and regretted knowing the little he found out. Kendrick surveyed the room, noticing a scruffily dressed man in the rear of the room, holding a small note pad in one hand and waving his other hand to be called on.

"Yes?" Judith Martin said, acknowledging him.

"My question is for Mr. Black. I'm curious how he thinks leaking a sex tape is going to square with the release of *It Is What It Is?*"

Kendrick straightened himself in his seat. "Pardon me?"

The man grinned with satisfaction that he had everyone's attention. "Better still, I'd like to know if you thought leaking a sex tape to coincide with the release of the film would help give you publicity since you're considerably less known than your co-star."

"What sex tape? There is no sex tape," Kendrick said, annoyed with the underhandedness of the question and its implications. There was no Brenda or entourage to steer him from trouble. Kendrick felt alone, sensing an even greater distance between himself and Shannon, who he knew was pissed because she was no longer the center of attention.

"Shannon, what do you have to say about your co-star employing such tactics to become known?" the man asked.

She looked at Kendrick, hoping for some indication as to how he would like her to answer the question, but he never met her gaze. Instead he nervously picked lint from his shirt.

Shannon glared at the reporter. "Is this some sort of joke?" she asked. "If he says there's no tape, then there's no tape!"

Kendrick rose to leave the table. He cut down the middle of the room toward the double doors. The same media that sat around, not caring who he was before wanted to hear what he had to say and clicked frame after frame of his every step. Their collective chant of "Mr. Black! Mr. Black!" sounded cult-like.

The elevator opened the instant he pushed the button. He got in and repeatedly pushed the button to close the door. A heavy tide of media followed. A rush of gratitude overcame Kendrick when the doors closed just as reporters thrashed upon themselves like waves.

When Kendrick got to his room, he ran his key card along the lock sensor, and waited for the tiny red light to turn green. He entered the suite. The air conditioner did its job in cooling the room. Kendrick walked into the middle of the living room. "Sabathany!" he yelled. He glanced toward the bedroom, then at the bar. *I know this bitch hears me,* he thought as he poured himself a shot of the best whiskey they had. Downing the shot, he marched into the bedroom to find Sabathany exactly as he left her. He snatched the sheets from the bed, yanking Sabathany along with them.

"What the hell is your problem?" she screamed, dazed and groggy. It was the first time they spoke since landing in Miami.

"Did you record us?" Kendrick asked.

"What?" She peered up from the floor. Her disheveled appearance was alarming considering her usual vanity.

Kendrick chucked the balled up sheets at her. "Don't 'what' me like you're trying to come up with something to say! You recorded us fucking, didn't you?"

Sabathany put her head down. "What's the big deal? Look at Kim and Paris. No sex tape ever hurt them."

"The big deal is that I just had to answer questions about a sex tape I knew nothing about. I felt humiliated down there!"

"Nobody cares about sex tapes these days, Honey. It's about what comes *after* the tape that counts. Think of all the opportunities."

"I already know what you're trying to do. You're trying to kill my career before it's even made it off the ground."

"Baby, you know that's not what I'm trying to do," Sabathany said, trying to reassure him.

Kendrick shook his own head, offended by her duplicity. "Pack your shit. You're going back to L.A."

"Baby . . ."

"Shut up! I don't want to hear it." Kendrick stormed into bathroom and slammed the door.

SIXTEEN

"Can you believe it?" Kendrick mused, swirling Courvoisier in his snifter. Brenda held a glass of wine. Both were curled up on her sofa. A fire crackled in the fireplace.

"What else would you expect from a thirsty, fame-seeker?" Brenda said. She tossed her braids over her shoulder as though they were a nuisance.

"And what makes it so bad is she said Kim Kardashian and Paris Hilton have one, and now they're making millions. Like that makes it any better."

"The thirst is real, I'm telling you!"

"What am I going to do with her? I can't trust her as far as I can throw her."

"I told you that you need to stay aware, didn't I? Not everyone you keep around you wants you to do well. Or, if they do, it's because they have some stake in it." Brenda drank her wine.

"That's why I hate this place. Brings out the worst in people!"

"If I were you, I'd get rid of her. You just said yourself you can't trust her. Why would you wanna keep someone like that around?"

Kendrick thought about it. "I don't know," he said finally.

Brenda rubbed her hands together, shuddering at her perception of the nonsense. "How did it go in New York?"

"My head was so screwed up; I couldn't concentrate on the interviews. Nobody was interested in the movie. All they wanted to talk about was the sex tape. I've never been so humiliated in my life. And on top of everything, I get a call from my mother, wanting to know if everything she's been hearing is true. Took me three hours to convince her that I had nothing to do with any of it."

"Listen, don't worry about the tape. I've got people on it. The video is being yanked. And for those who got it twisted and think there's money to be made off this, we've got a cease and desist for their asses. "

"I appreciate it." Kendrick leaned back, again swirling his brandy.

Brenda clicked the TV off, then dimmed the lights. Having gotten his side of the story, much of her disappointment faded. Her overall energy was relaxed. She put her feet up onto the glass table.

Kendrick sat, warmed by brandy and the fire. He stared at Brenda Vaughn, taking all of her in. *She sure does pull it together for a big girl,* he thought, marveling at how shapely her legs were.

Kendrick's eyes moved to the lusciousness of her lips. He watched them make contact with the wine glass. He envied the wine glass.

Kendrick could easily fall into the seduction of her fetching eyes. He spied her ample bosom, thrust forward in her low-cut blouse. He fantasized about burrowing his face between them, savoring their fullness. Kendrick scooted closer to her and delicately rubbed against her knee.

Brenda smiled, but wanted to laugh outright. "Boy, what do you think you're doing?"

"Can't I sit close to you?" Kendrick asked, activating his powerful gaze.

"Kenny, come on. Stop all of that. You think because you get a few women to go crazy over that eye thing you do that I'll fall for it, too?" She spoke to him as though dousing the flames of a horned-up teenager.

"No, Brenda, seriously. I've been thinking about this a lot lately. You're the only one in this town who cares about me. I get that you work for me, but you've always been straight with me. I feel like everyone else out here in L.A is working angles— doing something because they want something."

Brenda found Kendrick's Midwestern innocent act cute. "That's because they do. All the time I hear people say they're tired of fake people, but they themselves are fake. That's just the way it is out here, baby. Ain't gonna change no time soon."

Kendrick's eyes revealed sadness and yearning. "Damn shame you're the only person I know who keeps it real with me. I know I say it all the time, but you've done so much for me. I owe you so much." Kendrick's glance dropped again to her breasts.

Brenda put her glass down to adjust her blouse, aware of the attention her breasts were receiving. "And you think I want some of that as payback?" She pointed to the visible erection between his parted legs.

Embarrassed, Kendrick closed his legs. "I don't know what came over me. I'm sorry."

"It's okay, I get it. You've just realized the person you've been sharing a bed with is untrustworthy. And it hurts. So you feel like reaching out."

Kendrick nodded.

"But it's a good thing you know what you're dealing with. Now you know what you have to do now, right?"

"But you're wrong about one thing. I didn't just realize she's ratchet. There's been red flags." Kendrick lowered his voice, looking around even though they were the only two in the room. "I think she was trying to get pregnant."

Brenda rolled her eyes at that old trick. "I'm not surprised."

Kendrick chugged the remaining brandy. It went down harsher than he thought it would. Standing up, he took his keys from his pocket.

Brenda rose from the sofa. "Did I upset you?"

"No, just gave me something to think about. Sorry about earlier."

"Don't be sorry." A slight flirt danced in her tone. Brenda moved in close to him, her chest touching his. She smelled beautifully. She placed her arms around his neck and imparted a kiss upon him.

Kendrick's knees buckled. Her lips were succulent. He instantly wanted to taste them again. "What was that for?"

"Luck."

"For what?"

"I don't get involved in mess, Kenny. Clean up the mess and there's more where that came from."

"Oh, it's like that?"

"It's like that."

Kendrick was quiet for two beats. He accepted her words as a challenge, one he gladly planned to rise to. He stepped in for another kiss, but Brenda placed a hand to his chest to stop him. The warmth in her eyes was replaced by an eerie seriousness.

"No. I said, clean up the mess first." Brenda opened the front door, and stepped aside to allow him a clear path to leave.

Wanting to show that he could either take it or leave it, he left without saying another word. By the time he got to his car, he gave a final wave, but Brenda had already closed the door.

During the ride home, Kendrick thought of how he planned to break it off with Sabathany. As soon as he pulled up to the house, his stomach fluttered as though attacked by a million butterflies. There was no easy way to say the thing that would ultimately be best for both of them when he finally said it.

Kendrick called out to her but there was no answer. He went into the master bedroom and observed that things had been moved around. *She must've come by to grab a few items when she knew I was out,* he thought.

Last he saw her, she was getting into a cab destined for the Miami airport to fly back to Los Angeles. Before that, she had sequestered herself to a dark hotel room at the Fontainebleau. Sabathany refused to get out of bed because the memory of being molested overwhelmed her. He didn't want to believe that the same woman who had displayed such vulnerability, had also leaked a sex tape meant for her gain.

The time Kendrick spent alone in the house, he wanted to expel all the nervous energy buzzing inside him. He resented his peace of mind being contingent on the whimsy of the wrong woman. He was going to force her to own up to the truth of what she did, even if he had to trudge through her lies to get to it.

The morning of the premier, Sabathany finally sent a text announcing that she was on her way.

Kendrick held little faith that, "I'm on my way" was written with any intended urgency, but was relieved to finally have some communication from her. That didn't stop him from lurking about the foyer, awaiting her arrival, like a dog anticipating its owner's return. When he heard keys jingle, he threw open the door with the confidence of an "I gotcha." The two stared into each other's eyes before Kendrick finally said, "Where the hell have you been?"

"I was staying with Tammy," Sabathany replied. "Tammy Boone, meet Kendrick Black."

Tammy behaved like the usual star struck fan. "Oh my goodness, hi!"

"Hey," Kendrick said. He was not expecting company. Turning his attention back to Sabathany, he said, "Can I talk to you alone?"

"Tammy was good enough to let me crash at her place. She's a survivor, too."

"Survivor of what?"

"Survivor of sexual abuse."

Tammy confirmed with a sad nod.

"I'm sorry to hear that."

"I sort of figured after Miami that I needed to talk to someone," Sabathany said.

"But you know we have some talking of our own to do . . . alone."

"And we will. But right now we have company." Sabathany extended her hand to her friend. Tammy took it.

"Ask your company to wait for you in the other room."

Sabathany ushered Tammy further into the house. "Don't be rude. As soon as she leaves I'm all yours."

Tammy smiled awkwardly as she was led into the house. Kendrick remained at the door, watching the two women disappear around the corner. *She thinks she's slick,* Kendrick thought. But, Sabathany's bringing a friend over would not save her from what Kendrick had to tell her. In fact, it changed nothing at all.

Kendrick felt the light tapping of small fingers against his back, waking him from his nap. The tapping was followed by a gravelly, childish voice. "Hey, Mister," the voice said.

Kendrick rolled over to find Kayla Jones grinning malevolently from the foot of the sofa. She wore a pink dress, with pink and white butterflies clipped to her pigtail.

Frightened, Kendrick bolted upright, finding himself sur-rounded by an otherworldly stillness. "Why are you looking at me like that? Why are you bothering me?"

"Because you're a liar," the child's voice croaked. "And I hate liars."

"What did I lie about?"

"You said you're sorry."

"I am."

Excited to be haunting him, Kayla's grin broadened. "I can't tell."

"I swear I am."

Kayla stopped grinning. Her face became serious, and there was a sudden maturity in her voice. "Then turn yourself in."

Kendrick felt his stomach roll. "I can't. I've got too many people counting on me. But I promise you, I'll find a way to make this right!"

"You forget, I see everything. Just remember, in the end, there's only one way this is gonna end."

"What does that mean?"

"You know exactly what it means. Do the right thing, Mister; otherwise, I'll just keep coming back until you go crazy."

"Please." Kendrick pleaded, "Leave me alone!"

"Leave you alone? Mister, I'm just getting started!" Kayla gurgled a shallow sound from her dirt-filled throat. Her arms broke from their sockets like stumps of wood, and disintegrated into dust. Kayla's body ruptured open as it did in the forest. Kendrick wanted to run from the loud munching sound of the maggots as they enjoyed the girl's innards; however, his body refused to move, paralyzed by fear . . .

Kendrick jumped up, gasping for breath. His drenched shirt clung to his chest. Sweat rolled down his temples and forehead. The television flickered in front of him, bringing him back to the real world. Kendrick heard voices, and followed those voices to the master bedroom. Pausing in the doorway, he discovered both Sabathany and Tammy laughing with expensive clothes all around them. The sordid details of their sexual abuse seemed the furthest thing on either of their minds.

"Oh, hi. You're awake. Tammy was just helping me figure out what I'm wearing for the premier tonight," Sabathany said. She wore a pink jumpsuit with pink and white swirl-print heels.

Tammy sat on the bed, holding an iridescent white cocktail dress. She smiled and waved hello, but Kendrick ignored her.

"Why didn't you wake me up?" Kendrick asked.

"I don't know. I figured you must be tired. So I left you where you were."

With all the traveling, yes, he had been tired. But he knew it was nothing more than a convenient excuse allowing Sabathany to avoid talking to him.

"Listen, we need to talk."

Sabathany passed Tammy a look. "We're almost done," she said.

Kendrick remained in the doorway, almost as if he were waiting for disobedient teenagers to do what he asked them to do. He eyed the massive amount of pink in Sabathany's off-the-shoulder jumpsuit. And the side ponytail topping off the look was too similar to the dead child's. Kendrick wanted to know if Sabathany was taunting him, even though he knew that was not possible.

"You're wearing that?" Kendrick asked.

"What's wrong with it?" Sabathany replied, giving her image in the full length mirror another check.

"Don't you think that color is a tad childish?"

"Not for what I paid for it, I don't."

"I think it's cute," Tammy said.

Kendrick gave Tammy the side-eye. "Sabathany, you wanna tell your friend that you'll talk to her later?" Kendrick didn't look at Tammy full on, but motioned for her to take a hike.

Sabathany pursed her lips, her eyebrow arched. "I said we'll be done in a minute."

"You know, I really should get going," Tammy said.

"You don't have to go anywhere."

"I know, but I bet Craig is wondering when I'm gonna bring my ass home. I say you'll look beautiful in whatever you decide to wear, girl. Have a good time at the premier!" Tammy hugged Sabathany quickly and rushed past Kendrick, leaving with a less than pleasant impression.

"You know that wasn't called for," Sabathany said.

"How else was I going to get you alone? You know I've been wanting to speak to you. But I like how you tried using your friend to avoid me."

"Oh, you liked that, huh?"

Kendrick finally entered the room, but came to a halt in the middle of it. He expected her to say something meaningful, and behave as though she actually cared.

"Shouldn't you start getting ready?" she asked.

"You don't think there's anything wrong with taping an intimate moment without the other person's consent? And then you went ahead and leaked the damn thing."

"Will you relax? This ain't old Hollywood. The world's not gonna turn against you just because you like to have sex with your girlfriend. Hell, R. Kelly can piss on underage girls and he still has a career."

"Allegedly, and that's not the point. You made a very private moment public. And for what? To get on some reality show?"

"You've got your success. I'm just trying to get mine," Sabathany said, having made her peace with it. "Hell, sometimes you have to make opportunity happen for yourself.

Folks will be talking about us. They're gonna be talking about *me!*"

She checked to make sure the highlight under her eyes was just right, then slid the shoulder of her jumpsuit down a little further to reveal more of her bare skin. Her eyes became locked with Kendrick's reflection through the mirror.

"I'd really appreciate it if you'd find something else to wear," Kendrick said.

"Are you asking me or telling me?"

"I'm telling you."

Sabathany continued to stare. "Would it help if I wore it in black?"

"Let me see it first."

Sabathany left the vanity and disappeared inside the walk-in. After changing into the black version of the jumpsuit, she reemerged, dropping a pair of black heels to the floor and slipping her feet into them. "Better?"

"I guess."

"What's your damage? You told me to change, so I changed!" She made her way back to the vanity, then reached into her jewelry box to fish out a chunky, gold necklace to wear.

"Because you refuse to take responsibility for anything you do." Kendrick watched as Sabathany went about her business of getting ready. If she heard what he said she seemed unaffected by it. Kendrick shook his head and sighed deeply before he went into the bathroom. He removed his clothes and got into the shower, hoping to wash away the failure of the last year and a half. Time wasted on a woman whom had been slowly peeling back the layers to who she really was. All the while he refused to see it.

Kendrick lathered his work of art body. The years of weight training had paid off. He was on his way to becoming the object of America's affection, a thought which brought him back to thinking about the premier. And thanks to Sabathany, he was unable to enjoy the accomplishment.

"Yeah, she's definitely gotta go," he said, though he barely heard himself because of the pelting water over his words.

When he finished his shower, Sabathany was gone. He was thankful for the few moments alone, dressing in a dapper, sleek black suit, black shirt and silver tie.

Kendrick met Sabathany downstairs in the living room. She was looking at her phone, uninterested in how sexy the movie star thought he was. She also failed to notice his shaky hands from nervousness. He clasped them together in hopes of getting rid of the trembling, but to no avail.

"Guess there's no good time to tell you this," he said, shoving his hands into his pockets.

"Tell me what?"

"I can't do this."

"Do what?"

"This! You know, I used to ask myself why I felt so empty when it came to how I felt about you, why imagining a future with you never seemed authentic. Now I know. There's no way I can be with someone that I've always gotta be wondering what she's up to. I'm not going to force myself to be in love with someone like that."

"You're leaving me for someone else, aren't you?"

"No, there is no one else. I'm just not feeling this. I'm not feeling you." Kendrick's revelation was freeing. The trembling in his hands began to subside.

"This is all because I want the world to know who I am, too?"

"Yeah, that and the fact you tried to get pregnant when I first came back to L.A. from seeing my family."

"And you picked the night of your premier to drop your little bombshell? How long have you been planning this?" There was a mix of surprise and hurt in her voice.

"I don't know, for a while now. Listen, I have no doubt you'll find someone. I just don't see it for us. Period."

The way he said, "period" sounded wobbly, especially when he dropped his gaze and began to fidget. Sabathany sensed his uncertainty the way a canine sensed fear.

She could only produce a smile because trying to argue would have been futile. She toyed with the necklace around her neck. "We're gonna be late."

Kendrick looked baffled. "Did you hear what I just said?"

"Yeah, I heard you."

"And you're still going to the premier?"

"And miss your big night? Not a chance," she said, breezing past him.

In the limo, Sabathany spent most of the ride posting photos of herself on social media. Kendrick stole a few glances of her. He had to admit, she looked ravishing.

It's too bad things didn't work out between us, he said inside his mind. He would have liked to have put one on her right there in back of the limo.

Knowing her own allure, Sabathany faced Kendrick with twinkling eyes. Her entire face lit up when she erupted into girlish laughter.

"What are you laughing at?"

"Just thinking about what you said earlier."

"And that's funny?"

Sabathany squinted. "No, the fact that you think I'm going to just let you walk away is funny."

"You had your chance to talk back at the house," he said, refusing to be drawn into another argument.

"But you've already gone ahead and set the tone for the evening."

"What tone?"

"You go sit next to Blondie on a talk show, and now you think you're mister big time."

Kendrick rolled his eyes. He wanted to put her out by the side of the road. "I'm not doing this now."

"Oh, I get it. You're too good to engage in my foolishness. Am I right?"

"Look, you chose to come along. Fine, whatever. But don't think you get to ruin my night."

"But I wouldn't dream of ruining your night. You're about to become America's Prince Charming. Though, I'd be curious to know what America will think once they find out you ran down a child in the street."

Kendrick felt something collapse inside his stomach. "What did you say?"

"Oh yeah, I know all about that. Actually, I overheard you talking to your sister." Sabathany enjoyed seeing the guilt appear on Kendrick's face. His eyes twitched. "You're not going to waste both our time denying it, are you?"

"It was an accident."

"Of course it was."

"I suppose this is the part where I beg you not to say anything."

"You catch on quick."

"What do you want?"

"I want you to set the date."

"There's no way in hell I'm marrying you," he said.

"Kenny, Darling, this doesn't have to get ugly. It doesn't even have to become difficult. If you play nice with me, then I'll play nice with you."

The limo slowed to a halt. Paparazzi swarmed the car, cameras clicked and clacked as flash bulbs popped off. The chauffer opened the door. Both Kendrick and Sabathany peered out onto the endlessly long tongue of red carpet.

"We'll talk about this later," Sabathany said, playfully tossing her side ponytail forward before stepping out. "In the meantime, why don't you be a good boy and smile for the cameras?"

SEVENTEEN

"Sabathany knows, Lenox. *She fucking knows!*" Kendrick practically cried into the phone.

"How did she find out?" Lenox asked with urgency in his voice. The last thing he needed was for Kendrick to have a moment of regret in making the call.

"It doesn't even matter at this point."

"It does matter."

"The night you dropped Paris off at the apartment, I'd had a bad dream and went into the kitchen. Paris came in later and we got to talking about everything. I couldn't keep it in. I guess Sabathany overheard us."

"You guess or you know she overheard you?"

"Oh no, she told me she did."

Lenox glowered on his end of the phone, realizing the family trait—neither Kendrick nor his sister were capable of keeping their mouths shut. "I told you not to say anything. You should've denied it, especially to that bitch!"

"I admit it, I messed up," Kendrick said.

"Okay, so what do you want to do now?"

"She wants me to marry her."

"Man, stop playin'."

"I'm serious."

"But you ain't, right?"

"If I don't, she'll go public."

They discussed the possibility of making Sabathany sign a confidentiality agreement, stating that once married to Kendrick she was prohibited from discussing anything having to do with him—past, present or future. If she breached the contract, she relinquished all claim to financial settlements in the divorce.

"I like the sound of that. But can you get her to sign it?" Lenox asked after hearing the full idea.

"That's where you come in. I'll tell her if we're going to move forward as a married couple then we're doing it my way. I'll have the papers drawn up and sent to Minneapolis. It'll be explained to her that I'm putting her on a plane. You'll see to it that she signs them."

"Why don't I come out to L.A.?"

"No, no. I need to get her as far from me as I can. I need time to think."

"What if she refuses to sign?"

"Sabathany is greedy. She might give you a little lip at first, but I know her. She'll sign them."

"Okay, let me know when you get everything done on your end."

"Will do. Thanks."

There was something soothing in Kendrick's tone. Lenox felt as though Kendrick were speaking to him as his friend, not just an errand boy he could throw orders at. Lenox wanted desperately to settle back into the comfort of their friendship, to be close again—close enough to broach an uncomfortable subject.

"Listen, about me and your sister . . ."

"I don't want to talk about that."

"Wait, hear me out. I just wanted to say that I broke it off with her. No female should come between our friendship. That includes Paris."

"That doesn't fix things. I keep asking myself if you're the same person I knew in high school who had all those Pam Grier posters all over his walls, and how you you'd go on and on about fantasizing about putting a baby in her."

"So what?"

"So, you were running around trying to act like the big man."

"You act like your shit is perfect. Am I clowning you on your choices, and the fact that your girlfriend is blackmailing you?"

"No, but I'm not screwing your sister either. And at least my girlfriend has . . . never mind."

Lenox's heartbeat quickened the moment he realized that he misjudged the timing of mentioning any of it. But it was too late to take it back. He became stumped for something to say.

"Dude, you didn't even have enough respect for our friendship to be truthful with it. You hid the fact you were in a relationship with my sister. This isn't something you just slipped into. You've been messing around for years!"

"Yeah, but I told you I broke it off."

"And?"

"I thought with everything you've got going on maybe we could move past this."

"Tell you what . . . you get that bitch to sign the papers and I'll think about it."

"I will. You don't have to worry about it. I'll take care of it," he promised, hoping it would make the difference.

It was the sincerest declaration Kendrick never heard. After Lenox finished speaking he waited for a response, but got the sound of a dial tone.

Later, Kendrick found himself back on Brenda's sofa. After two glasses of wine, he had the liquid courage to open up about everything. When he finished saying all he could say, Brenda rubbed his shoulder.

"Thanks for telling me. You did the right thing."

Kendrick wasn't so sure, but felt lighter having confided in Brenda about everything—from hitting little Kayla Jones, up through the moment Sabathany threatened him with what she knew.

"And you think marrying her is the answer?"

Kendrick took a sip of his wine, which gave Brenda the excuse to sip hers. He shrugged. "I guess I'm trapped."

"Yes, you are," Brenda said with a wink. "But you don't have to be."

EIGHTEEN

Sabathany's arms overflowed with bridal and wedding magazines; she didn't think she would make it into the house. The magazines spilled and trailed onto the floor as the landline rang. Sabathany let the remaining magazines fall where they did to reach across the kitchen peninsula. The number flashing on the phone had a 612 area code. Though she knew the call originated from Minneapolis she didn't recognize the number, and let it go to the answering machine.

"Now I see why you didn't promise not to say anything. You couldn't wait to go run your mouth to Lenox, could you? Hope you're happy, because he left me. Thanks a lot! It's really messed up how you two think you're the only ones who get to have the happily ever after. Like no one else gets to find love besides you! And the thing is, you know how difficult it is for someone like me to find someone who's not afraid of commitment. But that's all right. I've got something for both of you. You didn't think about that, did you? You didn't think by you putting your nose where it doesn't belong that you started a whole lot of mess. Well, what I've got planned for the two of you, you'll have no one to blame but yourselves. Good looking out, brother of mine. I hope you're satisfied."

Sabathany smirked. "She's got heart. I'll give her that much."

She spent the next couple of hours snacking on sesame sticks while flipping through the magazines. She placed colored tabs on the pages of dresses and wedding ideas she fancied. At one point Sabathany rose to stretch her legs. She needed a second pair of eyes, but Tammy was at work. All of Hollywood, and Tammy was the best she could come up with to be her maid of honor? She was pitiful at best, cursed by a lack of curves and gangling limbs, pockmarked skin, and nappy roots. It would be a waste of good money to make Tammy over because she would never commit to the upkeep. However, that worked out perfectly because whenever Sabathany wanted to feel better about herself, all she needed to do was stand next to Tammy.

"That settles it. After the wedding, I'm kicking Tammy to the curb. She ain't ready to roll in the big leagues." Sabathany returned to the computer and typed in "celebrity weddings." As far as her choice of potential dress maker, she decided on Vera Wang or Michael Costello. The wedding was to be the height of opulence, serving as inspiration for weddings to come. She envisioned Oprah and Beyoncé standing in line to wish her and Kendrick luck. Sabathany wanted to pack the church with five hundred people even though she didn't know five hundred, but she would settle for two hundred. Dinner would consist of three choices: Argentinean beef filet, wild striped Bass or mustard grilled chicken, all served with grilled asparagus and roasted rosemary potatoes. And for dessert, a seven tiered, red velvet cake so moist that it dissolved on the tongue.

For the honeymoon, the newlyweds would climb into a limo and be whisked away to the airport to board a private jet for Bali. And on this honeymoon, she planned to become pregnant with the first of six children—three boys and three girls.

When Kendrick came home from Brenda's, Sabathany was imagining the fabulous gifts they would receive. He had no idea he was about to burst her dream bubble.

"Good, you're home," he said, standing in the doorway of her office.

"Hey Sweetie! I was just thinking about the wedding. Have you come up with a date yet?

Kendrick noticed all of the magazines strewn about. "Yeah, about that. There's something I need you to do first." He left the room, hoping to have piqued Sabathany's curiosity.

She followed him to the kitchen. A bag of fast food rested near the house phone, which reminded her that Paris called.

"What do you need me to do?" she asked.

"I'm having a confidentiality agreement drawn up. I'll need you to sign it before we get married."

"What? No prenup?" she asked, flippantly.

"Oh, that's coming. Don't you worry."

"I don't understand the purpose of this," she said, jolted from the assumption her threat would have gone unchallenged.

Kendrick was strident. "Come on now. You're too smart to play this dumb. The papers should be done in a couple weeks, at such time you'll board a plane to Minneapolis. Lenox will meet you at a determined location and you're going to sign the papers. And I don't expect to get any calls that you won't sign them."

"You seem to forget who's holding all the power."

"Oh, is that what this is?" Kendrick said, tickled by her overconfidence. "You'll sign the papers or there won't be any wedding. Period." Then he walked away.

"So, it's like that?" she muttered. She looked over at the answering machine. Kendrick seemed elated to have found his testicular fortitude. Why spoil his rediscovered manhood with an angry sounding message from Paris?

"I think I'll keep this one to myself," she said, and hit DELETE. She would sign his silly papers if it meant having the wedding of her dreams. She needed this wedding to fulfill the two things she longed for—security and not being alone.

Kendrick may have been angry, but he would grow to love her. For his sake he had better, because if for some reason Kendrick decided to renege, Sabathany would remind him that she had a little something on him that might serve as an incentive to keep his promise.

NINETEEN

Paris checked her cell phone, hoping to hear from her brother. He had not returned any of her calls. It broke her heart that he had become one of those judgmental-type people he used to shake his head at, who never walked a moment in her shoes.

Paris moved to the corner of the loveseat, hoping to disappear all the while knowing it was impossible. She craved a hug from the one person who gave the best hugs—Lenox. His hugs were all encompassing; they blocked out fear. They were a rare and tender reminder that he had once opened his heart to her.

Paris focused her attention toward the blank space just above the flat screen TV. Memories hovered, dense like storm clouds.

Paris turned off the generic noise of the TV and forced herself up from the couch. She knew that once the confrontation began there would be no turning back. Still, she hoped to find even the smallest trace of love behind his eyes when they met face to face. Lenox needed to see her heartbreak up close if he was going to realize the folly of denying his feelings. He needed reminding that he had loved her first. Hopefully that would be enough. But in case that did not work, there was always good ole fashioned revenge to fall back on.

The neighborhood was different from the way Paris remembered it. Craftsman-style homes sat on reasonably maintained lots, framed by jack pine trees.

Paris was surprised she even remembered the general area. She was drunk the night Lenox met up with her at Delilah's Cabaret. They were on their way to her place when he decided to stop at his house to make up with his wife while Paris waited in the car, struggling not to pass out.

I should've seen the disrespect then, she thought, continuing down the winding, narrow streets, lined on either side with SUVs and station wagons.

Daylight had begun to slip away, with just enough light left to make out the houses. They all looked alike, yet different at the same time.

Lenox was in the yard out front of a gray house with maroon trim. He was smiling, something Paris rarely saw him do. The twins were on their knees playing with a small tan, floppy-eared puppy. The puppy ran circles, enjoying the attention it received. It yipped excitedly into the coming night. Then Paris noticed the wife, a light-complexioned, short haired woman who seemed to be enjoying her life. There was no indication that Lenox stepped out on her, or had any intention of leaving.

Paris was startled by the toot of the horn from an oncoming car, warning her that she had veered too far over. She swerved, allowing the car to pass, and ignoring the glare of the passing driver. She continued down the block, and pulled into the next available parking spot.

Turning the car off, she was hit with the compulsion to weep into the steering wheel. What she had just witnessed bore no resemblance to what Lenox told her. That woman in the yard did not look like someone who nagged her husband into a loveless, sexless marriage. The warmth in both their eyes proved love was still very much alive in their relationship. The realization that he had no intention of leaving his family hit Paris like a fist.

"It's not fair!" she sobbed. She checked her phone to see if he answered the text stating she wanted to talk to him.

"Can't you take a hint? Leave me alone!" Lenox's reply read.

Delirium set in, as Paris didn't know whether to laugh or cry at the cold response. She felt like an irritant—a gnat being swatted away.

"Why should I be the only one who has to sacrifice? Why does he get to have it all?" she asked. Anger replaced drying tears and sadness. Before she lost the nerve, Paris got out of the car, activating the auto lock on the car. She charged down the sidewalk, her steps long and purposeful. She could see the Hunter family's jovial movement down the street. She was angry with herself for giving her heart to a man who selfishly ruined her life. If she was going to be declared the loser of this, she would make sure Lenox fared no better.

Paris approached the front of Lenox's house. The family interaction played out like a scene from a movie. The children rolled on top of hardened grass with the tan puppy, it licking its new playmates. Laughter permeated their perfect world. The wife looked on, happy because they were happy. She looked up from their frolic to a distressed woman, standing at the steps of the house.

"Hi, there! Can I help you with something?" she asked, extending her smile to the woman.

The wife's voice sounded different then Paris imagined, the few times she tried imagining it. It was sweet and trusting, the antithesis of a woman unhappy with her marriage.

Lenox's face froze from alarm when he followed his wife's gaze to Paris.

Paris paused herself, unable to do what she had come to do. She had been looking forward to staking her claim, but the bravado that had been building since the walk from the car disappeared. Suddenly, the idea to wreak a little havoc was less appealing in light of what he stood to lose. Paris hated that she even cared. She no longer wished to become the reason behind the breakup of a family, or these children crying out for a father who could no longer be with them.

Paris spoke up, "Hi! I've been trying for the life of me to find this bakery that sells really big chocolate chip cookies. Do you know where it is?"

The wife relaxed her eyes. "Oh, yes. You want Ruby's bakery. It's three blocks over," she said, pointing in the direction Paris should go.

"Thank you so much," Paris said, forcing a smile.

"You're welcome. The cookies are delicious. I know you're gonna love them!"

"I'm sure I will. By the way, you have a lovely family."

"Oh, thank you," the wife said. "Do you have children?"

Paris's eyes jumped to Lenox, who moved closer to his wife, placing a protective arm around her, making it clear that he made his choice. His eyes carried a warning in them.

"No. I'm afraid I don't," she said, backing away as though she suddenly became aware of the danger. "Thanks again for the directions. Have a great night." Then she quickly proceeded back to her car, resisting the urge to give Lenox a parting look.

As soon as Paris returned to the car and fastened her seatbelt, she laughed uncontrollably. It was as though she had stuck her head inside the mouth of a lion and lived to brag about it. Just as she turned the ignition of her car, she received notification from her phone of a new text. Tapping the icon, she retrieved the message.

"Thought you were smarter than that. You really don't wanna fuck with me!"

Paris grinned. "No, Lenox, you don't wanna fuck with me," she said.

Getting a rise out of Lenox redeemed the visit. As a treat to herself, Paris made her way to Ruby's bakery.

And the wife was right, the cookies were delicious.

TWENTY

November 18, 2013

3:20PM

"Your champagne sucks," Sabathany said to the flight crew as she exited the aircraft. "That's if you can even call it champagne." She chuckled to herself as she walked the jet bridge like a diva.

Other than the crappy sparkling wine, the flight had been a smooth one, though she was surprised Kendrick had not rigged it so that she rode with the luggage. Sabathany expected her driver to be outside waiting with a popped trunk to slip her luggage into it. The sooner they could get moving the better before she got anymore of "the look."

The sex tape thing blew up in her face. She hated the double standard, which in her opinion allowed white women to survive leaked tapes by sitting down with publicists and executives to discuss brand expansion, whereas she was just another dehydrated, fame-thirsty whore trying to dig her claws into any kind of notoriety available. She read the magazines, and online gossip blogs. All of them said the same thing—Kendrick Black needed to kick her to the curb. Public opinion being what it was, she could not go anywhere without getting dirty looks from people.

Outside on the arrivals deck, Sabathany waited for her ride. Five minutes became ten, then fifteen to twenty. She took

132

out her phone, surprised with herself for waiting that long to see what was keeping her ride. There were moisture spots on the phone's screen that expanded as she pressed her thumb into them. She had no idea where they came from. When she attempted powering off the screen changed from black to deep purple, followed by the faintness of a familiar chirp. Sabathany looked around for someone to lend her a cell phone when she realized she had no idea who to call in Minneapolis.

More and more people got picked up and drove away. Soon, there were no cars left, except for one far down by door one. Sabathany was at door twelve. She dragged her carry-on toward the car, praying the driver had mistakenly parked at the wrong door. Drawing nearer, she saw how beat-up the car was. No way it was her driver, and even if it were, she would never be caught dead getting into the rusty car, BMW or not.

"Where's my car service?" she whined aloud. "Where's Lenox?' she wondered. Wasn't he the one witnessing her signatures? At the very least he could have been the one to pick her up.

Sabathany became startled by the blast of a techno ringtone, which was not the ringtone she set but she was grateful the phone worked the little it did.

"Hello?"

"How was the flight?" It was Kendrick, sounding overly enthused to speak to her.

"Where's my driver?"

"Aren't there cabs sitting out there?"

"Why are you playing with me, Kenny? You know damn well that I don't do cabs!"

"That's right, I forgot. Well, there's also a lightrail tram that leaves from the airport. You better hop on it."

"You think this is a joke?"

"This whole relationship is a joke."

She ignored his last statement. "Where's Lenox?"

"No idea."

"Will you call him and tell him to come pick me up. Or, if you can't be bothered, give me the number and *I'll* do it."

"He doesn't work for you. He works for me." The line went dead.

"Oh, so you wanna play, Kenny? Sabathany asked, staring at CALL ENDED flashing on the phone. "Fine. Let's play."

There were no cabs sitting idle as Kendrick suggested. Sabathany proceeded back inside the airport in search of signage pointing to a taxi stand. As she walked, her blood boiled. Kendrick's flippant way of dealing with her was not the beginning she expected, or felt she deserved.

After taking the escalator to the lowest level she approached a bunch of Somali and white drivers chatting together outside their cabs. Conversations quieted with all eyes on her. Some of the drivers scampered to their vehicles, wanting her to cut the line and select them.

"Where you go, lady?" a driver with a heavy accent said to her from his first spot in line.

"I need to go to Loring Park."

The man scowled. "Too much gay at the park. You gay?"

Sabathany laughed. "Uh, not at all."

The driver's face calmed. "Ok. Get in."

Sabathany waited for the driver to assist with her carry-on in the trunk, but was shocked when she saw the trunk pop open and the driver remained inside the car. She gave the other drivers an incredulous glance, but received no sympathy for choosing him. Sighing, she placed the luggage in the trunk herself.

"Thanks for the help."

"Where in Loring Park you want to go?"

Sabathany read the address from a piece of paper.

"Oh," he said in a pleasantly surprised tone.

"Oh?" Sabathany asked. "*Now* it's worth your time?"

The driver did not respond. He turned on the radio. Sabathany was unaccustomed to the prayer music blaring whiningly from the speaker. She would have preferred the local R&B station or Top 40 at the very least, but decided not to protest, doubting the driver would care. Instead, she crossed her arms, bit her lower lip and slinked into her corner of the back seat, hoping for a quick trip to Kendrick's penthouse.

As the ride went on, strange terrain and landscape passed her by. Without Kendrick there to nuzzle and make out with, she could pay attention to the environment around her. Thankfully the view provided a temporary comfort from the blaring music.

When they arrived out front of the building, the driver popped the trunk, but again made no effort to assist her. A doorman came out of the building and began taking Sabathany's bags.

"That's all right. Just don't get mad when you get squat for a tip," she said after reading the meter. Sabathany counted out exact change and let it drop wherever it fell into the front seat, not bothering to hand it to the driver.

"Say, wasn't he supposed to charge me a flat fare?" she asked the doorman. But before he responded she said, "You know what? Never mind." She was glad to be rid of the useless driver. After the professional greeting and assistance from the doorman, she gave him what she would have tipped the driver, and then some.

The apartment felt cold without Kendrick there. She second-guessed how she played her hand. The intent was to get Kendrick to love her, not drop her like Michael Wray did. Any deceit and machinations stemmed from self-preservation. Since there were no guarantees in life, sometimes people had nothing but their hustle to get through it. Kendrick should have understood that and cut her some slack.

LLOYD JOHNSON

Sabathany moved toward the sofa where they made love for what she guessed was the last time. But as much as Sabathany liked to think on what could have been, she realized there was no going back. Kendrick made it clear that he had no intention of working on their relationship. What remained between them was nothing more than a business arrangement. But what would she gain by signing the documents? An allowance? Trinkets when he saw fit? The only thing he had given her recently were cold eyes and an emotionally vacant heart.

Sabathany hung on to the thought as she rolled the luggage into the master bedroom. Then she ran herself a bath. There was something about the relaxation from soaking in a tub that opened her mind and sent ideas her way. When the water was just right, she poured herself a glass of wine and slipped into the water.

Any marriage to Kendrick would be loveless on his end. She understood. So again, what was the point? Since she was unable to win his heart, then at the very least she wanted all that she could get from him. But he was far more valuable to her if he thought she could spill the beans on him at any time.

"I want that son of a bitch to know that I own him. He won't be able to take a dump without me knowing about it!"

TWENTY-ONE

It was a little after one o'clock when Kendrick met Brenda at the outdoor café on the corner of Santa Monica Blvd. and Robertson. Kendrick wore jeans and a red and white striped button-down shirt. His pectoral muscles squeezed the fabric nicely.

Brenda wore a powder blue sundress; her braided hair was coiled into a bun centered on the top of her head. Her lips were glossed to perfection.

Kendrick noticed them immediately.

"Thank you for meeting me," Brenda said, watching him ease into the seat like only he could. The server waited patiently for Kendrick to get settled before taking his drink order.

"The iced tea is really good here," Brenda said. "They spiked mine with a little lemonade and a splash of vodka, in case you're interested."

"I like how you think," Kendrick said, matching Brenda's mischievous smirk with one of his own. He glanced at his watch. It was too early in the day for him to drink. "I'm going to be boring and take a regular iced tea."

The server nodded. "Very good, sir. You'll find the list of specials inside of the menu in front of you." Then he left them to get the drink.

Brenda took off her sunglasses and checked for smudges. "I received a couple of interesting phone calls today."

Kendrick's eyebrows raised. "Really? How interesting?"

"Truly change your life interesting."

"I'm intrigued."

"For starters, the pre-release reviews coming in for your movie have been fabulous. If the public agrees, that'll only help your bankability. I guess I should let you know that there has been some interest in you for a couple of future projects. One is a heist film where you'd be co-starring with Mark Walberg. The second is a buddy comedy. You'd get second billing to Kevin Hart, of course, but the good news is that he personally asked to get you."

"You're joking."

"Nope. You're really hot right now."

"I guess I am." Kendrick became thoughtful. "Any talk about money?"

"You're looking at seven figures per movie."

"How deep are the seven figures?"

"Last I heard, they were talking five million. But if box office receipts for the new film are on point opening week, it's possible we could get you more."

"I like the sound of that." Kendrick acknowledged the server when he brought his beverage. Then, looking back at Brenda he said, "Are you ready to order?"

"They make an awesome turkey club Panini with a Cajun potato salad."

Kendrick passed the server his menu. "Sounds good. I'll take that."

"Me, too." Brenda said, following suit.

A few people passed their table, giving Kendrick the stare he had become accustomed to. They accepted his polite smile as invitation to approach the table and ask for autographs and selfies. He delighted in giving them what they wanted. Brenda sat quietly, smiling at her latest creation.

When the last of the fans left, she said, "Feels good, doesn't it?"

Kendrick could not deny that, yes, it did feel good to be recognized. "Thankfully I haven't gotten tired of it yet."

"Believe me, you'll have those days when you want to tell people to leave you the hell alone. Just do your best to stay centered, and be gracious. And remember those of us who helped you to get to where you are."

"I would never forget you," he said before his face dissolved into a look that read he had been wrestling with something.

"What's wrong?"

"I keep thinking what if this is too good to be true?"

"Kenny, when good things happen to you, just say thank you. Don't ask a whole lotta questions. You've worked very hard in the time that I've known you, and it's paying off." Brenda could tell her words were having little effect, especially when he stared off toward Santa Monica Blvd. She stroked his forearm.

"This is supposed to be a happy time. What's going on with you?"

Kendrick tried to smile, but it felt weak at best. Disheartenment settled in.

"I still have nightmares about the girl. I think she's haunting me."

Brenda listened, unsure whether the confession was for her benefit or his.

"I don't think that little girl is going to let me have any peace of mind unless I turn myself in."

"Kenny, you don't have to turn yourself in," she said quietly, scanning to see who was around them.

"Yeah, I do. It's the right thing to do." He quieted down as soon as the food came.

Brenda waited for the server to leave before saying, "Then, why don't you hop your ass on a flight to Minneapolis and turn yourself in?"

"I don't know. Maybe I should."

"Look, no one here at this table is going to jail. You hired me to do a job, and damnit, I'm going to do it."

Kendrick didn't appear convinced.

"Okay, I understand that you feel terrible for what happened. You should feel terrible. But doing the right thing doesn't necessarily mean doing prison time. Here's what we'll do. I'll set up a press conference. You'll say that you're a native Minnesotan and the family's story touched your heart. In fact, you can say that your thoughts and prayers go out to the family, and you'd like to create a foundation in the child's name. In effect you're paying restitution. This way, you can address the issue without placing yourself at the center of an investigation. How does that sound?"

"Eat your Panini."

"You're not even going to consider it?"

"I didn't say that. We can talk about this back at the house."

Brenda did a double take. "I don't remember being invited."

"Eat your Panini," Kendrick said again, this time with a wink.

Brenda had no idea how she could allow herself to be enticed back to Kendrick Black's house. Sure, she had dreamed about the sexy actor ever since he showed up at her office five years before requesting representation. She had a mental rolodex of fantasies, and two worn out vibrators to show for it. Now, here she was, in Kendrick's personal space, clearly because he wanted her there.

"Are you going to give me a tour?" Brenda asked, accepting a glass of blush from her host.

Kendrick poured a glass for himself. "You really want me to show you around this place?"

"Why not?" Brenda asked, then sipped.

Her eyes lit up after the first taste, though Kendrick guessed that any alcohol would have gotten the same reaction.

Kendrick led Brenda through the modern-style house, decked out in warm neutral colors and a lot of glass. Brenda noticed they were passing through much of the house without explanation, though it was obvious to her what the living and dining rooms were.

Brenda followed to the bedroom, where Kendrick moved into the middle of the room. He stopped and inhaled deeply, then exhaled, proud of the room's serenity as light brown and white window sheers danced against the breeze coming through an open window.

Brenda remained at the tip of the doorway. Poking her head in she asked, "What's in there?"

"It's called a bedroom."

Brenda gave a playful side-eye. "I know that. I mean, why are you showing me your bedroom?"

"Because you know how people say their homes are their sanctuary? My bedroom is mine."

Brenda stepped into the beautiful room. White orchids adorned both end tables by the bed, and dresser, along with jasmine-scented candles. Oversized, but tasteful mirrors were strategically placed throughout the room. A giant painting of a 1970s black, afro'd couple making love hung just above the bed—a housewarming gift from Lenox.

Brenda admired the touches. She was intrigued by the window view that expanded beyond the infinity pool.

"I'm a sucker for a decent view, but this is ridiculous," she said in awe.

Kendrick came up behind her, placed his large hands on both her arms and squeezed. "I'm glad you like it." He spun her around to face him. "And this view?"

"Come on, Kenny." she stepped back and nervously sipped wine.

"Is there something between us, or am I making this up in my head?"

"What do you think?"

Kendrick took the wine glass from her, and placed it on the dresser.

"That's going to stain."

"I don't care. Answer my question."

Brenda's whole being stirred. It was a guarded stirring. She knew sleeping with Kendrick would lead to a deepening of her feelings, and after Kendrick gave her gratitude sex, he would ultimately pick someone thinner and prettier for his image. She did not want to experience that kind of hurt.

"We shouldn't do this," she heard herself say. Though, she was unsure she meant it.

"You kissed me, remember?" Kendrick proudly threw that fact back in her face.

"So?"

"So, you told me if I clean up my mess there was more where it came from."

"And that was a mistake." Brenda was exposed and vulnerable. Yet, a part of her wanted to share that vulnerability with him.

"Is *this* a mistake?" Kendrick held her face as he kissed her. The kiss was full of many things. It conveyed gratitude, lust and hope, and was as overpowering as it was tender.

Brenda's legs were like mush. Kendrick grabbed her, saving her from a tumble. Taking her by the hand, he guided her to the bed. He possessed a confidence in how he led the way, like he intended for her body to know immense pleasure that afternoon. Brenda guessed that Kendrick enjoyed taking his time, or at least making it appear to last forever.

He snatched the straps of her dress. She bashfully pulled back.

"What's wrong?"

"Ain't found a diet plan that works yet."

Kendrick kissed her left brow bone. "You're beautiful," he said, still in whisper.

He reached again for the strap. This time Brenda did not resist, but the look on her face as she turned away was of shame. Kendrick put his index finger to her chin to meet her gaze. He kissed her again, twirling his tongue with hers. Then he worked his tongue to her neck, where her fragrance was strongest. He inhaled her scent, offering delicate bites to her ear and neck, which melted into smaller kisses along her shoulders.

Brenda's dress tugged away from her. She kept her eyes closed, imagining his grimace at the sight of rolls and dimpled flesh. No man who looked as good as Kendrick Black would settle for what she offered unless he suffered from low self-esteem, right?

Brenda opened her eyes to see Kendrick move away. He removed his clothes. The look in his eyes was serious and committed. It said that no amount of cellulite scared him away. Brenda watched his pants drop to the floor, witnessing what lie beneath his grey boxer briefs had the makings of something special.

Brenda was transfixed. His skin's sheen was luminous in the natural light. Brenda began to salivate, watching him slide the boxer briefs down to reveal the most beautiful penis she had ever seen. It was the perfect size, wagging with a firm bounce from side to side. Kendrick gently inched Brenda further back on the bed, which creaked as the mattress gave into her weight. Shame flooded her face. "Oh my God, I'm so sorry."

Kendrick climbed onto the bed and crawled toward her like a Chippendales dancer. "It's okay. Will you please relax?"

Brenda squirmed, her dress pulled up to just over her breasts. *Why did I have to kiss him?* she asked herself, as Kendrick pulled her dress over her head. Tossing it aside, he maneuvered about her. He kissed and licked as her body's response guided him to her sexual core which erupted with anticipation as he made every inch of her feel like perfection.

The thought of Kendrick making love to Sabathany in this very room, *in this bed*, came to Brenda 's mind. She bolted up. "Wait a minute . . . wait just one minute! When's the last time you slept with her in this bed?" She wanted to know.

A kneeling Kendrick was perplexed. "The day you picked me up from the airport."

Brenda killed the mood with her questions. "And you think I'm gonna let you stick that into me in the same bed you sleep with her?"

"But I'm not sleeping with her anymore. And there are a lot of other things we can do that don't involve penetration . . . hot things," Kendrick said, glancing down at his still bouncing erection. "To tell you the truth, I'd rather wait on the intercourse until after all the Sabathany drama is behind us. Then it can mean something."

"Well, then, we can stop this now because you're never going to get this behind you if you plan on marrying her."

"On paper, yes. But we would live separate lives."

"And you'd be fine with that?"

Hearing himself say it out loud made him unsure. "Yes . . . I mean . . . I guess . . . I mean . . . I don't know."

Brenda laughed. "Didn't you think this through?"

"I'm just trying to keep her quiet. If I marry her I can keep my eye on her."

Brenda thought for two beats. "Okay, what if there was a way that you could keep her quiet without having to marry her."

"How do you figure?"

"I told you I received two phone calls this morning. The second was my dumb eighteen-year-old nephew, Jook."

"What did he want?"

"He asked me to get him the best attorney I can find. He killed someone."

"Aww, man! I'm sorry to hear that."

"Yeah, well, I'm not surprised. Everybody in my family knows that Jook was never going to amount to anything. The reason I'm telling you is because I know the name Lola Morris means something to you."

"Yeah, that's . . . I mean . . . that was Sabathany's mother." His tone was not sad; it was more matter-of-fact.

"Jook killed her."

"What?"

"Jook said Sabathany hired the hit."

Kendrick's jaw dropped.

"You know what this means, don't you? Sabathany has in effect been neutralized. That paper you had her sign is null and void."

"Is Jook going to name her?" Kendrick cracked a smile.

Brenda sighed. "Yeah, he thinks by naming her he'll get some sort of deal. Even I know that's not going to happen."

Although Brenda lay there next to him, Kendrick reflected about the last year and a half. Had there been clues that Sabathany was capable of such evil? Had he chosen to ignore them?

"Look on the bright side," Brenda said, bringing Kendrick's attention back to the conversation. "You don't owe her anything."

"You're right. Sure is a shame, though. I wasn't a fan of Lola's, but she didn't deserve that."

"Yeah, I know. Especially not for a measly two hundred bucks."

"Two hundred bucks? That's how much a life is worth nowadays?"

"Apparently. Jook told me that Sabathany had been sitting outside her mother's house, watching the comings and goings. My nephew sold drugs to Lola, and so he was supposed to make up some excuse about how she owed him money. Sabathany was going to give Lola the two hundred, and Jook was supposed to kill her anyway for not having the right amount, when all along the two hundred was the right amount. Lola basically handed her killer the fee to end her life."

Kendrick dropped his head. "That's foul. Now I know why she didn't tell me when Lola died."

"Yes, but the good news is, you don't have to go through with that ridiculous plan to marry her."

"I guess not. But now what?"

"I don't know. You know her better than I do. Do you think she'll leave you alone now that you got dirt on her?"

"I think so. Still, with her it's best to be prepared for anything."

A conspiratorial twinkle entered Brenda's eyes. "Well, you know, I could just call a source I have over in Compton and have the situation dealt with for you if it's all that."

"Oh, God no! That's the last thing I need. I'll figure something out before she gets back." He kissed Brenda on the forehead.

Brenda gladly received the kiss, followed by a kiss on the lips. She could not wait to savor this man and if he was willing, have him all to herself. As far as Kendrick's lack of action plan in dealing with Sabathany Morris, she was less sure.

TWENTY-TWO

The drive to the penthouse to meet with Sabathany allowed Lenox alone time to think. There was still a part of him that wanted Paris to have the happiness she longed for, but he was not cut out to be a part of her life. He had no interest in being judged from any direction, or for any reason. After making the decision not to engage her, the text messages and voicemail piled up. He promised himself he would ignore her, but his curiosity and the bothersome chirping of his phone got the better of him. Lenox pulled over to the side of the road and scrolled through his phone. Bracing himself for what he was about to read and hear, he could only imagine what await him.

The immediate response to the last text he sent her the night she showed up at his house said:

"That's an all-time low. All I wanted was to know why you left me, and you're gonna sit there and threaten me? Do you really think you ought to be doing that?"

Then the next:

"I'm sorry. That was completely uncalled for. I already know I shouldn't have come by your house. I wasn't going to say anything. Just wanted to see you. I miss you."

Lenox scrolled down a little further until . . .

"Okay, this doesn't make any kind of sense. I figured I would compromise and not call you directly, but hoped you'd at least be decent and answer my texts. You need to start answering the damn texts!"

And . . .

"I think you're trying to make a fool of me. If you don't want me to walk away with that impression, then I advise you to text me back."

Lenox almost dropped the phone from the chill creeping through his hands. Thankfully, it was the last of the texts. He needed to *hear* her voice. With dread, he dialed the voicemail. There were fifty-four messages.

Message one:

"You know what? I'm done trying to be civil about this. Because the truth is I can't be civil with a clown. You act like you can just walk into my life, use my body all up, and then keep it moving without having to answer for yourself. You're wrong if you think that. You need to call me so we can talk about this, and see where we're gonna go from here. Bye."

Message two:

"You're fucking worthless; you know that? A real man owns what he did . . . good or bad. See, you think that you get to do your dirt, then go hide. But you can't hide. You better call me. That's not a request."

Message three:

"You're all that matters to me! What don't you understand about that? And it really makes me sick because I hate myself for loving you. You don't deserve my love. You can't even love yourself!"

And on and on it continued, most of which brought a sickened feeling to Lenox's stomach.

"What the hell did I get myself into?" he pondered aloud. Many of the messages were non-sequitur frantic ramblings.

One minute she professed love and understanding of what he must have been going through, and called into question his manhood and integrity the next.

And as Lenox listened, his pity for her rivaled the anger in his heart.

"I should just call her and get it over with," he said, putting on the earpiece and dialing Paris's number, before pulling back into traffic.

Paris answered on the third ring. Her voice sounded like a creaking door. "Yeesss?"

"All right, you got my attention. Now, talk," he said with a calm command while focusing on the road.

"It's a shame I gotta act a damn fool to get your attention."

"I don't have a lot of time, Paris. Say what you gotta say."

"How have you been?"

Lenox sighed his exasperation. "I've been good. And you?"

"Like you even care."

"Look, you wanted me to call you, I called you. What do you want?"

"You mean you still don't know?"

"Should I?"

"You were always the selfish one. Even the way you make love is selfish. And the sad thing is, you *still* think it's all about you. You think you can do whatever it is you feel like doing and not have to answer for it."

"I'm about to hang up."

"I wanna know why you didn't bother to say goodbye! You told me you needed me to know how you felt about me. Was walking out the door your way of telling me?"

"You can't understand what this has been like for me, Paris. Okay, I'm an asshole for leaving, and I'm sorry I didn't return your calls, but I got a family to think about. Playtime is over with."

"Playtime? That's what I am to you?"

Lenox bit down hard on his lip, regretting his words. By diminishing her role in his life, he knew he had just prolonged a conversation he was uninterested in having.

"Is that all I am to you?" Paris asked again.

Lenox said nothing. Instead, Paris heard the ambient noise of honking cars.

"Okay, well, since you obviously care nothing about me, I see no reason to go on caring about you," she said.

"You're a grown-ass woman, remember? Go do what you gotta do."

"Oh really? Is that really what you want?"

"Look, all I'm saying is that you're more than welcome to feel any which way you wanna feel . . ."

Paris cut in. "I'm glad *you* feel that way, because I'll be telling your wife everything."

Mildly amused, Lenox said, "You tried that already."

"Oh, I'm not done. I'm planning on telling the cops what I know about your involvement with Kenny killing that little girl."

Amusement changed to seriousness. "If you rat on me, then you'll be giving up your brother, too. You wanna do that?"

"Seems like a fair trade. Kenny turned his back on me, so I don't feel I owe him a damn thing. As for you, what makes you think you get to go back to playing the family man? You don't. Frankly, I'd rather see you behind bars."

"You really should keep your nose out of things that don't concern you."

"It concerned me the moment Kenny told me everything. I especially like the part where you insisted on getting rid of the car. Pretty damn clever if you ask me."

Lenox paused, his heart thumping. "Paris, I mean it. Don't give me a reason to come over there and put my hands on you, okay?"

"You said it yourself, playtime is over with." Paris hung up.

"Aww shit!" Lenox screamed, shaking the steering wheel, while trying not to swerve off the road. Pulling up to the red light, his mood was shot. However, he still had a job to do. He would worry about Paris later.

At 5:00PM the elevator doors opened into the penthouse.

"Well, well. You get a gold star for being on time," Sabathany said, dressed in a pair of blue jeans and a tight fitting pink sweater. Her hair swept to one side.

The two had not hit it off the first few times they interacted. Despite thinking she was just one more user with a vagina Kendrick had grown fond of, Lenox opted to keep the tone of the conversation professional. Maybe if she saw him less as a threat and more like someone with a job to do, the meeting would move smoothly. Extending his hand, he said, "Sabathany, good to see you again."

She looked haughtily at him, shaming his politeness. Her tortoise shell, thin-framed glasses accentuated the arrogance in her eyes. "Come in."

Sabathany's being there alone carried a different energy throughout the room. It was obvious to Lenox from the moment he stepped into the apartment that Kendrick was not there.

"Can we get this over with?" Sabathany asked, walking him over to the kitchen area. She appeared vexed, as though she had been made to go along with something against her will.

"Of course," Lenox said, trying to maintain his composure.

"Is that it?" Sabathany pointed at the packet of papers in his hand.

Lenox nodded and slid the packet down the kitchen island toward her. "Read it very carefully."

Sabathany skimmed the document, almost defiant of Lenox's instruction. It boiled down to say that she was not at liberty to discuss anything pertaining to Kendrick Black, and that failure to comply would result in immediate divorce where she walked away with absolutely nothing.

"Care for a drink?" Lenox asked, sensing Sabathany's ferment.

"Only if you're having one."

Lenox smiled crookedly as he reached beneath the island counter. He brought out some whiskey and a couple of tumblers.

Sabathany watched him, a little put off that he seemed to know his way around the home, and that he had not bothered to ask if she preferred something else to drink.

Sabathany eyed Lenox's pour closely. "Is this all there is to the document?"

"Yep. It's pretty straight forward." He slid a glass over to Sabathany. Without saying another word, Lenox drank.

The recessed lighting caught the gleam of the single staple in the packet of papers as Sabathany breezed through them. Her face soured.

"Make sure you read all of it."

"You said that already."

"Well, from the way you're flipping through it like it ain't nothin', it looks to me that I have to repeat myself."

"Maybe that's because it is nothing." Sabathany decided the whiskey's taste was tolerable.

"You sign it, you're bound by it, is all I'm saying. You can't turn around and say you didn't know."

Sabathany cocked her head and squinted cunningly at him. "Say I sign this thing, what's in it for me?"

"Kenny won't kick your ass to the curb."

"Besides that?"

Lenox had not been briefed on anything outside the four corners of the contract. "Look, I don't know what kind of beef you two got going on, and I don't care either. But, my ass is in a sling. Will you please just sign the agreement so I can go on about my business?"

Sabathany smirked. "Wow. You're the best thing Kenny's got in his arsenal? You really disappoint me, Lenox. I was expecting a more formidable foe."

There was a coldness in Lenox's eyes that forced Sabathany to take notice. She knew she was driving the ridicule to a dangerous edge. But, she enjoyed pushing Lenox's buttons.

"I think you better be careful who you start conflict with. Remember, your issue is with Kenny, not me. Try and keep it that way."

Sabathany was turned on by the warning. She continued to meet Lenox's gaze, certain that something else was behind it. What, she didn't know.

"Let me ask you something." With a swing of her hips she came from behind the island. "Did it ever occur to you Kenny sent you here knowing full well that I have no intention of signing?"

Lenox looked confused.

"Of course it didn't. He hates your guts right now, so much so that he sent you here to do the impossible. That way he can justify kicking *your* ass to the curb. Not mine. Because whether or not I sign those papers, I'm going to be just fine."

Lenox sensed that Sabathany enjoyed hearing herself speak. But if it meant getting her to sign, he intended to indulge her.

"Ain't no beef between me and my boy. Like I told you the first day we met, he and I go back *years*. We're family. "

"Oh yeah, and he's thrilled to know you were screwing his sister the entire time?"

Lenox looked away.

Satisfied that she hit a nerve, she announced, "You know, I'm not much of a whiskey girl. I prefer wine." There was a victorious musicality in her movement as she crossed the kitchen to the cabinet for a wine glass. After pulling the

Sauvignon Blanc from the refrigerator, she paused before pouring her own. "Would you like a glass? Yes? No?"

Lenox's eyes remained hardened. His shoulders tensed as well as his grip of the tumbler.

"In a way, I almost feel sorry for you. I'm sure you had no way of knowing Kenny's loyalty to you would go bye-bye."

"Are you going to sign it or not?" He did not believe in striking women, but Sabathany moved dangerously close to that happening. He began to breath and count to ten in his head.

"I don't know. I think these terms are negotiable."

Lenox slammed the glass so hard he thought he cracked its bottom. "Ain't gonna be no negotiations. Sign the damn papers!"

"Easy," Sabathany said calmly. "No need to throw a tantrum."

Lenox snatched the documents out of her hand, and slapped them down onto the island. He roughly placed the pen on top of the papers.

"Sign it," he said again, his eyes threatening. Lenox walked over to the paper towel dispenser by the sink and tore a long piece from it. He blotted the sweat beading on his brow. *This bitch is making me lose my cool,* he thought to himself. Lenox could barely ignore the smug look Sabathany wore. He picked up the glass of whiskey and checked the bottom to see if he cracked it. Realizing he didn't, he drank from it.

The two stared each other down. Lenox broke the stare by asking, "Are you going to sign it?"

Sabathany shook her head.

"Aww, man!" Lenox hurled the glass to the floor; its burst found its way all over the kitchen. A shard cut Lenox on his chin. "I don't need this shit today!" As he paced, his long, leather coat flapped behind him.

Unmoved by his histrionics, Sabathany stared blankly at him. "Now that you've gotten that out of your system, I want to talk to Kendrick."

"Why do you think he sent me here to deal with this? He doesn't want to talk to you! Don't you get that?"

"I want to talk to him," she said, feeling good about her power play.

"Jesus Christ!" Lenox's glare reduced to pleading. He dabbed his stinging chin with the paper towel, realizing for the first time he was bleeding. "Hold on!" Lenox took out his phone and dialed.

"Hey," Kendrick answered.

"We got a problem."

"What kind of a problem?"

"She won't sign until she speaks to you first."

"Oh yeah, about that. Change of plans."

"What?" Lenox asked, annoyed with Kendrick's casualness.

"I said change of plans, so don't worry about it."

Lenox stared at the phone as though a foreign language came through it. "Exactly when were you planning to tell me this?"

"I'm telling you now. But don't worry, I'll deal with it when she gets back to L.A."

"What am I supposed to do now?"

"What are you, a retard? You don't have to do anything. Just take the document and leave!"

Lenox flinched as though he had been slapped. "Like I said, she wants to talk to you. She's standing right here." Without looking at Sabathany Lenox passed the phone to her.

"Say, Kenny, the next time you wanna send one of your goons over here to do your bidding, you gotta send better. Lenox has practically pissed his pants. A few seconds more and I'd have the poor brotha crying," Sabathany said. "I want to go over the terms of this nonsense you call an agreement."

"We won't be discussing the terms of anything, because you're not going to sign anything," Kendrick said.

"See? Even you realize how silly it is. You had no business asking me to sign it in the first place. What are you trying to do, waste more of my time?"

"The jig is up, Sabathany."

"Jig? What jig?"

"I mean the jig of you thinking you have something to hold over me."

Sabathany nipped the game playing in the bud. "If there's nothing for me to sign, then there's nothing for us to talk about. I'm hanging up now."

"That was really foul what you did to Lola . . . your mother."

Silence.

"I'm guessing by the quiet on your end that you know exactly what I'm talking about. So here's what's going to happen. Tomorrow when you come back to L.A, all of your things will be packed and ready for you. Should you fail to come get them, I'll consider them abandoned and have them disposed of. I know how much your labels mean to you, but they don't mean quite as much to me."

Sabathany took a deep breath, swung her hair from her shoulder, and tried to sound unbothered by what Kendrick said.

"I don't know what you think you know, but make no mistake, you have no idea what you're talking about, and you might wanna be careful with the accusation that I had my mother killed. That's called slander. People get sued for that sort of thing."

Kendrick broke into laughter. "Sabathany, I didn't say anything about you having your mother killed. All I said was it was foul what you did to her. You basically just told on yourself."

"I still don't know what you're talking about." Her voice sounded so thin, she doubted that Kendrick believed her. After another pause she said, "Okay, tell me what you want?"

"What I actually want is for you to fling yourself off a building. What I'll settle for is you getting the hell out of my life. You know my secret and I know yours, I'd call that a wash."

"Fine. You win."

"I win?"

"I'm not going to fight you, Kendrick. As much as it sucks hearing myself say this, I know I can't beat you, so, I'm not going to embarrass myself." She handed the phone back to Lenox just as a smile found its way on her face.

"So what now?" Lenox asked, noticing the mischief in Sabathany's expression.

After a long pause Kendrick said, "I'm going to direct deposit your severance pay into your account."

"Severance pay? For what?"

"The only reason I'm giving you money is because you've got kids. Consider us squared-up for everything you've done up until this point. Let that bit of money also satisfy any urge you might have to talk about things you shouldn't talk about."

Paris came to Lenox's mind. "I'm glad you said that. We've gotta talk about your sister."

"For what? You're the one who decided to fool around on your wife. If Paris decides to expose you, then that's what you get."

"Yeah, but I'm not talking about . . ."

"You know, I wasn't going to ask, but now I gotta know. Who did who? Did you do her or was it the other way around?"

Alarm passed through Lenox's eyes. He turned his back to Sabathany, who had returned to her glass of wine. "How can you ask me something like that?"

"Hey, I get no enjoyment from asking. But you must admit, it's a fair question. I mean, you've known about my sister since back in the day. One could assume you liked it enough to stay after all this time. But then, you insisted she have the surgery to get it wacked off. Oh, wait, you must've been doing her, right?"

"I never told her to have the surgery. She's the one who was insecure about it."

"Man, this just gets better and better. So you *like* the fact that she has a penis?"

"Fuck you, Kenny!"

"Well, I'd say back at you, but clearly you prefer someone else to do the job!"

"Can't you see that I'm trying to make this right?"

"Trying is for pussies. If you were a real man, you would've told me. I don't keep backstabbers around. Don't call me again." Kendrick hung up.

"Well?" Sabathany asked. Her tone was more subdued.

Lenox shrugged.

"I think we both could use a drink."

"Man, I don't want no drink, especially from you."

Sabathany grabbed a Post-It and jotted something down, then stuck it on the first page of the documents before folding the packet in half. "Here," she said, standing with her arm outstretched, the document hanging from her extended grasp.

Lenox snatched the documents from her and turned to leave without saying goodbye.

"This isn't over," Sabathany yelled from across the room.

"Whatever."

"Oh, that's right. You think this no longer concerns you."

Lenox spun around. His eyebrow arched, which feminized his otherwise rugged-looking face. "That's because it doesn't."

"You're dumb if you think things are going to clear up between you two."

Lenox pressed his index and middle fingers against his temple. A headache was coming on. "He's mad now, but he'll be all right."

"Of course. What do I know?"

Lenox left without saying anything else. He figured her spouting nonsense was to save face from having lost her angle. The elevator was still on the penthouse floor. As he rode it down, he breathed easier. Thankfully, Lenox had his family to go home to.

As soon as he got into his car he unfolded the document to see the yellow Post-It on top. It had Sabathany's phone number on it and underneath read:

"Let me know when you're ready for that drink . . ."

TWENTY-THREE

As soon as the woman of the house opened the door, Paris stared finality in its face. She knew this little stunt killed even the slightest chance of getting Lenox to reconsider a future with her. However, that no longer mattered. It was just as important that he lose the "respectable" future she lost him to.

The woman remembered Paris asking for directions to Ruby's bakery. Her smile acknowledged as much, as a brightness flashed in her eyes. The twins Lenox spoke so much about—Keyshawn and Toya, clutched their mother's legs.

"You're Ashley, right?" Paris asked with an antagonistic swing in her voice.

"Who wants to know?" Ashley's friendliness went out like a pilot light.

"I'm Paris, and I just thought you should know that your husband and I have been having an affair the entire time you've been together."

The woman dropped her gaze to her children. "Keyshawn, Toya, why don't you two go on back into the living room and color while mommy's talking."

The children did as they were told.

Ashley sized Paris up. "Now, I have a question. What is the purpose of you telling me this?"

Paris hardened her stance. "I just thought I would come to you woman to woman and let you know what's going on."

Ashley bit her lip. "You call yourself a woman?"

"I'm all woman!"

Ashley laughed heartily. She continued studying Paris through the screened door. It was a slow, deliberate examination that made Paris uncomfortable.

"Just because you allow another woman's husband to make you his mistress doesn't make you a woman. It makes you a whore!"

"Hold on, I came to you with intentions of having an adult conversation, and you're going to disrespect me?"

Ashley wanted to tear through the screen door. "Let me get this straight. You expect me to reward you for telling me that you've been undermining my marriage? Girl, I ought to stomp you right now for bringing that shit to my house!"

"Bring it then, bitch!"

"Oh, I can do so much better than that."

With two unattended five-year old children sitting inside, Paris figured Ashley would not come anywhere near her. "You don't have the guts to put your hands on me. Tell you what, Lenox tells me you're the most boring lay he's ever had. What does that say about you?"

"I can't be all that boring, I've got two kids with him. Ashley paused to rub her belly. "And one on the way. But I bet Lenox didn't bother to tell you, did he?"

No, he didn't, Paris thought to herself. She wanted to kick Ashley in her stomach out of spite, but she resisted the urge. The sting of the revelation brought up a truth she thought she had made her peace with. She would never be able to become pregnant.

The encounter was not going as planned. She thought Ashley would become a blubbering mess, pleading with her to leave Lenox alone. But this woman acted as if this was all a joke.

"Now, if you'll excuse me, I've got children to attend to! I'd advise you to get the hell outta here!"

"Lenox is gonna dump you the first chance he gets, especially now!"

Ashley became unglued. "You think my husband would leave me for the likes of you? Grown-ass woman my ass!"

Ashley's shift from nice suburban mother to a girl from around the way surprised Paris. Not knowing what to do next, Paris froze when she heard a man's voice pipe from behind. She turned to see Lenox looming over her with hatred in his eyes.

"Paris, what the hell are you doing here?"

Ashley came outside. Tears welled in her eyes. She pounded on Lenox's chest with her fists. "Tell your clownish bitch to leave!"

"Ashley go back in the house," Lenox instructed, bringing his voice down. Then he focused back on Paris. "You better get outta here!"

Ashley, like a chained rabid dog, moved back and forth in the yard. "You mean to tell me this is what you've been messing with?" Ashley pointed her finger right in Lenox's face.

"Baby, please get in the house."

Ashley lunged at Paris, taking a series of swings that would have connected had Lenox not pulled her toward the house. He shot Paris a look that told her what to expect the next time they were alone.

"Well, looks like my work here is done," Paris said, having gotten the response she hoped for. As she retreated down the walkway toward the sidewalk, Ashley continued to thrash about as Lenox held her at bay.

Walking to her car, Paris afforded the drama playing out in front of Lenox's house one last glance.

Ashley screamed at him, "Why would you disrespect me like this?" before slapping him multiple times. Embarrassed, Lenox bowed his head, refusing to strike back.

Suddenly, the rush Paris craved gushed forth like water from a cracked dam. She balanced herself to keep from falling over with laughter. Once inside the car she doubled over, cackling over the sense of victory. She regained her composure, her stomach muscles hurting from laughing hard. Paris started the engine and drove away into the almost freezing night.

TWENTY-FOUR

The following morning, Kendrick awoke in time to catch the sunrise. He decided then and there that it was a sin to own one of the best views in Los Angeles, but could only count that morning as the third time he had been able to enjoy it. And yet, he could not enjoy it the way he wanted to. His mind was jumbled. The preview of what was to come in the bedroom department with Brenda had not gone as he would have liked; in fact, it was out right embarrassing. He did not expect Sabathany to come up in conversation. Only she could manage to ruin the mood from 1,535 miles away.

He wondered if Brenda was right. Was there a better way to handle Sabathany? Just as heavy on his heart lay the decision to end fifteen years of friendship with Lenox, his supposed best friend.

Kendrick relied on the one thing to get his focus back on track—his morning jog. Something about jogging through the neighborhood and allowing his mind to completely empty itself made him feel good. Usually by the end of the run a solution to whatever was bothering him manifested itself.

At 9:30AM Kendrick returned from his run, ready for a shower and some breakfast. He was pleasantly surprised to see Brenda waiting in his driveway.

"After what happened yesterday, I wasn't sure you'd come back," he said, toweling sweat from his face.

They both looked toward the street. A nice-looking white couple jogging side by side smiled at them. Kendrick and Brenda smiled back and waved.

Joining Brenda by her Porsche, Kendrick waited until the couple was out of earshot. "Gave some thought to what you proposed yesterday."

"Yeah?"

"If you can get me a big check on either project, I'll do the press conference and put some of the money towards a foundation."

"I'm glad you've come to that decision."

"I was just going to make myself some breakfast. Then, I'm going to get started with packing Sabathany's stuff. I could use an extra set of hands if you're up for it. You'll get free breakfast out of it."

Brenda checked her watch. The very sight of Kendrick standing there, flexed and glistening was tempting enough of a reason to stick around. "I've got to be over in Pasadena for a meeting, but I think I have some time to kill."

"Yeah, okay, cool. I've got to make some calls first, then we can get breakfast going."

"Are you cooking, or am I?" Brenda asked, breaking the spell his eyes cast on her. She felt slightly foolish, having promised herself that she would be the last to succumb to his eyes' powers. After all, she had seen them at work with other women.

Kendrick, a beacon of masculinity, thrust his hardened chest forward and walked into the house, knowing Brenda was as much his weakness as he was hers.

Kendrick changed his mind, deciding to cook before placing his calls. He scrambled some egg whites and slapped a few slices of turkey bacon onto a skillet. After preparing Brenda's plate, he excused himself and headed to his home office. A call to Lenox's cellphone went straight to voicemail.

Lenox always answered his phone, and usually after the first ring. Kendrick tried Lenox at home. Ashley answered the phone, sounding as though she were crying.

"Hey, Ashley, is Lenox around?"

"Who is this?"

Kendrick hesitated. "It's me . . . Kenny."

Ashley sucked her teeth. "What do you want?"

Kendrick never understood Ashley's hostility toward him. If not for him, she and her husband would still be paying hospital bills resulting from a surgery that saved her life. Now Kendrick regretted letting Lenox talk him out of taking credit for the money; rather, he agreed to transfer the funds into Lenox's account, allowing Ashley to continue to think Lenox took care of it. Maybe if she knew who her real benefactor was she would not act so high and mighty.

"Look, is he home or not?"

"Hell no, he's not here. Probably ran off with that sister of yours!"

"Why are you taking it out on me? I just found out about it myself."

Ashley sucked her teeth again. "Because it seems like whenever there's trouble you're always connected somehow. I used to tell him to stop hanging around you, but he wouldn't listen!"

"You ungrateful bitch! The reason you're even alive is because of me!"

"What are you talking about?"

"That tubal pregnancy you had before you got pregnant with the twins? Lenox came crying to me that you needed an emergency surgery. I paid for that out of the money I got when I snagged that sitcom. I put fifty thousand in his account so he'd be able to save face as your husband and pay the damn bills!"

"You're insane."

"You're telling me you've never had surgery?"

"Sure, to have my tonsils taken out when I was a little girl. That's it."

The phone call to Ashley posed unexpected questions and answered none.

"I have to go."

"Do me a favor. Tell the low-life he'll never see his kids again. He can make new ones with that scag of his!"

Kendrick ended the call, angry by what he had just learned. He quickly speed redialed Lenox's number again.

"Hey, Lenox, it's me. We need to talk. Call me when you get this message."

The previous evening Kendrick had a nightmare that Paris had gone public with his involvement in the hit-and-run. Although it was just a dream, he got an urge to check in with her. It was three hours later in the Twin Cities so he figured she was awake and carrying on with her day. Perhaps Lenox had gone there, but when he called, that, too, went to voicemail.

"Damn, don't people answer their phones anymore?"

Later, in the bedroom, Kendrick and Brenda sat in a sea of Sabathany's personal effects.

"I'll say this, she's got great taste," Brenda said, carefully folding an Yves Saint Laurent blouse and putting it on the sizeable pile of designer clothes.

"You don't have to be so delicate. Throw that shit in a bag and be done with it."

Brenda laughed. "You're getting what you want from her. She's leaving. No need to be nasty."

Kendrick stuck out his bottom lip. "If there's any justice she'll get what's coming to her. By the way, when you spoke to your nephew, was he already locked up?"

"He's waiting to be arraigned. He said he'd been laying low, but someone identified him as leaving Lola's place around the time of her murder. He called me as soon as they granted him his phone call. The poor idiot still thinks he can score some points if he gives Sabathany to the detectives."

"Hmm," Kendrick said, his face filling with doubt.

"Yeah, I'm not sure about that myself."

A tranquil chiming of the doorbell interrupted them. Without saying anything else Kendrick went to open the door. Two serious-looking men stood on the other side.

"Kendrick Black?" the younger of the two said.

"Yes," Kendrick replied, his voice layered with concern. He quickly sized up the two men. He could tell the younger of the two knew who he was by the glint of recognition in his eyes. The older man either did not know or care who he was.

"I'm Det. Daryl Trueblood, and this is my partner Det. Matthew Howards. We're here because we understand that a Ms. Sabathany Morris lives here."

"Uh, she does . . . well, she did. She's coming back today to get her stuff."

"Where is she now?

"She had to go to Minneapolis for something?"

"Do you know what for?" It was Det. Howards first time speaking.

"She and I aren't exactly on the best of terms right now. She's been sort of coming and going as she pleases. It's one of the reason's she's moving out."

"Do you know when her flight is scheduled to get in?"

"I'm sorry, gentlemen, just out of my own curiosity, what is this about?" Kendrick asked.

"We're conducting a murder investigation," Det.Trueblood answered.

"Oh my God." Kendrick placed a hand over his mouth, pretending it was the first time he heard the news. "And you think she's involved how?"

"Do you know when her flight is scheduled to arrive?" Det. Howards repeated, ignoring Kendrick's question.

"I think she said evening sometime. I'm pretty sure she'll get her lapdog of a friend Tammy to pick her up."

The two detectives shared a look between themselves. "You wouldn't happen to know this Tammy's last name, would you?"

"I want to say, Boone."

Det. Trueblood passed Kendrick a business card. "Just in case something else comes to mind."

Kendrick glanced at the card. "Okay, great."

"I'd like to thank you for your time, Mr. Black."

"I'm sorry I couldn't have been more helpful."

Det. Trueblood became bashful. He waited until his partner got into the driver's seat of the car. "I hope you don't mind if I break from professionalism,"

Kendrick flashed his movie star grin. "I won't tell if you don't."

"My wife's a really big fan of your movies," the detective gushed.

"Oh, yeah?"

"Yeah. She's even managed to drag me to a couple of them."

"Hope it wasn't a total waste of your time," Kendrick said, wondering if the detective was the big fan.

"Nope, not at all. Enjoy the rest of your day, sir."

"You do the same." Kendrick continued grinning.

Once the door was closed, Kendrick leaned back against it. A wave of relief moved through his body. When he opened the door, he was certain those cops were there for him. He had never been so happy to be so wrong about anything in his life.

TWENTY-FIVE

Sabathany Morris glided through the apartment, her latte in one hand and the morning paper in the other. It was 1:30PM, a bit late to be just getting up, but after the long evening she had it was worth getting her rest. Placing her latte down on the table, Sabathany sat on the sofa, propping her feet up.

The front page article immediately grabbed her attention. The serial killer responsible for the deaths of women seeking non-committal hookups had struck again. She wondered if the police were doing all they could, or barely doing anything at all.

Sabathany noticed movement through her peripheral as Lenox emerged from the bedroom wearing a pair of Kendrick's blue and white striped pajama bottoms. He seemed discombobulated as he rubbed his eyes and yawned into the afternoon.

"What time is it?" he asked.

"It's late."

"Damn."

"Yep."

Lenox shuffled behind the sofa. He leaned down to kiss the side of her face. "Thank you for last night. I needed that," he said, becoming seized by the intensity of the memory.

"You definitely took care of business."

Lenox swung around the arm of the sofa and fell into the crevice next to Sabathany, barely fitting. "I may not know how to do much else, but I know how to make love to a woman."

"I don't recall any love making in that at all."

Lenox laughed, and ran his hands down the length of his face. "But you enjoyed it, right?"

"Very much."

"Better than Kenny?"

"Maybe," Sabathany replied, wondering how long Lenox had been in competition with Kendrick.

Lenox was like a contented child. It was a small victory, but he would take it. "Say, where'd you get off to in the middle of the night? I got up to take a piss and you were nowhere to be found."

"When I can't sleep I go for a run. I took a jog around the park. Have you been inside that park? It's nice."

"Even I don't go into the park at night. That's asking to get my head knocked in. Nobody tried to bother you?"

"Nope."

"I'm starving. Did you eat?" He leapt from the sofa and headed for the kitchen before Sabathany responded.

Her eyes followed, but her mind traced back to the events of the previous evening . . .

Lenox had returned to Sabathany's door at almost nine. His dour expression told Sabathany things had not gone well, though none of it was a surprise. She had warned him of the outcome, especially with Kendrick. Lenox bulldozed his way into the penthouse.

"Are you going to tell me what happened, or just push your way into people's homes?" she asked, adjusting her raw silk, red Japanese robe. Her hair was pulled up and pinned in place. A few stray hairs fell down either side of her face. She wore no makeup, but was naturally very pretty even without a smile.

Lenox paced the room, much like he did before he left. It was more frenetic energy than Sabathany needed.

"Been driving around for hours. I don't know what I'm gonna do. Ashley ain't gonna let me see my kids."

"She's angry now. Maybe she'll come around."

"No. I know how she is. She's vindictive as all hell!"

"What did you expect?"

"I love my kids. Ashley can't take my kids." His voice shook.

"How did it go with Kenny?"

The mere mention of Kendrick's name made Lenox's feelings go from bad to worse. "He fired me."

"This is what happens after we outlive our usefulness. Kenny's good for doing people like that. He'll make you think he's not like everybody else in L.A, but he's no different. The whole year and a half we were together, I'd watch all sorts of people come into his life, and as soon as they couldn't do anything for him, they would suddenly stop coming around. The few people I was allowed to meet, anyway. He sits there and talks all this crap about getting out of L.A because he can't handle the shadiness of the industry, but he's just as shady. Now, he wants to run because the bodies are piling up."

Lenox looked dismayed. "What bodies?"

"It's a figure of speech, silly. I'm saying he's screwed a lot of people over."

Lenox took a seat, burying his face in his hands. When he looked back up he said, "Right now, I can't think about him. I just don't want to lose my kids."

Fair enough, Sabathany thought. She really could not have cared less. Considering her own past with a cheater, she had little sympathy for a man who in her opinion was willing to step out on his family.

Sabathany went into the kitchen and reached for the whiskey. Lenox certainly looked as if he could use it.

"Here," Sabathany said, reaching around to hand Lenox the glass. "This'll calm your nerves."

Lenox downed the whiskey like a shot. He closed his eyes and waited for the warmth to fill his chest. "Too much is happening. I need to think."

"Some of my best ideas come to me while taking a nice hot bath," Sabathany said.

"I'm more of a shower person myself. Lenox got up and began removing his leather coat. He slung it over the arm of the sofa. Sabathany caught a whiff of the thick leather mixed with stale cigarette smoke. By the time he made it to the hallway, he had stripped from his black sweater. The recessed lighting caught the definition of his trapezius muscles. She wondered if a front view would be as glorious.

Sabathany bit her lip as impure thoughts beckoned her to follow him. After a moment, she walked toward the sound of the running shower. Taking a deep breath, she began to disrobe, leaving a trail of clothes throughout the hallway leading to the bathroom. She slowly opened the door to find Lenox nude, the bulk of his muscles covered in lather. She watched his slow 360 degree turn beneath the rain forest showerhead. He was oblivious to her presence as she quietly opened the glass shower and got in.

"May I join you?" Sabathany asked, helping him spread the soap across his back.

Startled, Lenox jumped. "What the . . . what are you doing in here?" He ran his hand over his eyes, flinging water from them, then cupped his groin area.

Sabathany leaned against the door, the full view of her naked body encouraged a look.

"I say we do something to really piss off Kenny," she said, her words floating over the falling water.

"We can't. This ain't right."

Sabathany arched a wet eyebrow as his lower region belied his protestation. She moved in to touch it, affirming that what she held in her hand was proof that his words meant nothing.

Lenox, despite his tall, hulking physique, stood timidly. He knew if he crossed the line it could never be undone.

"Why don't you stop being Kenny's butt boy for just one moment. I don't know, maybe you like the way Kendrick's treating you."

Lenox glared at the insinuation, then stepped forward with a grunt. He pulled Sabathany deeper into the shower and shoved her against the opposite wall. She was briefly taken aback. Seizing her face in his hands, the kiss was hungry, a tad over-compensating. He felt he had something to prove.

The sex began in the shower, trailed into the hallway, and climaxed in the guest bedroom. Sabathany allowed this brute of a man to take out his sexual aggressions on her. She had given him what she knew he wanted from her the moment they laid eyes on each other.

Sabathany was barely able to shake the memory when Lenox appeared with just a towel wrapped around his waist. He stood before her, proudly revealing his erect penis.

"I've seen it already," she said, unimpressed.

Lenox remained confident. "Thought maybe you'd like to see it again."

Sabathany fed his ego with a bat of her lashes. "That can be arranged, but first I'd like to talk to you about something."

Lenox reclosed the towel and sat on the end of the sofa.

"I just wanted to know what your plans are from here on out."

"You're gonna think I'm a dog for what I'm about to say, but I want to try and fix things with Ashley. If for no other reason but the kids."

"You think there's a chance?"

"I gotta keep telling myself that. Is that crazy?"

"Not at all."

"You think you can patch things up with Kenny?"

"After that son of a . . . ," Sabathany caught herself. "No, too much has happened to ever go back." Sabathany got up from the sofa before she lost control of her emotions. "I'm going to take a shower and get ready. After that we can head on out. I think you'll like what I have in store for you."

TWENTY-SIX

Lenox was quiet most of the drive to his house. Sabathany questioned whether he was capable of going through with what they discussed.

"Have you ever had something you ain't thought about in years suddenly hit you out of the blue?" he asked.

"Of course."

"I was at the Smiling Moose bar in Uptown. I had to be twenty-three or twenty-four at the time. Anyway, I was talking to this dude from Bosnia. Ever met anyone from Bosnia?"

"No," Sabathany said.

"Yeah, he told me a couple of guys forced him to watch as they killed his wife and kids. Shot each of 'em in the head, execution-style."

"He just up and volunteered that story to you?"

"We'd been talking for a while, but I remember at one point he got up to go to the bathroom. When he came back his mood was different. He started talking about all kinds of messed-up stuff."

"I see."

"He told me that he'd pay me whatever I wanted to kill him."

"What did you say?"

"I told him to move around with that. I mean, I tried to be nice at first. I couldn't imagine someone killing my family like that. He said he wanted to join them in Heaven. And he kept pushing and pushing, to the point where we could no longer have a decent conversation. I finally cussed his ass out and told him to stop bothering me with that."

Lenox's eyes were distant. "Anyway, that just came back to me. Ain't thought about it in a long time."

"How much longer until we get to your house?"

"We're here." Lenox pulled into a parking space directly in front of the house.

"Now, remember what we talked about."

Sabathany got out of the car. Lenox trailed behind her as they headed up the walkway. For all of his command between the sheets, he seemed unsure of himself and how this might play out.

While Sabathany knocked at the door, Lenox said a silent prayer that Ashley would have a change of heart, though he knew she probably would not. When Ashley opened the door, her face was expressionless.

"Hello, Ashley," Sabathany said.

Ashley looked over Sabathany's shoulder. Lenox remained steps behind her, hands in pockets, shifting from foot to foot.

"And who are you supposed to be?" Ashley asked as flatly as her face expressed. "Oh, let me guess, you're his latest piece?"

"No, my name is Sabathany Morris. I'm the girlfriend of Kendrick Black . . . you know, the actor."

"And? What do you want?"

"I'm here because I know for a fact that Paris and Lenox have not been in a relationship."

"Oh? And how would you know that?"

"Paris is mentally ill. She has it in her head that she's in a relationship with your husband. The only reason Lenox was even civil to her was out of respect for his friendship with Kenny."

Ashley came outside. "Is that true?" she asked Lenox.

"Baby, you know how I feel about you and my kids. I don't know what kind of craziness Paris is on. But Kenny's my boy. He's the only reason I would even speak to her."

"Listen, I'm not gonna sugar-coat this. Woman to woman, I think you have every right to feel angry with Paris trying to make a play on your man. Believe me when I tell you, if Lenox was doing what you think he was, I'd offer my help in whoopin' his ass. But, I've seen Paris's craziness for myself."

"Mama, can we have cookies?" the twins called from the house.

Hearing his children's voices made Lenox perk up.

"Wait here," Ashley ordered before disappearing into the house. Lenox had seconds to see his children before watching them being led from view. Soon, Ashley returned holding Lenox's phone. She smiled. "You know, I might've believed all of that, except, you forgot this last night."

The guilt on Lenox's face was immediate.

Ashley grinned. "If you're dealings with Paris were so casual, then perhaps you can explain to me why the bitch sent you pictures of herself spreading her ass open?" She held the phone up to show the picture, which had a caption that read, *"Waiting on you to put something in it, Daddy."*

"Oh, and there's more where that one came from." Ashley kept smiling as though she were enjoying herself. She scrolled through the pictures, all capturing Paris in all levels of undress. "Now, this one here is real cute," she said, holding up another, this time showing a picture of Paris tugging at her nipples with a look of ecstasy on her face. It read, *"Want milk?"*

"And you want me to believe that you weren't sleeping with her?"

Lenox turned to Sabathany for needed support, but received a blank stare. He moved bashfully from behind her and said, "Yeah, she sent those to me. But only because she thought she could use them to seduce me. "

"Uh huh. There were texts, too. But of course, you knew that, right?" Ashley again scrolled. "Here we go, '*Thanks for laying it on me tonight, Daddy. I can't believe your wife can't handle all that meat. Oh well, more beef for me! LOL!*' Does that sound like someone merely fantasizing about being with you?"

Lenox looked sheepishly at his wife, unsure of what else he could say that she would believe.

"But the real doozy is this one. '*Hey, Baby! Can't wait to get my pussy! And I bet when you try it out for the first time, you're gonna leave that bitch you got at home! Say goodbye to this monstrosity between my legs, because I'm getting ready to become 100% realness!*' "

"You mean to tell me you've been messing around with some transsexual?" Sabathany asked.

"He sure was. I sure hope it was worth it, because he'll never see Keyshawn or Toya again."

Lenox could feel heat radiating from the glares of both women. "Wait! You can't take the kids. I'll do anything, but please, let me see my kids," Lenox begged.

"I already know you'll do anything. You made that abundantly clear by carrying on with whatever that is. I'll be damned if I'm going to let you expose our children to your choices."

"Can I have my phone back, please?" Lenox asked.

"Absolutely not! I need evidence for when I take your black ass to court!" Ashley marched into the house and closed the door, leaving a dejected Lenox and a confused and angry Sabathany standing in the cold. Seconds later, the door opened once more. "Oh, and your friend, the movie star, called. He'd like to know why you lied to him about needing money for a surgery I never had. Thought you'd like to know." Then, the door closed.

"You're into transsexuals?"

"No! I mean—not really!"

"Does Paris have a penis?"

Lenox did not answer.

"All right, then. That means she's a transsexual, idiot! Hell, if I'd known that, I wouldn't have bothered with any of this! That was a complete waste of time!"

"I didn't know she had my phone," Lenox said, keeping an eye on the house, hoping Ashley would reemerge at the door ready to forgive him.

"And what money is she talking about?"

Lenox followed Sabathany to the car, but offered no answer to the question. Instead, he watched his children cry and bang on the living room window as they reached for him. The demonstration of their love brought tears to his eyes. But suddenly, the window curtain was yanked shut.

Lenox started the car. "Boy, this just ain't my day," he muttered before driving away.

"I want to go home," she said, making sure it sounded more like a command than a request. "I don't know why I even wasted my time on your stupid, lightweight ass!

Again, Lenox did not respond. He was still embarrassed from Ashley having seen the pictures of Paris. Squeezing the steering wheel, he slammed his foot onto the gas pedal, making the car lunge forward into reckless speed.

"Will you please slow down?" Sabathany clutched the dashboard.

Lenox eased on the break, but soon his adrenaline kicked in and he sped again. He was a man on a mission. Sabathany braced herself for an inevitable impact.

"I said I want to go home!" she shrieked, though she may as well have been commanding the air.

After some time, Lenox slowed down to normal speed. Sabathany removed her hands from the dashboard.

"I'm gonna take you home. But there's something I gotta do first." Lenox parked behind a low-rise apartment building. "I'll be right back," he said, leaving the car running.

Lenox stormed up the stairs to the fourth floor, prepared to pound on Paris's door. Upon finding the door cracked open, his eyes narrowed at the odd occurrence.

"Yo, Paris," he called out, while rapping his knuckles against the door. But there was no answer. He pushed the door in further, not knowing who or what awaited him on the other side.

There was a stillness in the air despite the living room being in disarray. Thousands of beads and rhinestones bedazzled the hardwood floor. Her fabrics had been ripped from the shelves. And some of the dress forms were knocked over.

Lenox passed the small lit kitchen. He noticed the piled dishes in the sink in need of washing.

Lenox entered the dark bedroom. An eerie chill blew over his face. He turned on the light, unprepared . . .

Paris was lying on her bed, her nightgown raised to her waist. She was saturated in blood from being stabbed repeatedly—mostly in the chest and stomach. There were also deep slices along the arms and hands. The most grotesque of the mutilation was Paris's hacked male genitalia stuffed in her mouth.

On the wall in bloody smudged letters read: *"The nigger wanted a cunt, so I gave it one."*

Lenox shook his head, keeping clenched fists at his side. His anger was belied by memories of good times between the two of them. Slumping to one knee he took one of Paris's blood streaked hands in his.

"Oh my God!" Lenox's head bobbed listlessly, the shock of it all taking much out of him. "Feels like I was just talking to you," he sobbed.

When Lenox emerged from the apartment, he adjusted his coat. His face was sorrowful. Sabathany got out of the car.

"What's wrong?"

Lenox became still. Staring at the pavement he said, "I think you should drive."

"Okay, but I don't know where I'm going." She looked very intently at Lenox's expression—that of someone who had just witnessed something unspeakable. "Why do you look funny?" she asked, leaving the passenger door open. She walked to the driver's side and got back in. Lenox got into her vacated spot and stared ahead.

"Are you going to tell me what's wrong?"

Lenox continued to stare forward, tears glistened the rims of his eyes. Sabathany shrugged, put the car into drive, and pulled out of the parking lot. He waited until she came to the first stop light to turn and face her.

"Paris is dead," he said with an eerie calmness.

"What?"

"Please don't make me say it again."

"What do you mean she's dead? What did you do?"

"I didn't do anything. She was like that when I found her."

"What happened to her?"

"Somebody stabbed her—a lot." Lenox placed his bloody hands on the dashboard.

Sabathany did a double take when she saw his hands. Her heart thumped loudly in her chest. "Is there something you're not telling me?"

"What the hell kind of question is that?"

"I'm just saying. I kinda find it hard to believe you even care that much. I mean, unless I'm mistaken, didn't you go over there to do the same thing?"

"Ain't no way in the world I would do something like that! Yeah, I was gonna rough her up a little bit, but what I saw . . . that shit there was evil!"

"What else was there?"

"Somebody cut off the things that once made her male. Stuffed dick and balls in her mouth! Seemed like they stabbed her everywhere they could. Then, they wrote some sick shit on the wall."

"What did they write?"

"Something about the nigger wanting a cunt and giving her one."

Sabathany grimaced. "Yeah, that's frickin' overkill. They didn't have to do all that to her," Sabathany said. Her face brightened. "Say, I don't know if you've heard, but there's somebody out there killing the women he meets online and through those dating apps. Maybe that's who's responsible. Maybe they met up and he found out she had the same business going on below that he did."

"I know one thing, whoever did this is gonna pay! I'm calling the police when we get back to the penthouse. In fact, give me your phone."

"I don't think we should get involved."

Lenox turned sharply. "What do you mean we shouldn't get involved?"

"I'm just saying . . ."

"Well, I sure as hell ain't gonna just leave her in there to rot! I think I have to call Kenny and let him know what happened!"

"Are you stupid? After he fired you and told you he wants nothing else to do with you? You do that and Kenny's going to start asking all sorts of questions. No, I think he needs to find out another way . . . from someone else."

Sabathany backed off, deciding to focus on the drive back to the penthouse. She sensed the complexity of Lenox's emotions which were a medley of anger, disgust, and sadness.

"Sorry for your loss," she said, pulling up to a stop sign. "I'm sure you cared about her in your own way." She squeezed his arm in support before driving away.

By the time they arrived back at the penthouse, Lenox's tears had stopped, but the mood was still melancholy.

Sabathany reached under the kitchen island for the whiskey and a couple glasses which was like Déjà vu. Considering the heinous thing they both knew, a drink seemed appropriate, if only to squelch the shock of it all.

"Where are you going to live?" Sabathany asked, bringing focus back to Lenox's original dilemma.

"I dunno. I was thinking about hanging out here until Kenny changes the locks. You won't tell him, will you?"

"Get serious. What do I look like?"

"Do you need me to take you to the airport?"

"I was thinking about staying on a few more days. I'm not in any hurry to get back to L.A."

"Looks like we're gonna be roomies."

Sabathany shot back the whiskey, then poured herself another. Shifting uncomfortably, she said, "Look, I think there's something I should tell you."

"What?"

"I lied about where I was last night."

Lenox's eyes narrowed. "Okay . . . so if you didn't go for a jog in Loring Park, where'd you go?"

Sabathany dug her fingers into the kitchen island. She knew once she began there was no turning back. "After you fell asleep, I called Paris and asked if I could come over. I took a cab to her place."

Lenox's body stiffened. "Why?"

"I wanted to convince her to change Kenny's mind about everything. I wanted her to get him to give me another chance."

"What did she say?"

Sabathany could not bring herself to look at Lenox.

"What did you do?"

Still looking away, and with a hint of regret dangling in her voice, she said, "I'll say this much . . . things got a little out of hand."

TWENTY-SEVEN

"Did you kill Paris?" Lenox asked. Part of him wanted to punch Sabathany in the mouth before she had the opportunity to lie.

"Of course not! When I left, she was very much alive."

"Then what did you mean by 'things got a little out of hand'?"

"She became belligerent." Sabathany raised her index and thumb, showing a slight distance between the two. "I was this close from kicking her ass."

Lenox loomed over Sabathany. "You look me in my eyes and tell me you had nothing to do with what happened to her."

"I swear I didn't." She began to fume. "Wait a damn minute! All this talk about me, how do I know *you* didn't kill her?"

"I already told you, I was gonna beat her up, but I wouldn't have killed her."

Sabathany quieted down. "Anyway, she was in a bad mood when I got there. I was finally able to get her to calm down a little, and that's when she told me to leave because she'd been talking to a guy all evening before I got there."

"What guy?"

"I don't know, some guy from one of those dating apps. She said since you obviously moved on, she didn't think it was fair that she be lonely. If she hooked up with him, maybe he's the one who killed her."

Lenox became agitated, shaking his head. "Exactly! All the more reason why we should've called the police, so they don't come suspecting us," he said, stomping off. "I'm gonna take a shower. I need to wash that scene off my body."

Sabathany watched him disappear down the hallway.

As Lenox took his shower, Paris came to mind. He remembered the first time they had sex, the first time he made her cry, and the first time he told her he loved her.

After his shower, Lenox went to the kitchen to sit in solitude and make finishing the whiskey his goal. Memories from two disparate halves of his life began to overlap as the last of the booze took effect. The memories were precious, evoking both tears and smiles. However, those memories carried certain truths he was not ready to face.

Despite the previous and dramatic thirty-six hours, Sabathany managed to fall into a hard sleep as soon as her head hit the pillow. She had nothing to worry about—nothing some deep thought and faith in herself would not fix.

Sabathany's body lay awry on the perfectly made king-size bed when a sharp and grating chirp woke her up. She squinted at the caller ID and saw Tammy Boone calling.

"Hello?"

"A couple of detectives came by here looking for you."

"What?" Sabathany sat upright on the bed. "What did they want?"

"They're investigating the murder of your mother and they had some questions for you. Then they asked if I was picking you up from the airport."

"What did you say?"

"I told them I didn't know you'd left town."

"Good, good. That's great thinking, Tammy. Thank you."

"When does your flight get in tonight?"

Sabathany closed her eyes to concentrate. "I'm going to stick around Minneapolis for a few more days. But I need you to do me a favor . . . actually two."

Tammy huffed, annoyed at having become more involved than she wanted to be.

But Sabathany was her best friend, and unlike most of the posers in Los Angeles, Sabathany was *actually* making something of herself. And if her friend did well, then she stood to benefit from Sabathany's generosity. In fact, Tammy enjoyed riding Sabathany's coattails, but she had not expected the ride to include murder. She was beginning to question whether her best friend was all she presented herself to be.

"Tammy, do you hear me talking to you?" Sabathany's words yanked Tammy back into the moment.

"Uh, yeah."

"Come on, girl, I need you to do two favors for me," Sabathany repeated.

"What do you need?"

"I'm going to need you to go by Kenny's house and pick up some things he's packed up for me because he'll throw them out if nobody comes for them."

"Okay, and what's the other favor?"

Sabathany giggled innocently. "How do you feel about going on a little road trip?"

TWENTY-EIGHT

Kendrick nor Brenda intended to make love. However, their powerful energy pulled them in that direction. They could only surrender to it. The sex was blissful—void any unnecessary acrobatics. It was simple and honest, comfortable and unpretentious, as though this first time was one of many. That was how well they fit together.

Brenda relished being made love to by a movie star, and Kendrick delighted in making her feel like his leading lady—the way he imagined Diana Ross responded to Billy Dee Williams.

There was no need for idle chatter afterward. Rather, they welcomed the quietude. Brenda remained in Kendrick's embrace. Both stared into the tray ceiling. Neither had any idea what the other was thinking, but they shared the question of *what now?*

"I could lay here with you all day," Kendrick breathed into Brenda's temple.

"You can lay here if you want to, but unfortunately I have a meeting to get to."

"I dunno, I kind of like the meeting we've got going on right here." He followed those words with a gentle kiss.

Brenda could bend to his will if she allowed it. Spending this time with Kendrick Black, the man, restored her sense of desirability as a woman. She longed to stay in bed with him and lavish upon him her gratitude for the restoration, but if she did not get up at that moment she would never leave.

Kendrick watched her jump up from the bed and gather her undergarments.

"Can I use your shower?" Brenda asked, disappearing into the en suite. She already expected a yes answer.

Kendrick got out of bed as well. Pausing in the entrance-way of the bathroom he asked, "Need any help?"

His hard, naked physique caused Brenda's breath to quicken. "No, I think I can handle it on my own."

"Are you sure? I'm really good with my hands."

"So I've noticed. But I won't be in here too long. I'll be in and out."

"Aw, come on."

"Mr. Black, if I let you in this shower with me, we're gonna wind up back in that bed, and I'll miss my meeting."

"Well, we can't have that happen."

The doorbell interrupted them before Kendrick's words changed Brenda's mind. He tossed Brenda a wink before crossing the room to the walk-in to grab a white robe. After making sure it was securely hiding his personal business, he answered the front door. He was surprised to find Sabathany's plain looking friend Tammy standing there.

"Hi there." Kendrick offered a mildly confused grin.

"Hello! Sabathany asked me to stop by and pick up some things you packed for her."

"Sure, give me just a minute. Why don't you come on in and wait in the kitchen?"

"Thank you." Tammy entered. "I never had the chance to tell you the last time I was here, but you have a really pretty house."

"Thanks. So, you must've just talked to Sabathany."

Tammy smiled. "I had no idea she'd left L.A."

"Really?"

"Yeah, she called me to say she was going to be in Minnesota a little longer than she'd planned."

Kendrick's eyebrows raised. "Did she tell you the reason she's staying on longer?"

"No, why?" Her tone was defensive.

A few more minutes and her defensiveness would turn into an inferno of hostility, Kendrick guessed. He eased back a bit, and changed direction. He fixed his eyes into her, deciding to disarm her with his best Kendrick Black charm.

"You know, I can see why Sabathany is so jealous of you. You're way prettier than she is." Kendrick moved in for a seemingly closer inspection.

Tammy frowned. "She said that?"

"She laughed about it."

"That bitch!"

Kendrick casually licked his lips. "And I have a feeling that I owe you an apology. I wasn't very nice to you the first time we met. But if you'll let me, I can explain what that was all about." He happily refocused Tammy's anger. As far as he was concerned, Sabathany had this coming. "First of all, I couldn't act like I was too happy to meet you because then I'd have to hear her mouth. I'm sure you can imagine what that's like. And also, I was a little pissed off about some things she'd already done up to that point. But what really made me mad was that she'd managed to pull yet another poor, unsuspecting person into her lies."

Tammy crossed her arms, tempted to leave Sabathany's precious labels to be thrown in the garbage. "Oh yeah? What else did she say?"

"Just that she thinks you're stupid and that getting you to do things is as easy as shooting fish into a barrel."

"She can go straight to hell. Forget I even came by to pick up her crap."

"I think you're finally seeing her for what she is."

Tammy's head dropped feebly. "I guess so."

Kendrick put a supportive arm around Tammy. His eyes, once smoldering and seductive, chilled to a compassionate friendliness; his embrace was meant to take Tammy back to that first day when she first laid star-struck eyes on him. But he still sensed her hesitation, as though whatever remaining loyalty she had to Sabathany implored her to remain true. His hand fell to the mid-section of her back, just to put Tammy more at ease with the betrayal he intended for her to commit.

"Did she tell you when she was coming back to L.A?" He was certain he had Tammy on his side.

She nodded.

"When?"

"She has no intention of coming back to L.A."

Kendrick faced her, once again cranking up the seduction in his gaze. He placed both hands on her shoulders, hoping to lock in his effect on her. "She's going to be sorry for ever thinking she could play you. Where is she going?"

Tammy's shoulders straighten under his touch. A sudden anger flashed in her eyes. "I was supposed to rent a car and drive to Minneapolis to pick her up. Then, I would take her to LaJolla."

"She wants to go to San Diego?"

Tammy nodded again.

"Is she paying you?"

"Five thousand, but she can forget that now."

"No, no. I say you give Sabathany what she's asking for, except I'll pay you twenty thousand to let me know when the two of you get to San Diego."

"You're going to surprise her by showing up?"

Kendrick nonchalantly brushed his hand against her cheek. "Oh, she's definitely in for a surprise. Do we have a deal?"

Tammy was mesmerized again, despite knowing what he was doing at the beginning and fighting against being drawn in by him. But there in a kitchen, she stood in Kendrick Black's super nova-like star power. She could not say no.

When her lips parted to say yes, a full-figured woman appeared in her peripheral view. The woman came from the rear of the house, adjusting her green and white printed wrap dress. The only blemish on her otherwise pretty face was embarrassment. By contrast, a frown wound its way back to Tammy's face. She stepped away from Kendrick's grasp, breaking his spell on her.

"I didn't realize you already had company," Tammy said, still looking at the woman.

"Brenda is my agent. She just stopped by for a sec, right, Brenda?"

Brenda managed to keep the disappointment from showing on her face. Was she supposed to be another one of Kendrick's best-kept secrets? Swallowing what felt like her pride, she stopped fidgeting with her dress and forced a thin smile. "Yes, that's right. Thanks again for letting me use your bathroom."

Tammy rolled her eyes. "The bathroom . . . right."

After an uncomfortable moment, Kendrick spoke up. "I guess I'll go get Sabathany's things." He left the two women alone, hoping they would be on their best behavior in his absence.

"His agent?" Tammy asked with disbelief.

"Yeah, his agent," Brenda replied sharply, but kept smiling to soften the tone.

"You ought to tell your client that if he expects the ole leading man seduction routine to work, it helps if the woman he just got done smashing doesn't come out of the bedroom."

"I don't really see how that is any of your business."

"Oh, honey, he made it my business by offering me money to double-cross my friend." Tammy looked sad. "*Former* friend."

It took Kendrick six trips to the bedroom to bring out all of Sabathany's clothes, shoes, perfumes and cosmetics. By the sixth time, Kendrick had changed into a pair of sweat pants, a navy wife-beater and flip-flops. Between the three of them, they filled up Tammy's rented SUV.

Brenda went back into the house, desperate to talk to Kendrick about something. Kendrick wrote down his cell number.

"Look, I don't know how much you know, but Sabathany is dangerous. And I don't think you want to be anywhere near her when things start catching up with her." He handed Tammy the piece of paper, but did not let it go. "Like I said before, twenty grand, and all you have to do is let me know when you've made it to San Diego and the exact location." He finally released the paper when the distrust thawed from Tammy's face. He remained hopeful that she would take him up on his offer.

"You ain't gonna try and kill her, are you?"

"Hell no, I'm not going to try and kill her."

"So, you'll make sure I'm long gone before you do whatever it is you're gonna do?" Tammy asked, folding the already small paper into a smaller half, then tucking it into a compartment of her purse.

"You have nothing to worry about."

Satisfied with his answer, Tammy got into the vehicle and started the ignition. Kendrick ran around to the passenger window and knocked on it. He watched it glide down. "So, do we have a deal?"

Tammy's once dead eyes now twinkled. "We'll be in touch."

When Kendrick went back inside his house, Brenda awaited him with folded arms, tapping her high heel against the floor.

"Your agent? That's all I am to you?"

"Don't be silly, you're more than that."

"Oh, my bad. I'm an agent who'll give out her pussy when you ask for it, right?"

"I think I made a mistake telling Sabathany that I knew about her mom. That's' why she isn't coming back to L.A. I was trying to convince her friend to help lure her to me."

"And you thought flirting with her would get her to do it?"

"It helps."

"And if it came down to it, were you prepared to sleep with her to sweeten the deal?"

"I was playing her, and doing a good job of it until you came out of the bedroom. Thanks a lot."

"So, now it's my fault? Or were you just embarrassed that your ole fatty-fat side piece came out the room and killed the perception that you only sleep with skinny girls?"

"Is this what being with you is going to be like?" Kendrick huffed.

"See that? You're already looking for a way out!"

"No, I'm thinking that you're too old to be this insecure. Look, Brenda, I like you a lot . . . as you are. But if you're going to be one of those people who expects me to boost your busted self-esteem every chance I get, then you're going to be disappointed. Now, I'm not saying there's anything physically wrong with you, but you clearly have issues with how you look. If you don't like it, then change it. It's as simple as that."

"I'm going to be late for my meeting."

Kendrick forced an embrace that left her stiff in his arms. He remained quiet during the escort to Brenda's car. He hoped their parting kiss would say the things that words could not.

TWENTY-NINE

Tammy Boone exited Interstate 105 on to Crenshaw Boulevard when she called Sabathany.

"Hello?"

"Hey, girl. I'm on my way home from getting your stuff."

"Really? And what condition is it in? I bet he threw it all in a couple of trash bags,"

"No, actually, I was impressed. Looked like they put everything nicely into your luggage. Now, all of your makeup, perfume and shoes they put in some plastic grocery bags."

"Great, my Louboutins are most likely all bent out of shape. Wait a minute . . . you said 'they.'"

"Oh, yeah," Tammy laughed. "He had some thick chick over there. My guess is she was helping him and he humped her as a thank you. Told me the lady was his agent."

"Ah, so Kenny's humping his agent now? How original. How did they treat you?"

"He was decent. She acted like I was cutting in on her action, though."

Sabathany giggled.

"Okay, here's the deal. I'm going to leave L.A. the day after Thanksgiving. If I keep it moving and don't stop too much, I should be in Minnesota in a few days."

"Sounds good."

"When will I get my money?"

"Didn't I tell you that I got you? We're best friends, remember?"

"That's all fine and good, but with me taking off work to come get you, I'm going to need to make that money up somehow. I need to know that you're going to have it for me like you say you are."

"I would never screw you over like that."

Tammy pondered for a moment. "Okay, as long as we're on the same page."

"We are. Now, I've got something I need to take care of, so I'll see you when you get here, okay?"

"Okay. See you in a few days."

Sabathany was about to hang up but said, "Look, I know I can be a bit much to deal with sometimes, but I do appreciate everything you're doing. You know that, right?"

"Yeah."

"Good. So, don't take any of this personally, okay? I don't know what I'd do without you."

"We're good. See you in a few days."

Sabathany hung up the phone, satisfied she managed to allay Tammy's worry. And Tammy was more than happy to let Sabathany have that impression.

THIRTY

November 28, 2013

Thanksgiving Day,

Lenox woke up to suicidal thoughts. The day would be difficult to get through without Ashley and the kids. On a day meant for giving thanks, there was little to be thankful for.

Lenox looked soggy from the all-night whiskey guzzling. He sat at the window, watching the world callously continue as snow quilted the ground.

Sabathany noticed, but chose to leave him alone. She had things to do, plans worth looking forward to, as long as Tammy kept up her end of the deal.

Sabathany googled the travel time from Los Angeles to Minneapolis. Knowing Tammy as she did, and factoring in the number of predicted stops she would make, it would take her a day and a half to two days to make the drive. It gave Tammy a buffer, and Sabathany plenty of time to get things set up.

Later, Sabathany changed into a black cashmere sweater, black pants, and a winter white coat with an exaggerated, floppy lapel.

"I really wish you'd get cleaned up and come with me to Kenny's family's house," she said, closing the clasp of her coat.

Lenox refused to look at her. "You know good and well he don't want us over there."

"Yeah, but he's in L.A. Not much he can do from there, is there?"

"Why do you wanna go and make things worse between you two?" Lenox shifted just enough to raise the whiskey to his lips.

"It's Thanksgiving and I'm hungry. Besides, his mama won't turn me away." Sabathany shook her head. "You're gonna just sit here all day and kill your liver?"

Sweat-faced, Lenox squinted his eyes to better focus. "My choice if I do."

"Have it your way. Will you at least write down the address, please?"

Lenox scribbled the address onto a piece of paper, handed it to her, and settled back into his gloom. "And don't think we're done talking about what you were really doing over at Paris's," he said just as the penthouse elevator doors closed behind Sabathany.

A young Latino doorman Sabathany had never seen before was startled when she emerged from the building. Embarrassed, he quickly extinguished his cigarette.

"Oh, you didn't have to put that out on my account."

"It's all right. Anything I can do for you, Miss?"

"I don't suppose you could get me a cab, could you?" Sabathany asked with a dash of helplessness.

"Of course." The doorman stepped into the street, ready to hold out his uniformed arm to hail a taxicab.

Sabathany picked through her oversized purse to get her tip money ready. When a cab arrived, the doorman opened the backdoor for her. She pressed a tip to his chest and let her eyes settle upon his for slightly longer than usual.

"What's your name?"

"Javier."

"Well, Javier, that's for being a gentleman," she cooed.

He was charmed by her attractiveness. His face blossomed red, like a school boy with a crush. "Thank you, Miss," he said.

See? I'm not a total bitch, Sabathany thought as the doorman's eyes lit up after discovering the twenty-dollar tip she gave him.

"Where are we goin', lady?" the portly driver asked, sounding like he was doing her a favor for having stopped. It was a brash contradiction to the way she had just been treated by Javier.

Sabathany held her breath to avoid the stench of underarm and cigarettes. After she belted herself in, she told him the address.

She imagined less offensive aromas tapping her nose in the Black home. The very thought transported Sabathany back to the days when she lived with her grandparents. Anyone who had the privilege to break bread with her family at Thanksgiving never left the house hungry, not with Cornish hens, ham, potato salad, sweet potatoes and marshmallows, and cornbread stuffing to fill them up.

It was not just the food that assaulted Sabathany's senses, it was the memory of how her grandparents looked and smelled, and the only time in her life that she ever felt truly loved and cared for by anyone.

Sabathany arrived at the house expecting a warm smile, not the empty stare she received from Kendrick's mother when she answered the door. She braced herself for another rigid embrace from the older woman.

"Good to see you again, Mrs. Black."

Diane allowed herself to be hugged. Disappointment flagged her face when she realized Kendrick was not accompanying Sabathany. "What brings you here, honey?" she asked.

"I'm in town on some business, and it dawned on me that I couldn't go back to L.A without seeing you," she said, attempting to draw out Diane's smile.

Sabathany proceeded inside and sniffed the air. There was no bouquet of delectable holiday dinner smells, though it did smell as though someone had cooked. Sabathany entered the living room. She was greeted by the faces of forlorn-looking people sharing a familial resemblance.

"Why does everyone look as though they've just come from a funeral?" Sabathany asked, balancing curiosity with light-heartedness.

"No ones' heard from Paris," said a collection of solemn voices.

"Not to be rude, but who are you?" asked the young lady who bore the closest resemblance to Kendrick.

"She's Kendrick's special friend, Arlene," Diane said.

Sabathany assumed the man staring at her was his father. "Have you called Kenny? I know they're close," Sabathany asked.

Diane shook her head. "Today his movie comes out. I don't want to bother him. Besides, Alex went to check up on her. We'll find her."

Sabathany put a comforting hand on Diane's shoulder. "I know you will." She shared memories of her first encounter with Paris.

"It's not even that serious, you guys. I mean, if I was banned from being a part of this family I wouldn't answer my phone either. She's fine. No need to worry. Now, can we please eat?" Arlene said.

Relief passed through the room like a breeze. Arlene stood up, signaling the end of her involvement in the conversation. Everyone else followed her.

"Young lady, you're more than welcome to stay and have something to eat," Wallace said.

"Thank you, I'd like that."

Sabathany took a seat at the dining room table. Dinner was offensively basic—Sloppy Joes. Sabathany expected down-home cooking, not something from a can. Conversation was minimal, and the sound of loud chomping made Sabathany think of a pride of lions feasting upon a kill.

"I don't mean to be nosy, but . . ."

"Yes, you do," Diane interrupted.

"Go ahead with your question," Wallace said.

"I was just curious why you and Kenny don't get along."

Wallace stopped chewing. The welcoming gleam in his eyes cooled. "Ask his mother." "Can't we just enjoy our meal?" Diane asked.

"Fine." Wallace said before taking another bite of his sandwich.

Sabathany quietly observed the family dynamic play out like live theater. Despite their crabs in a barrel mentality, at least Kendrick had a family to come home to.

"So when are you heading back out to L.A?" Carl, Arlene's husband, asked with a flirtatious lilt in his voice.

"Not sure. Got some business to tend to," Sabathany replied, feeling Arlene's and Diane's dagger-like glare.

"Yeah, you make sure you handle that!" Arlene said.

Between Paris and jealousy, the mood in the house was sour. Sabathany announced that she was going to call a cab, thanking them for the meal. She politely declined Wallace's and Carl's insistence that one of them give her a ride back to the penthouse.

Fifteen uncomfortable minutes passed before the cab showed up. Sabathany was glad to escape the hostility. As Sabathany headed toward the front door, Diane gently tugged at her arm.

"Next time you decide to drop in, it might be better for everyone if my son accompanied you, don't you agree?"

"Of course, I completely understand."

"Also, I'd appreciate it if you didn't say anything to Kendrick about his sister. Ain't no sense in getting him all worked up over what's probably nothing."

Sabathany gave Diane a kiss on the cheek, knowing the matriarch would most likely wash the kissed area clean after she left. Sabathany smiled, but promised nothing. She had every intention of saying something—and she would do so happily.

Sabathany entered the penthouse. The smell of over-nuked spaghetti hung in the air. Lenox was sitting at the counter, eating greedily. Sabathany was happily surprised to see a glass of juice had replaced the whiskey.

"How was your Thanksgiving feast?" Lenox asked after slurping a noodle.

"Wasn't a feast. We had Sloppy Joes. Anyway, there was too much bad energy flowing. Both Kenny's mama and sister were upset because both their dogs for husbands paid me too much attention. Plus, they were upset about Paris."

Lenox looked surprised. "You told them what happened?"

"No. They'll find out soon enough. They said Alex went over there to check on her."

"They're good people. Wouldn't have hurt you to tell them."

"If that's how you feel, why don't you tell them?"

"You told me not to."

"Yes, and for a very good reason. Look, I know it sounds cold-blooded, but I don't involve myself in things that don't concern me. I'm going back to California and don't need to get caught up in any investigations. Hell, I've got my own stuff to worry about. But you feel free to do what you gotta do."

"You wanna run that story by me again about why you went over to Paris's?"

Sabathany cleared her throat. "I already told you. I wanted her to help me change Kenny's mind. When I got over there, she was drunk. I asked her what was wrong and she told me she didn't want to talk about it, so I went ahead and asked for her help. She told me that her mother didn't think I was trustworthy."

"And you wonder why you walked into so much hostility?"

"Anyway, from that point on she got really bitchy. I wish I would've known about the gender thing because I would've used it to make her feel really low about herself."

"Why? She was just being true to who she was."

"What do you care? You said she ruined your marriage."

Lenox stabbed into his spaghetti.

"Speaking of which, after everything that's gone down, I think it's best if I spend the next few days at a hotel."

Lenox put down his fork. Despite Lenox's intimidating size, his confidence was on par with an awkward teenager. "Did I do something?"

"Oh no. I'm actually thrilled to learn that I slept with a sexually confused man."

"I ain't confused."

"If you say so."

"I'm not!"

"Besides that, I need to cut my ties to Kenny. This is *his* place. You're *his* friend."

"Don't you mean *was* his friend?"

Sabathany shrugged. "You know what I mean."

She was about to leave him standing in the heat of her rejection. His feelings had not mattered up to that point, and would never begin to.

"You're right. I am confused about my sexuality. Didn't used to be. I always saw myself as a straight man. But being with Paris for so long put doubt in my head. I figured it would be easier to go the normal route with my wife and kids, than to stand around holding some banner. Where I come from, nobody would understand that." He searched Sabathany's eyes for sympathy, but was shaken by the coldness he found in them.

"Guys like you go on your merry way, thinking it's all about you. And while you're busy finding yourselves, you don't think about the women who get sucked up into your messes. You never think about the lives you destroy!" She turned to leave again.

"Look, I know you can't stand the sight of me right now. Hell, I can't stand the sight of myself. But will you please stick around? You can call me names and tell me what a piece of shit I am. I just can't be alone."

There was a desperation in his eyes. Sabathany chose her words carefully. "Lenox, the plan was always going to be that I return to California. So, no matter how awful you feel, and I get that you feel awful, I'm not going to be here to babysit you."

"I never expected you to babysit me. But you said yourself we've been abandoned."

"Yes, I did. And I'm learning to get over it. You need to do the same."

"I'm not sure I can."

Sabathany turned on her heel, determined to go on her way. "Well, you'd better figure out a way."

An hour later, Lenox had fallen asleep on the sofa. Sabathany could hear his breath steady to an even-rhythmed snore.

She quietly packed her belongings into her roll-on luggage. As she packed, she began to question the wisdom in telling Lenox she had paid Paris a visit, especially after the look of disbelief he had given her. Something told her he still didn't believe her. When she finished, Sabathany glanced out the window overlooking the park. Snow swirled about the evening.

She put on her coat and grabbed the key and cell phone laying on the kitchen island.

During the ride down in the elevator, Sabathany leaned against the elevator wall. She fought to quiet the many thoughts in her mind of how bad her involvement in this looked. When the elevator doors opened, Sabathany passed through. Javier was outside, sneaking a cigarette. This time he smiled and continued smoking. With his free hand he held the door open for her.

"Could you hail me a cab again?"

"Certainly, Miss." Like a magician waving a wand, he extended an arm out into the oncoming stream of traffic, gesturing for a taxicab.

When one finally showed up, Javier put out his cigarette and placed Sabathany's luggage into the trunk. She handed him another twenty dollar bill and surprised him with a kiss on the lips. It was willful and forward, but she did not care. She would never see him again anyway.

"That's for being so kind," she said before slipping into the backseat of the cab.

This cab smelled like synthetic cherry—a sickeningly sweet aroma—but the tradeoff was an interior one hundred times cleaner than the last cab ride. As Sabathany rode to the hotel, she checked her watch, reminded that she had to give Kendrick a call. She was convinced he would want to hear what she had to say.

THIRTY-ONE

It was the sixth movie theater of the day and twelfth showing of *It Is What It Is* that Kendrick sat through. It had become his ritual, his way of knowing if he starred in a hit or a flop.

Hot, buttered popcorn and soda replaced any number of Thanksgiving meals he had been invited to partake of. Kendrick always enjoyed spending the day and well into evening of opening day, incognito, sitting in the shadows of the back row, corner seat, watching the audiences love or hate his films. But thankfully in this case, the responses were consistently positive, which told him all he needed to know . . . Kendrick Black had a hit movie on his hands.

Shannon Dwight was Hollywood gold, but if the movie did well, he wanted it to be as a result of collaborative talent, not because he rode her coattails.

Someone could have recorded a laugh track using every audience attending the showings. His comedic timing was impeccable. Every audience laughed at the same places in the film. He was also thrilled to see the theaters filled with people who were not offended by the interracial coupling of the characters.

Kendrick was watching Shannon Dwight's character decide how to discreetly leave personal items in his character's medicine cabinet, when his phone rang. The back of his neck warmed as he scrambled to silence the ringer. Moving to his feet, he ignored the glares and groans from the paying moviegoers. He scurried to the lobby. Seeing the number made him want to turn the phone off altogether, but curiosity brought the phone to his ear.

"I had no idea your father was such a dirty old man," Sabathany said.

"And how would you know that?"

Sabathany was tickled that Kendrick had not bothered to defend his father's honor. "Because I thought with it being a holiday, I would pay your mother a visit. He was there."

"What possessed you to go to my family's house?"

"I thought they might've been enjoying a real Thanksgiving dinner since you ruined the other one they had for you."

Kendrick gritted his teeth. "You better stay away from my family!"

"Listen, I didn't call to argue. Something happened to Paris. No one knows where she is."

"How do you know?"

"Because I was there when your family talked about it. The whole vibe in the house was depressing. I didn't stay long after I ate."

"Nobody thought to go by her apartment?"

"Supposedly your brother Alex went over there. I feel bad, actually. I like Paris."

"Save it. You just called to gloat."

"Is that what you think of me?" Sabathany quivered her words hard for effect. "Honestly, I didn't call to fight with you, Kenny. I called because I'm worried."

A young mother with two children came from the bathroom. She gave the large movie poster a glance and then Kendrick a long stare. Kendrick turned away, pulling his ball cap down to maintain his anonymity. "Maybe she went out of town."

"Maybe. I know she and Lenox had words before he came to crash with me at the penthouse. Maybe she felt like getting away from all the drama."

"Whoa, my penthouse?"

"Where else was he supposed to go, Kenny?"

"A hotel."

"I felt sorry for the guy. You would, too, if you'd seen how pitiful he looked."

"Get him the hell out of my house! Neither one of you have any business staying there."

"Calm down. I moved to a hotel."

"And where is he?"

"How the hell should I know?"

"Was he there when you left?"

"Yes. As a matter of fact, he was sleeping." Sabathany gasped. "You know what, what if he did something to her?"

"He wouldn't do anything to my sister."

"His wife left him, and promised to keep the kids away from him. How can you be so sure? You know what? You're right. It's none of my business anyway."

"That's right, it's not." Kendrick received an in-coming call. He looked at the phone. "I gotta go, my mother is calling me now."

"Give your family my best," Sabathany said. But it was too late, Kendrick had already clicked over.

"Hello?" Kendrick said, happy to hear from his mother. She would provide reassurance. There was commotion on her end of the phone. Kendrick pulled the ball cap from his head as though it would help him hear better on his end.

"You gotta come, Kenny! You gotta get here!"

Wailing resounded in the background on his mother's end, forcing him to strain to hear.

"Why? What happened, y'all?" Kendrick asked, dropping the crisp, perfected grammar Hollywood taught him.

"Somebody killed Paris!"

THIRTY-TWO

Alex sat in his mother's favorite armchair, the one by the window facing the street. Yellow police tape, booming voices from the homicide detectives ordering him to leave the premises after he forced his way through, and Paris's brutally stabbed body played themselves like home movie footage in Alex's head.

Alex watched his mother breakdown as she spoke to Kendrick on the phone. He resented his brother's phoned-in sorrow. He thought it was typically convenient and removed. Alex also blamed Kendrick for putting it in Paris's head that he was ashamed of her, and while that was true in the past, Alex regretted the lost time he could have spent in reconciliation with her.

Wallace did his best to remain stoic. However, Alex could tell from the way Wallace chugged the remaining swigs contained in the Remy Martin bottle, that despite all the horrible things he had said about Paris, he was having a difficult time with the news. Wallace finally took the phone from his wife.

"Son, it's me, your father."

"What? Put mom back on the phone."

"Your mother needs a minute. You can talk to me." He had no intention to argue, only to listen to what Kendrick had to say.

"Daddy, what's gone down between us doesn't matter at this point. Paris is dead. And I know you'd like to think that Paris died the moment she revealed her truth to you, but that's still your child," Kendrick said, taking the conversation out to his car, and leaving the scripted world of *It Is What It Is* playing on the cinema screen.

"I know, son," Wallace said. It hurt Wallace's pride to make such a concession.

"Daddy, I love you," Kendrick blurted out. The sentiment surprised both men.

"Let me give you over to your mama," Wallace said. Unease moved through the old man. No one ever showed Wallace how to embrace the emotions that brought about vulnerability. Wallace refused to do vulnerable.

Diane took the phone. "I'm back."

"Mama, I'm taking the next plane out."

"Why would someone do this? Huh? Why would they do this to my baby?"

"Mama, I need to call you back in a little while. Stay by the phone, okay?" Kendrick said, ending the call before Diane answered. He dialed Lenox's cell number. But as before, the call went to voicemail. "Lenox, something's happened to Paris. I know you two had a fight. I need you to call me back right away. Please."

Kendrick was too emotional to return to the movie theater. Sabathany's seed had been planted; the insinuation of Lenox's involvement continued to roll around. He breathed deeply and ducked when someone passed by his parked car.

Easy breathing helped Kendrick find the clarity to call Brenda at her office. She only needed to hear his voice to know something was dreadfully wrong, and offered to meet him wherever he wanted. He decided on meeting at her house because it was closest from the movie theater.

Because of his emotional state, Kendrick took his time driving, much to the chagrin of fellow drivers. His speed was consistently slow. He hoped to give Brenda enough time so they would arrive at approximately the same time.

He timed it perfectly, making his way down her street just as Brenda turned into her driveway. He parked next to her. As soon as they were both out of their cars she embraced him. All of the tears welling inside of him released. It did not matter that in the hour and a half moviegoers spent immersed in the fictitious world of his film, he had reached a new fan base, or had become the swoon worthy, up-and-coming prince of Hollywood.

Brenda stood with him in the middle of her driveway, allowing him all the time he needed. She stroked his back, like a mother comforting a distressed child. She still had no idea what created this level of sorrow, but once Kendrick separated himself from her and stood on his own, she escorted him inside the house.

After the first glasses of wine were poured and they settled on the chaise lounge out by the pool, Kendrick shared what he found out from his mother. He paused for moments at a time, taking large gulps of air to keep from retching. Brenda listened intently.

"I can't believe someone could be filled with that much hate," Kendrick said.

Brenda, too, was filled with wonderment as to who would do this to another human being. "What if it was less about her and more about the killer? Maybe the killer had some unresolved issues, some self-loathing that made him lash out this way."

Kendrick thought about Lenox and the numerous calls that had gone unanswered. "I don't give two shits about their issues. They've got therapy for that. And I don't care if it was as simple as having a bad day. You don't do that to someone."

Brenda looked down at her empty glass, but made no move to refill it. "I'm not sure if there's anything I can do to help you, but if you can think of something, please let me know."

Kendrick appreciated Brenda's offer although he had no idea what she could do.

"Should I call someone to help with the arrangements?"

"I think my mother has it covered. I'm going to pay for everything, of course. My family doesn't need this financial burden."

"I'm sure they'll appreciate it."

"Considering this is all my fault, I'd say it's the least I can do."

"How do you figure it's your fault?"

"It's all karma for me walking around here scot-free. This is God's way of getting me back. My family is being made to suffer for what I did to Kayla."

"No, no. It doesn't work like that. Look, I know you're sorry for what happened. I can see it in your face. And you're taking care of it."

Kendrick refused to be consoled. "It's not just the money. I keep telling you, Kayla comes to me in my dreams practically every night. And things are happening to her in these dreams that shouldn't happen to a seven-year-old."

Brenda sighed. "Well, like I said before, whatever you need from me, let me know."

The two fell quiet. Brenda used the lull in conversation as opportunity to refill her empty glass.

"I just figured out what you could do to help," Kendrick said upon her return.

"Anything."

"Come home with me to attend the funeral."

Brenda's eyes fluttered with surprise. Accompanying Kendrick to Minnesota to bury his sister would mean meeting his family. Meeting his family would be nice, but under these circumstances the idea did not sit well with her. Plus, if anyone were to ask, she had no idea how to define their burgeoning relationship.

"Um, I don't know what to say."

Kendrick looked quizzically at her. "What do you mean, you don't know? I thought you were willing to help in anyway."

"I am, but you have to admit, my meeting your family like this is a little weird, and don't forget your mom just met Sabathany. How would you explain that to her?"

"Evidently the whole family just met her."

"Even worse."

Kendrick's face brightened from an idea. "You're still my agent and publicist. We can tell them that you're there to help navigate the story before it hits the tabloids."

There it was again. *Agent and publicist*—Kendrick's way of minimizing her presence in his life. She thought back to Tammy's drop by at his place, and how awkward Kendrick behaved when throwing the agent-publicist line out there.

"If you're ashamed to say that you're banging a heavy-set woman, why don't you just say so?"

"Not this again! You know what? Forget I said anything. I'll go by myself!" Kendrick set the glass of wine down and rose from the chaise.

Brenda was stunned when Kendrick stormed from the patio and into the house. She realized her paranoia was bound to sabotage whatever they had before it blossomed into anything deeper. She got up to apologize for making it about her when he needed her support, but by the time she reached the front door, Kendrick was already gone.

THIRTY-THREE

December 2, 2013

The pandemonium stretched from LAX to the Minneapolis/ St. Paul International Airport. Had circumstances been different, Kendrick would have relished feeling like a rock star.

It had been an overwhelming feeling, being in a fish bowl with everyone watching. Kendrick thought he could handle people clamoring to get close to him for a selfie or autograph. And he thought it would be a piece of cake to pretend to be charmed by the thousandth story of so-and-so's daughter, girlfriend, or wife having the biggest crush on him as though it was the first time he heard such a story. Then there were the women, and few men, brazen enough to flirt with him. He feigned flattery, when all he wanted to do was get to his destination, and be with his family. He had no choice but to stand there as the fans got too close, ignoring cues like tears raining from his eyes, because a selfie was more important to them than the brutal murder of his transgender sister.

Kendrick did not have it in himself to act like a Hollywood brat because he had heard horror stories about the actors, without half the film credits he had, behaving as though they were onstage night after night receiving Emmys and Oscars. Even the so-called reality show personalities were in on the diva routine. But, Kendrick refused to behave like them because he was grateful to finally be on Middle America's radar. No,

Kendrick would give the fans what they wanted. He could always cry in the backseat of a limo later.

Besides the fan madness, Kendrick spent much of the trip worrying about what Paris's body would look like once it came back from the coroner. Apparently, his mother made up her mind to have an open casket. Diane told him she wanted the world to see what evil did to her child. He understood her frustration, but was unsure of the appropriateness of that decision.

There was also the unrelated worry of what sleeping with Brenda would do, not just to their working relationship, but to his career. Her incessant fishing for reassurance was off-putting, an unpleasant surprise from an otherwise strong and together woman.

Kendrick instructed the driver to take him to the funeral home. When he arrived, his sister Arlene greeted him with a hug.

"How's Mama holding up?" he asked.

"She's devastated," Arlene said, breaking their hold. She led Kendrick into a sitting area where their mother waited on a burgundy-colored velvet bench, flipping through a thick catalogue of caskets. "I'm going to see if I can track down the man so he can show us some of the models they have on the premises."

Kendrick embraced his mother, but she pulled away in agitation. "I told those people over at the medical examiner's office not to take forever and a damn day with my child."

"It's a murder investigation, Mom. Let the people do their job."

"Well, they can start by telling me who did this. Never mind all that other stuff. What good does it do to know how many times she was stabbed? Won't bring her back. No, best thing to do is get this over and done with. A quick burial is the best thing we can do for her and for ourselves." She looked down at the catalogue and continued flipping through it.

Kendrick decided not to argue with the grieving woman. "See any you really like?"

"You know, these are beautiful, but I never understood the point of spending all that money on something that's going six feet into the ground."

Diane scooted over to allow Kendrick space to sit. She placed the book between them so that he had a better look.

"Listen, I don't want you and Daddy worrying about money. I got this covered, so spare no expense."

"Thanks, son. Your father and I appreciate it."

Kendrick stared at his mother's profile. The skin below her eyes puffed from crying.

"That's a nice one," Kendrick said, pointing to a gleaming, silver casket.

"Costs too much."

"Mom . . ."

"I know what you said, but for that kind of money you could buy a used car."

"Paris deserves it."

Diane's eyes wrinkled when she spoke, "Yes, she does, doesn't she?" She closed the catalogue, slapping both hands on top of it. In an instant, she became taken by fury. "It's not natural for a mother to lay her child to rest. I tell myself that God must have some plan I don't know about."

"It's okay to be angry, Mom."

"Oh, you better believe I'm angry. If it had been anybody else, they'd have the SOB in custody by now."

"Don't even worry about it. I plan to stay on them until they find whoever it is."

Diane appeared relieved, gripping her son's hand. "I know you will. You're a good son, Kenny. I've never had to worry about you because you always do the right thing. I'm so proud of you."

Kendrick took an anxious breath, lacking the words to disabuse his mother of her unspoiled perception of him. She still had no clue of the secret he kept, and this made his heart jump. Because if Diane knew of his involvement in the death of Kayla Jones, she would have looked at her son quite differently.

THIRTY-FOUR

Tammy called an hour before her arrival. There was something different in Sabathany's voice when she answered the phone. The sweet-as-pie tone Sabathany rolled out when she needed a favor had been replaced by a tone Tammy was better acquainted with—the one from the bossy, self-entitled diva who wanted what she wanted, and could not care less about the broke backs and hurt feelings necessary to get it. Yes, Sabathany could be a lot of fun—inspirational even—but to enjoy that, Tammy had to put up with the lesser attractive qualities of Sabathany's personality. However, the five thousand dollars Tammy was making for the drive was enough anesthesia to dull Sabathany's best shot.

The trip was a good one—winding through Nevada to Utah, then on to Colorado, Nebraska, Iowa and finally Minnesota. Having made the decision not to rush, the journey took a little longer, but allowed Tammy some alone time to think about whether to proceed with Kendrick Black's offer. She even got to relish parts of the country she might otherwise have never seen, rather than mere glimpses of what whizzed past her from the car window.

The weather became challenging once Tammy crossed the state line into Iowa. Heavy snow skewed her vision, but conditions improved the closer she got to Minneapolis.

Once Tammy went inside the hotel lobby, she called to let Sabathany know she was there. She was proud of herself for having made the trip alone, and arriving in one piece. As far as she was concerned, she earned her five thousand bucks.

Tammy found a place to sit at the bar. Twenty minutes later Sabathany came down to find her nursing a cocktail.

"Where are my things?" Sabathany asked.

Tammy stirred her drink with her index finger and then licked the finger. "No hello or how was your trip?"

Sabathany sat down, gesturing to the bartender. "Yeah, I'll have a glass of your Pinot Grigio." She gave Tammy a tight smile. "How was your trip?"

"Don't you worry, your Louis Vuitton luggage and everything in them made it here safe and sound," Tammy said.

This again? Why do I have to finesse every damn thing I say to her? Sabathany thought. She winked at the bartender when he returned with her wine. Her tone became like saccharine, "Girl, I'm just anxious to get the hell out of here. I'm sorry. How was the trip?"

Tammy stared into her drink. "Weather turned bad when I got around Iowa, but other than that, it was nice."

"Good. Not often you get the chance to see the country. How many people can say they've done that?"

"True," Tammy said, smiling at the accomplishment. "When do you wanna get going?"

"Tomorrow afternoon. I figure you could use some rest in an actual bed."

"That would be nice."

"Okay. I say we get something to eat. I don't know if you're in a going out kind of mood, but I'm sure we can find someone who knows the best places to hang out." Sabathany stroked Tammy's back.

"I assume you've got my money, right?" Tammy jerked away, tossing Sabathany a side-eye.

"Look, didn't I say you'll get your money?"

"Yes, you did. But saying it and actually putting it in my hands are two different things." Tammy looked about the bar before leaning in. "I want my money, and I'm not playing with you."

Sabathany pursed her lips, stung by Tammy's moxie. "I see someone found her big girl panties during her little adventure."

Tammy knew she pushed a button, and for the first time she did not much care if Sabathany was offended. As far as she was concerned, it was long past time Sabathany received some of her own medicine.

"I didn't travel all those miles to get the runaround. The intent isn't to get out of character with you, but if you plan on screwing me over, I will." Tammy confidently sipped her drink.

The two ladies ordered dinner at the bar. Tammy looked forward to eating something other than fastfood. Lobster Cobb salad and side of hush puppies would do the trick. Sabathany ordered an arugula salad and linguini with Cajun tiger prawns.

When the food arrived, the women glanced at each other's plates, but ate in silence. There would be plenty of hours to fill with innocuous conversation during the drive back.

The suite was unlike anything Tammy had seen before. Contemporary-styled living room, kitchen, dining room, media room and two bedrooms with en suites. The colors throughout were taupe and white. The view from the window looked down on to Marquette Street on Nicollet Mall. Christmas lights were already strung along potted trees, lamp posts, and framed storefront windows.

It was early evening when Tammy showered and crawled into bed. Between the trip and the lovely dinner, it did not take long for her to dissolve into the most comfortable bed she ever slept in.

Sabathany poured herself a glass of wine from the bottle of Sancerre Sauvignon Blanc delivered to her room. Closing her eyes, she pondered Tammy's earlier show of defiance. Not wanting to create a scene at dinner, she allowed Tammy to have her moment. But, now filled to her chest with exorbitantly priced wine, she was tempted to march into Tammy's room, wake her up, and give her a piece of her mind.

Let the bitch sleep, she thought to herself, resisting the impulse to go into Tammy's bedroom. There was no need to begin miles of journey back to California with such negative energy. Besides, once Sabathany arrived safely in San Diego, she would be sure to remind Tammy who was boss, and more than happy to do so.

THIRTY-FIVE

Lenox Hunter awoke to the expensive, burgundy down comforter being torn from his body. The room was dark, his eyes unfocused. He had no time to react to the deadly heaviness crushing his larynx.

"What'd you do to my sister?" a thundering voice demanded to know.

There was something familiar about the voice.

"Answer me!"

Recognition of the voice came to Lenox as he struggled to pry fingers from around his throat. A heavy tingling coursed through his temples and forehead. His words came out in a panicked jumble. "Man, I didn't do nothin' to her! I found her like that!"

"I thought you said you broke it off with her!" Kendrick loosened his hold just enough to allow Lenox to speak clearly.

"I did!"

Kendrick removed his hands completely from Lenox's neck. His expression was one of manic astonishment. "Then what in the hell were you doing over there in the first place?"

Lenox rubbed his throat and tried to find steady breath. "Man, Paris went crazy! She was pissed that I dumped her, and wanted to get back at me. Plus, she was threatening to rat to the cops!"

"So you killed her?"

"Hell no! I went over there to beat her up! All right? I was mad that she ruined my life, so I went over there to get in that ass!"

Kendrick grimaced.

"I didn't mean it like that. I was gonna put my hands on her, yeah, but ain't no way I would've done that to her. That kind of thing ain't my style."

Lenox gulped his raw throat. "Everything started when I brought Sabathany with me to try and convince Ashley to take me back. But it did not go well. When we left, Sabathany wanted me to take her back to the penthouse, but my mind was on confronting Paris. She had no idea I was gonna go over to the apartment. When we got there, I told her to wait in the car because I needed to go in for a few minutes. I promised her I would take her home when I came back."

"Does Sabathany know?"

"She knew something was wrong when I came back out. I told her when we got back to the penthouse."

"And no one thought to call? You couldn't call my family?"

"That's the thing. Sabathany told me she was over there the night before. She said it was to get Paris to help change your mind about how you were treating her. But, when I told Sabathany that we should call you, she got weird. She said no, that you and your family would figure it out soon enough. That didn't make sense to me unless she had something to do with the murder."

"Yeah, but what reason would she have for killing her?"

"I don't know, man. She said things got a little outta hand. When I asked what that meant, she gave me some lame-ass excuse. I must've been asking the wrong kind of questions, because next thing I know, she's moving to a hotel."

Kendrick climbed off the bed to take in all of what Lenox had told him. Despite the look of sincere bewilderment on

Lenox's face, none of what he had said made sense, leaving Kendrick with a sense of both Lenox's and Sabathany's guilt.

Pausing in the doorway, he turned around to see Lenox still struggling to breathe. "Get your ass out of my bed and come into the living room," he said over his shoulder.

Lenox followed slowly behind, like a wounded puppy following its owner. He was wearing a pair of Kendrick's pajamas. He was embarrassed by the cluttered state of the apartment, recounting every lazy moment he could have taken to straighten up but did not.

Kendrick fumed, taking in the extent of disarray, and Lenox's appropriation of his clothes. "I guess you thought you were going to come in here and just take over, huh?"

Lenox had no response.

"When's the last time you saw Paris."

"Last I saw her, she was driving off laughing."

"Did she threaten to go to the police before or after you saw her?"

"She called to tell me she was doing it all—confronting my wife and going to the cops. Said she was getting back at me and at you for turning your back on her."

"I got another question for you."

Lenox's face expressed annoyance.

"Relax, you're doing so well."

Lenox broke into nervous movement, picking up items around the apartment. He knew the gesture looked empty, but it was better than meeting Kendrick's judging glance. "I don't know any more than you do about who might've killed her, Kenny," he said. "Swear to God."

"That wasn't what I was going to ask you. I want to know why you stole $50,000 from me."

"I mean, you always said how you'd do right by me when you started making money. But, it seemed like every time you came home, you were acting grander and grander. Hell, you even treat me like I'm some peon, not like the cat you've known for the last fifteen years. I figured you'd get so high and mighty that you wouldn't make good on your promise. That's why I told you that bullshit about Ashley so you'd have to give it to me."

Kendrick wanted to beat Lenox within an inch of his life for that nonsense of an answer. "And once again you didn't trust our friendship enough to be straight with me. So, not only were you smashing my sister, and trying to force her to have a sex change on my dime, but you sold me some crap to get into my pockets? And to top it all off, you let Sabathany convince you not to tell anyone Paris was laying up dead in her apartment? Anything else I should know?"

"The operation was her idea."

"Man, shut your lying ass up!"

"Dude, I ain't lyin'!" An unexpected jolt of emotion brought Lenox to his knees. He cried soft and muffled sobs, like someone crying into a pillow. Lenox held his head up, ensuring that Kendrick saw the grief on his face and throughout his entire affect.

Unmoved, Kendrick said, "From where I'm standing, I see two people who were the last to see my sister. At this point, neither one of you are looking too great."

Lenox picked himself up from the floor, offended by the suggestion. "How are you gonna say that to me? You've been knowing me since we were fifteen. You know I wouldn't do something like that."

"No, I don't know that. Just like I didn't know that after all those years of listening to you go on and on about Pam Grier, come to find out, you prefer your women with something extra. You sort of left that out about yourself."

"Your sister is dead and you wanna do this now?"

"All you had to do was be honest. My sister was the most courageous person I knew because she lived her life honestly.

And yeah, it was difficult for her being bullied in school while she was transitioning, and being separated from her family, people who were supposed to have her back. But you chose the easy way out—the coward's way. Admit it, you wanted your cake and to eat it too."

"Man, come on! You *know* where we come from! You mean to tell me you would've been down if I told you that Paris and I were hooking up? You would've been okay with that?"

Kendrick moved about the room to avoid answering the question. Lenox knew the answer, and Kendrick knew that Lenox knew.

"Man, you can't even look me in the eyes and tell me. *Now,* who's being a coward?" Lenox said.

Kendrick went to the kitchen island and took the penthouse key from Lenox's small key ring. "You won't be needing this. And you're going to return the money you took from me."

The finality of it all made Lenox's jaw drop. But if there was any doubt to the meaning of Kendrick's actions, it died when Kendrick said, "My family needs me right now. I better not find you here when I get back."

THIRTY-SIX

December 3, 2013,

Sabathany dreamed colorfully of Guadalajara, Mexico the previous evening. Something had manifested itself within her; it told her that San Diego was no longer the place to hide. She visited Guadalajara with her high school Spanish class, so it helped that she had a serviceable command of the language. She found its beaches to be some of the most beautiful she had seen. Now was her chance to enjoy them as an adult, while she basked in the sun with a tropical drink in hand, waiting for her mother's murder investigation to go cold.

Sabathany awoke to flurries, but by mid-morning that dusting transformed into heavy, wet snow. She was uneasy, worried about the potential difficulty in getting out of Minnesota without becoming stuck.

Tammy came out of her room, fully dressed and unsure of which of Sabathany's many faces had surfaced to greet her in the morning.

"I didn't expect you'd be up this early," Sabathany said.

"Good morning," Tammy said, eyeing the impressive spread of breakfast foods on the dining room table. Lifting the silver lids revealed a plate of still warm, fluffy buttermilk pancakes adorned with fresh berries, and another plate of applewood smoked bacon. Without looking at any of the other plates she piled the bacon onto her plate of pancakes and poured a ramekin of maple syrup over the entire mass of food.

Sabathany watched Tammy tear through the food. Clearing her throat, she said, "Boy, you're hungry this morning."

"Can't help it. This is so good," Tammy said after the last bit of strip bacon disappeared into her mouth.

"I didn't know what you'd like to eat. I'm glad it isn't going to waste."

"Now, you know good and well you didn't order all this for me," Tammy said.

Ignoring the dig, Sabathany asked, "Did you sleep okay?"

Tammy nodded with overstuffed cheeks.

Sabathany turned away from Tammy's shameless gorging, and picked through her fruit plate, opting for the luscious pineapple. She stopped chewing when a picture of Paris Black flashed across the screen from a local morning news program. The cops had a lead, thanks to the killer's sloppiness. Never had fingerprints been found at any of the crime scenes until now. Sabathany smiled as an information hotline number scrolled on the bottom of the TV screen. She crossed over to the desk and found a small note pad bearing the hotel's name. She jotted down the number before forgetting it.

Sabathany continued watching the news, waiting to hear of any improvement in weather and driving conditions. When the commercials came around, she looked back at Tammy. Though she hated to admit it, a pilgrimage across the country all alone would drive her crazy. Tammy already displayed a shift in attitude toward her. That alone warned Sabathany to proceed with some level of caution. Maybe if she wrote a check right then Tammy would lighten up a bit, which made it easier to control her later, she thought.

Without saying anything, Sabathany went into her bedroom. Shortly after, she re-entered the living room, holding her checkbook and a pen. Standing over Tammy as she ate,

Sabathany filled out a blank check with a dramatic sweep, wanting Tammy to be aware of the gesture. Tammy was unimpressed and continued enjoying her pancakes.

"Here," Sabathany said, watching the check flutter to the table. She hoped it would not land on the splotches of maple syrup left on the plate.

Having eaten enough, Tammy pushed the plate away. "Thank you," she said.

By 1:30, Tammy gathered their luggage by the door and called the front desk to send a bellhop up for assistance. The angry Tammy who met Sabathany in the hotel bar the previous evening shifted into the more biddable friend Sabathany had grown to know and use at her will. With the check in her hands, she was forgiving and ready to move forward.

A broad shouldered and modelesque bellhop showed up at the door. He helped Tammy place the luggage on a rolling cart.

"Here, this is for you." Sabathany handed him a tip. "Tammy, you two go on ahead, I'll be down in a little bit."

"I was thinking the best way to do this is to pull the car around front. You think you'll be down in enough time before they start waving me away?"

"Oh, sure. Shouldn't take me long at all."

Dealing with Sabathany for so long, Tammy knew that "a little bit" in Sabathany's world meant something else.

Sabathany headed for the desk and picked up the room telephone and dialed the hotline number.

"This is Det. VanDrunen," a voice answered.

"I'm sorry, did I call the hotline?"

"Yes, ma'am. Did you have information regarding the Paris Black homicide?"

"Yes, I do. Write this name down . . . Lenox Hunter."

THIRTY-SEVEN

The public toilet was repugnant, making Tammy rethink how badly she needed to use it. The acrid smell of piss violated her nasal cavity. She did what she could to avoid touching the splattered toilet seat with her ass, though precariously balancing herself between the wall and rusty sink was difficult. Her arms vibrated as she held herself up, careful not to slide across the tile floor which was slick from snow and urine. A florescent light flickering noisily above caught smeared boogers and obscenities on the wall.

"Who's got time to write this mess?" Tammy wondered out loud, attempting to shake the last of her tinkle. When she finished, she felt accomplished for not having fallen onto the squalor. The almost empty liquid soap was gunky. She filled it half-way with water, then squeezed diluted soap onto her palms, failing to lather the way she wanted.

"Better than nothing," she said, emerging from the re-stroom, gulping fresh air. She walked to the front of the service station, returning the key to the teenage male attendant sitting behind the Plexiglas partition. He was pimply-faced and bored, amusing himself by texting on his phone.

"You might want to get someone in there to clean that bathroom. It's disgusting," Tammy said. She picked a couple of chocolate bars and passed them through the slot along with the bathroom key.

The boy looked up from his texting and gruffly scanned the candy bars.

"Oh excuse me, you must have something more important to do," Tammy said, but the comment seemed to float over the boy's head.

Sabathany was awake when Tammy returned to the car. She was attempting to read the road map.

"You don't need that. I'm using the GPS," Tammy said as though she was a genius for doing so.

"Now you tell me," Sabathany said.

"If you bothered to stay awake you might've seen me using it."

Sabathany lowered the crinkled mess of paper. She glared in Tammy's general direction without making eye contact. "How long have we been on the road?"

"Four hours."

"Are we still in Minnesota?"

"Yep. We should be in South Dakota in a couple of hours."

"That long?" Sabathany shabbily refolded the map and stuffed it back inside the glove compartment. Eyeing the candy bars, she took one without asking permission.

Tammy scratched a thin patch of frost from the lower inside corner of the windshield with her fingernails. "I figured once we crossed the state line we could stop somewhere to eat."

"Yes, please," Sabathany said, munching the candy bar.

"Bet you wish you ate something besides that plate of fruit, huh?"

"Just drive."

"Don't go back to sleep because you're up next."

The women flipped through one weak signaled radio station after the next. Finally, Sabathany played music from her smart phone.

Tammy turned the volume down and asked, "Did you really do it?"

Sabathany blinked, stunned by the abruptness of the question. "Did I do what?" she responded, stalling for time to think of her answer. It was too late to act as though she had not heard it.

"Did you kill your mama?"

"Don't ask questions you can't handle the answer to."

"I wouldn't ask if I couldn't handle it. Okay, you want me to tell you what I know?"

"What do you think you know?" A million butterflies fluttered in her gut.

"I know that you've been given a raw deal all your life. I know Lola has disrespected you for most of it."

Relieved that Tammy was on her side, Sabathany let out a sigh. Her fluttering stomach began to subside, followed by relaxation of the muscles throughout her body. "Biggest lesson I've learned is that you're not going to cross the finish line with everyone you start with. Lola proved that she wanted no part of me. So, yeah, I finally got to the point where I thought if she's going to basically kill herself, then I'll put her out of her misery."

A sign decorated with faces from Mount Rushmore appeared suddenly, welcoming the women to South Dakota—a pleasant surprise because it hardly seemed like two hours had passed.

Tammy took the first exit, which led them into a small town that looked like a movie studio backlot. At the end of the road was a restaurant called, "Happy's Chow Cabin."

"You hungry?" Tammy asked.

"Yeah."

"Doesn't look like a fine dining joint."

"That's fine."

"You sure? I can hop back on the freeway."

"I said it's fine," Sabathany repeated.

"All right." She turned into the full parking lot. Tammy unbuckled her belt and moved to open her door when Sabathany stopped her with a gentle grab of her arm. Tammy looked down at Sabathany's grasp, offended by the violation of space.

"Hold on just a sec. You weren't planning on telling anyone about what we talked about, right?"

"Right," Tammy said, deciding a simple answer was better than a long declaration of loyalty.

Sabathany looked unconvinced.

Tammy smiled. "Girl, I won't say anything. As far as I'm concerned, you did what you had to do."

The two women went inside the restaurant. "Helloooooo, and welcome to Happeeeee's Chow Cabin! Eat up," the deer head mounted above said in a low, almost intoxicated sounding voice. Then it chuckled.

A group of restaurant employees were congregated at the hostess stand. Each had the hardened face of toilers.

The eldest of the pack was a plump woman. Her big teased hair, stiff from hairspray, looked like a throwback to 1987; her eyes were frosty blue and her pale pink lips shimmered. She sized up the African-American women, the only two she had seen in the flesh in all her years alive. She smiled the kind of smile that said she was not prejudiced. "Just two of you?"

"Yes, please," Sabathany said.

"Follow me," the woman instructed the ladies.

The restaurant fell to a hush as they were led to their table. They encountered a medley of facial expressions from the other patrons as they moved through the dining room. Some were merely curious, while others were stern, borderline hostile. Sabathany focused on the fire blazing in the fireplace, and then the log cabin motif of old-style rifles, pots, pans and plates hanging along the stained, eastern white cedar walls.

The ladies were seated in a small booth, tucked in the rear of the restaurant. The benches creaked as they sat down.

"I thought I'd let you ladies know that we're out of fried chicken," the hostess said, handing them each a menu. There was an assumption in how she said it. "Amber will be your server tonight."

Sabathany and Tammy exchanged a look between them.

"Oh, so because we're black we want fried chicken?" Tammy whispered.

"She doesn't know any better. I mean, look at her," Sabathany said, opening her menu.

Each woman shook her head and perused the menu. Tammy was in view of the front of the restaurant. She watched the woman go back to the podium and resume her conversation.

"She went back over there to run her mouth! Ain't no 'Amber' coming over here!" Tammy said.

"Give it five more minutes."

Tammy stared in agitation; her jaw stiffened and eyes became hard. She felt she had been punked, especially when the hostess turned her back after realizing she was being watched.

"I'm gonna say something," Tammy said, watching the hostess lean into the group and whisper something before they quickly dispersed. Still, no one came back to the table. Tammy bolted up.

Sabathany grabbed her arm. "Sit."

"But she's messing with us."

"What did I tell you? I said, give it five minutes."

"Can't believe you're . . ."

Sabathany put a finger to her lips, hushing Tammy as Amber approached the table. Each of the young woman's steps lacked urgency. She was blonde and blue-eyed, most likely the lone beauty queen of the small town. She probably had a boyfriend named Hank, her co-conspirator in getting out of such a retched place.

"Are you ready to order?" she asked, gazing lazily into her order pad, and scratching the crown of her head with her pen.

"What kind of wine do you have?" Sabathany asked.

"Red or white."

"I understand that, dear. I'm asking what type of wine is it. Is it Merlot? Cabernet? Chardonnay? Pinot Grigio?"

Amber looked as though she had been asked to do long division in her head. "We have red or white, so I dunno about any of those. To be honest, we don't get too many people asking for that around these parts."

"It doesn't matter. I'll have an iced tea. And the meatloaf."

"And I'll have an orange soda, and meatloaf," Tammy said.

"Okay. Be right back with your drinks." Amber's walk away was suddenly bouncy.

"This was a bad idea." Tammy said, hoping she was saying what Sabathany was thinking.

"You shouldn't let her bother you. She's like a lot of the young things in L.A. who get these sorts of jobs just to fill their time."

"Well, these kids better stop all that, because I know plenty of people who could use the work, and would do a better job," Tammy said.

Amber returned with the drinks. "Here you go, ladies."

Tammy took a sip from her soda. Sabathany tore open a packet of sweetener.

"So, um, I need to know if you seriously won't go running your mouth to anyone about what you know, because if you do I'll have to kill you."

Tammy laughed, coughing from her soda. "Girl, I told you I wasn't going to say anything." She cleared her throat, waiting for Sabathany to join her in laughter, but Sabathany never laughed.

THIRTY-EIGHT

After the memorial service at the funeral home, many of the attendees crowded themselves inside the Black household, trading heartwarming stories around the dining and living rooms. They enjoyed the mountains of food while toasting in honor of Paris. There were still tears, but the laughter filling the house was far more powerful. People moved about, most of them well-meaning, and some merely following the scent of good food.

Feeling claustrophobic, Kendrick went outside. He descended the rickety steps of the porch and walked from the yard into the street where he was met with thoughts of the little girl's body crushed beneath the wheels of the dumped Escalade. Blindsided by memories, Kendrick dropped to the curb directly from where the accident happened. Closing his eyes, a white light flashed behind his eyelids. Then, she appeared to him . . .

"Hey, you look sad, Mister," Kayla said.

Kendrick turned around to find Kayla, looking disheveled as she always did when she came to him.

"That's because I am." Kendrick said, avoiding her eyes. "And I'm ashamed."

Kayla ran her index finger along the tear trail on his face. "What does 'ashamed' mean?"

Kendrick chuckled. "It means I feel really bad about something I did, and it's been bothering me."

"What did you do?" she asked innocently.

Kendrick sobbed, clasping his hands together, and bowed his head. "Something really bad."

Kayla giggled. "I already know why you're sad." Then she put her hands on her hips. "But, I wanna hear you say it."

"No. Please don't make me!"

"I'm glad you're sad." Kayla walked out into the middle of the street. She looked directly at him. "You should be!"

Sitting between two parked cars, Kendrick lifted his head in time to see a black SUV hit Kayla Jones.

"No!" he screamed.

A hand shook Kendrick's shoulder, rousing him from his daydream. Kendrick jerked away to see his brother, Alex, standing there.

"Man, it's freezing. What are you doing out here?"

Kendrick jumped up and ran from his brother, into the street. There was no one there.

"I must've been daydreaming."

"In this cold?"

"Yeah, it was getting crowded in the house, and I needed my space. I guess I got lost in my thoughts. "

A grey Buick slowed to a stop, parking in front of the two men. A plain-faced, but pretty Latina got out of the car.

"I'm Det. Leticia Ramirez, I've been working the Paris Black murder investigation." The way she flashed her badge seemed like a timed trick.

Alex recognized her as one of the detectives that ushered him from Paris's apartment. He puffed his chest out. "What can we do for you, detective? "

"Can we go inside the house and talk?" Ramirez asked, clearly the in-charge type.

Kendrick stepped forward. "With all due respect, we've got a house full of people. I think bad news would be too much."

Ramirez's eyes smiled. "Actually, I have some good news. We received a tip that led to the arrest of a Lenox Hunter."

"What?" the brothers said in unison.

"We have evidence that places him at Paris's apartment."

"Well, he and my sister were . . ." Kendrick gulped and averted his eyes. "Were messing around, lovers, boyfriend-girlfriend . . . whatever you want to call it, so of course his prints would be all over everything. But anyway, I just saw him, and he looked me dead in my eyes and told me he had nothing to do with it. In fact, he thinks a woman named Sabathany Morris is responsible for it."

Alex spoke up, "Detective, after you kicked me out, I didn't leave right away. When you and your partner went into the bedroom, some old lady said she heard a female laughing like the devil."

Ramirez's eyebrow arched. "And how would you know she said that?"

"Because I was standing out in the hallway with her when she said it. Both of us watched the comings and goings of officers. She said it like she'd just remembered it. But it was like she wasn't speaking to anyone in particular. Maybe she was talking to herself. But I do know she said the laugher was diabolica, which is feminine.

"And do you even know what that word means?"

"I work with a lot of Spanish-speaking people at my job. I pick up a word here and there." Alex said.

"Really? What do you do for work?"

"I'm the general manager at the McDonald's out at the airport. Ninety-eight percent of my staff is Spanish-speaking—Mexican, El Salvadorian, Guatemalan, take your pick. I know some of them don't get along and we had one of the ladies who cleans the lobby say that another woman who she didn't get along with had worked some black magic voodoo on her or something. She used the word diabolica and it was explained to me by a translator when I had to have a sit down with the two women. That's how I know the word means devilish," Alex said, thinking he had passed over an important piece to the puzzle.

"That's very good to know. Thank you. Don't worry guys, when it's all said and done, someone is going down for this."

Four hours of nothing passed at the police station. Lenox sat in the chair, flippantly tossing off answers as though Paris was an inconsequential fleck in the universe. He told the detective repeatedly that he did not know her. But it did not matter what came out of his mouth by that point, Det.VanDrunen knew it was a lie.

"Look, you're starting to piss me off," VanDrunen said, trying to keep his anger under control. "Now, I'm not planning on sitting here with you all night, because my wife and I have been having difficulties. She called to say she wants to talk things through. And I'm really hoping we do, because I love my wife. And I'm hoping I can get laid after we're done talking, so you're not gonna mess that up!"

"Sounds like a personal problem," Lenox said, without making eye contact.

"Oh, so you wanna be a wise guy, huh? Okay, Mr. Wise Guy, do you wanna explain to me why if you don't know the victim, how come your fingerprints are all over the victim's apartment? Can you explain pictures of the victim and threatening texts going back and forth between the two of you?"

Lenox continued to avoid eye contact.

"What do you think we do all day, eat donuts and play Scrabble? We always get the bad guy, and you sir are a bad guy!"

Both the detective and Lenox's eyes were drawn to the opening door. Det. Ramirez stood in its doorway. "Can I have a word?"

VanDrunen studied the young woman's face. It was void of the assuredness it once held before she went to speak to the Black family. He had faith that he just managed to piece together the perfect narrative, but the look on her face took a sledgehammer to it.

"Spoke to two of the brothers. One of them I had to shoo away from the crime scene after he barged his way past."

"Yeah, so?"

"He told me the mother of the landlord, who actually discovered the body, was out in the hallway saying that she heard a female voice laughing the night Paris was killed. Apparently our perp told Kendrick Black a woman by the name of Sabathany Morris also had dealings with Paris the night before."

"No way a female did that kind of damage. Sorry, my money is on the asshole we've got sitting in the interrogation room right now. He's playing games, yeah, but we'll get the truth outta him."

"Could you live with yourself knowing you didn't at least check this out? We need to see where it leads."

"No, bullshit! We are *not* doing this! I've got a second chance to make things right between me and Lacey. I'm telling you, Lenox Hunter may act like he's too cool for school, but he's our guy!"

"Look, I want you and Lacey back together as much as you do, but we've got to cover all bases."

VanDrunen sighed wearily. He had a strong suspicion that he was not leaving anytime soon.

Both detectives reentered the interrogation room. Lenox seemed less angry and more pensive.

"You look like you want to get something off your chest," Ramirez said.

"I knew Paris. I was seeing her on the side."

VanDrunen sat back in his chair, the hind legs of it teetering. He extended his arms out, massive palms up. "See? Now was that so bad?"

"But you gotta believe I didn't kill her. I know everybody says that, but I'm telling you the truth."

"Right."

"When I found her, I wanted to call the police, tell Paris's family, even, but she told me not to."

Ramirez perked up in her chair as VanDrunen settled back on all four legs on his. "Who's 'she'?" she asked.

"Sabathany Morris."

"Any idea why she'd suggest such a thing?" Ramirez asked, but both detectives leaned in with anticipation of the answer.

"Because she's running from the law her damn self, and didn't want to get stuck having to answer any questions. *That's* who you need to be looking for!"

"Are *you* running from the law?" VanDrunen asked.

"Not exactly."

"I don't know what that means."

Lenox slapped a palm to his forehead in frustration. He could feel the cold beneath it. It was too complicated a story to try and unravel. The best thing he could do was talk slowly and try to answer everything in one take. He braced himself, ready to put it all out there. He felt in control of his captive audience. Lenox could not help but smirk. Judge Judy, and something he heard her say constantly on her program came to mind . . . *When you tell the truth, you don't have to have a good memory.*

"We're gonna get to the bottom of this one way or another. You might as well get comfortable, because you're gonna be here awhile," Ramirez said.

Lenox took a deep breath, having nothing more to lose. "Fine. I'll start from the beginning."

THIRTY-NINE

Kendrick made it home to the penthouse. Looking around the apartment reminded him of the backstabbing squatters that had been there. He knew where Lenox was, but wondered how far away Sabathany had gotten. His mind turned a dark corner, thinking what would happen if she went bye-bye permanently. At least then he would have the peace of mind of knowing where she was, and the worry that she would share what he had done would be gone.

A sharp pinging came from the intercom. Kendrick had only heard the obnoxious sound twice before. He darted to answer the wall device before it offended his ears again.

"Yes, Javier?"

"Uh, yeah, Mr. Black, I have a Ms. Vaughn here to see you."

An enthused smile pushed through. "Send her up," Kendrick spoke into the intercom.

The time it took Brenda to reach the penthouse seemed like eons. Kendrick stood by the elevator door to receive her. He could not think of a better surprise, or wait to kiss her before she uttered a hello.

"Get in here," he said, giving her that kiss.

"I, uh, thought you could use my, uh, help quieting publicity," Brenda said, breathless and flustered. It felt good to feel wanted, especially after the way things were left.

Kendrick took her luggage, setting them by the kitchen island. He gave her a full tour of the apartment. She was taken with how the sterile décor contrasted with the warmer, tranquil furnishings of his L.A. dwelling.

Later, Kendrick ordered in Chinese food for the two of them. After lunch, they spent much of the day in bed. Both welcomed the closeness.

"How's the rest of the family holding up?" Brenda asked, her braids tousled all over the pillow.

"My mom is taking it pretty hard. I couldn't tell you what's going on in my dad's head. And my brother Alex is acting like I came back with the sole purpose of grand standing at my sister's funeral."

"Emotions, no matter how misdirected, are still honest."

"I guess."

"We also need to get this press conference scheduled. I made some phone calls to the local media before flying out. How's the day after tomorrow?"

"That's fine."

"All right. I'll handle everything."

"You're gonna love my mommy and daddy," Kayla said, her words coated with a childlike exuberance. It was the night before the press conference. Kayla's timing was perfect. She must have sensed Kendrick's apprehension and need for reassurance that he was doing the right thing.

"I will? Why?" he asked.

Kayla sat at the edge of his bed, nodding. Her attention bounced from one corner of the room to another. Kayla looked alive and vibrant. Her jogging suit was cotton candy pink—before the blood ruined it.

"Because," Kayla said with the usual giggle. She played with the draw strings dangling from her top. To her the reasons were evident.

"Why will I love your mommy and daddy?" Kendrick asked, intrigued.

"Because they'll forgive you if you turn yourself in."

"I'm sorry. I can't."

Kayla stopped twirling the draw strings. Her face had a maturity in it. It was the first time she came to him without disintegrating before his eyes. "Wrong answer."

"I'm being honest."

Kayla shrugged. "Okay. Just remember that I tried to warn you."

Before he could answer, Kayla faded into the dark. What if he did what Kayla wanted— freed himself of a secret that ruined so many lives? Would there be forgiveness waiting from her parents? Could he finally forgive himself?

The day of the press conference, journalists were hastily gathered, armed with phones and tablets, ready to record everything said. When the actor came out, he was accompanied by publicist, Brenda Vaughn and Kayla's parents, Antwon and Yvette Jones.

Antwon's face was somber, having just returned from a traumatizing third deployment in the Middle East. He had not expected to come home to the personal loss of losing a child, or the public's whispering and pointing of fingers. Nothing prepared him to spend an inordinate amount of time defending his wife's insanity following the death of their daughter.

Yvette was the army wife, collapsing under the pressure of having to do it all mostly alone. For a long time, focusing on her children helped combat the recurring impulses of depression she knew as a teenager. Now that depression loomed over her like a bad habit she wished she could break. Coupled with guilt, she ate little. Instead, she was goaded by the powerful temptation to climb into a hot bath and slit her wrist.

Stepping to the podium, Kendrick tapped the head of the microphone. He read from a prepared statement: "Tragedy is tragedy, and while I cannot say that I understand the grief that has befallen the Jones family from losing a child, I do understand the hurt that's felt from losing a loved one. It's my fervent prayer they will find who did this—to begin the healing. I know the family has had a difficult time, so I wanted to extend a financial hand. And now, I believe Kayla's mother, Yvette Jones would like to say something." He stepped aside to make room for Yvette to come to the podium.

She walked shakily, as though she had been recently awakened, discombobulated, from a nightmare. The look in her eyes was unfocused and faraway, and her hair lay swept into her sunken face. She took a deep breath before speaking.

"It's been very difficult just getting up in the morning, looking at myself in the mirror, and knowing that I could have prevented my daughter's death."

Her husband moved to her side and clutched her arm.

Before continuing, Yvette sought strength by putting her hand over her husband's. " A few days before she died, Kayla asked me if she could spend the night at one of her friend's house and I'd originally said yes. But that day I was in a dark mood. I don't know, I felt trapped with all these kids, and I love my kids, but they were driving me crazy. It's a lot when you feel like you're doing it all by yourself." Yvette burst into tears, suddenly focusing on the people in front of her. "I'm sorry, y'all."

A collective look of sympathy showed on the faces of the journalists.

"The kids weren't doing like I asked them to. Kayla hadn't cleaned her room and I don't know, I just lost it. I told her she couldn't go to her friend's house. 'But, Mama, you promised,' she said. Those were the last words my baby ever said to me." Yvette erupted into a full wail. "I guess when I was trying to get the younger kids settled down she left. I didn't even know she was gone."

Kendrick could feel the tears well in his own eyes. Hearing Yvette's story pulled at his heartstrings. He had no idea what she was going to say beyond thank you for the money, but to hear of her struggle and guilt brought forth pangs of his own guilt. He passed Brenda a look.

"Everyone said it gets better. But it doesn't feel like it. And even if it did, I'm not sure I want it to. I don't deserve it to." Yvette dissolved into an unintelligible tangle of words.

Antwon stepped up to the microphone. "We're grateful to Mr. Black for his generosity," was his succinct answer.

Kendrick initially agreed to the press conference because there weren't going to be any questions allowed, but at the last-minute Brenda thought better of it, arguing the press had to think they were being given something to justify their attendance.

"I like how you changed it up midstream," Kendrick said, scoffing.

"Don't worry. I'll handle the questions," she whispered in his ear. "You go ahead and walk them offstage."

Not wanting to lie any more than he had to, and feeling he had no choice, Kendrick flashed a smile, though worry showed in his eyes. He had no idea what the press was going to ask, but he could only imagine.

"My name is Brenda Vaughn, Mr. Black's publicist," she said, stepping to the podium. "I will be answering questions on his behalf."

"Why isn't Mr. Black answering his own questions?"

"Mr. Black wanted to be a beacon of strength offstage for both Yvette and Antwon Jones."

"Is Mr. Black related to the Joneses?"

"No."

"Any developments in the hit-and-run investigation?"

"Actually, I reached out to the detectives working the Kayla Jones case. I'm sure they are more than willing to share their findings."

Kendrick had a split-second to wonder what Det. Ramirez and an older white man were doing there. Watching from a monitor backstage, worry continued to bubble in his gut. He felt ambushed, unsure of Brenda's motive for inviting the police to his press conference. He returned to the stage, joining Brenda at her side as the detectives approached the podium.

"My name is Det. Leticia Ramirez and this is my partner, Det. Blake VanDrunen. On behalf of the entire Minneapolis Police Department, we would like to extend our deepest condolences to the Jones family. We are pleased, however, to announce that there have been some developments in the case."

The journalists stirred with interest. Many of them double checked their devices to make sure they were recording everything.

"We were able to reconstruct fragments from a headlight lens found at the crime scene. By doing so, we could ascertain the make of the vehicle from the company logo and manufacturer's code number. As of now, we've compiled a list from the DMV of registered vehicles that fit the description of a 2013 black Escalade. An eyewitness's account also corroborates this. We believe it's just a matter of time before we find the perpetrator involved in the death of Kayla Jones. They *will* be brought to justice!" Ramirez said, turning to look Kendrick directly in the eyes.

Kendrick nodded enthusiastically while meeting the detective's glance, hoping she saw how thrilled he was with the latest developments. Brenda thanked the press and stepped away from the podium to signal the end of the conference.

Kendrick followed her backstage, swapping his charming smile with glaring eyes.

"Can I talk to you for a minute?"

"Sure," Brenda said.

"Excuse us for a moment," Kendrick said to the Joneses. He led Brenda off to a far corner. "What the hell was *that* about?"

"The police had to be here, Kendrick. Otherwise, what would've been the point? The press wanted answers. If no one is implicating you, don't worry about it."

"Yeah, but you had no way of knowing what they were going to say. You took a chance and it just happened to work out for me. I might not be so lucky next time."

"Mr. Black, can we have a word?" a voice said.

Kendrick turned to see both detectives approaching. His heart pounded. It was as he feared, the moment he saw them on stage. To spare the actor any embarrassment they waited until the very end, out of the view and earshot of the press to detain him, or worse, to arrest him. His forced smile did nothing to stop the pounding in his chest. "Of course. What can I do for you?"

"Are you okay?" Ramirez asked, eyeing him closely.

"Yes, I'm fine."

"You sure? You're sweating a little."

"It's a little warm in here. And I was nervous because I hate speaking in public. I didn't want to embarrass the Joneses or their daughter's memory. I'm just glad the conference is over."

VanDrunen's eyes narrowed. "For someone who makes his living talking in front of cameras, you were nervous?"

"Yes. This is real, detective, not scripted make-believe. There's a difference."

"Mr. Black, we were wondering if you've been in contact with Sabathany Morris?" Ramirez asked, getting to the reason they stopped Kendrick.

Kendrick shook his head. "Can't say that I have. Last I heard she was on her way back to L.A."

Brenda jumped in. "Listen, with all due respect, Mr. Black needs to get going. He has a nice lunch set up for Mr. and Mrs. Jones, and knows how eager they are to get back to their family."

"I completely understand," Ramirez said. "Would you mind giving us a call when you have a free moment?" She handed Kendrick her card.

"Sure will."

Kendrick watched the detectives until they were out of sight. Once they were, he leaned into Brenda and said, "I hope you're satisfied."

Javier, the doorman, had been advised to allow Diane Black into the penthouse to ensure lunch was ready by the time her son and his guests arrived. She brought with her a savory chicken stew and pineapple upside-down cake.

Kendrick sat at the head of the table. It was obvious both Antwon and Yvette would have preferred to skip the lunch, but acquiesced out of two million dollars' worth of gratitude. Diane's diffident attempt at small talk received polite responses from Antwon on behalf of himself and his wife.

Yvette managed to finish the bowl of stew. The check was secure in her husband's wallet. She did what was expected— showed the public a grieving mother, eaten more than she had in a while, and was grateful. Yvette left charming the hosts to her husband, while she sat heartbroken, gazing out a window toward the stretch of gray skies.

"Sounds like the police are doing everything they can," Diane said, wishing she could say the same about her own daughter's case. "The good news is they're able to figure out the vehicle. Shouldn't be too much longer until they have a suspect."

Kendrick felt his stomach spasm. "Maybe they should just give themselves up," he said, ignoring an annoyed look from Brenda.

Yvette shrugged. "I don't care if they find the person today or tomorrow; it still won't bring back my child."

The spasm in the center of Kendrick's belly ballooned to an audible rumbling, followed by nausea.

"Are you all right, Baby?" Diane asked.

The skin below Kendrick's eyes twitched. "My stomach's been acting up. I'll be okay."

Yvette took the moment to give her husband a look, signaling she was ready to go home. Secretly she wanted to die, and no amount of money was going to change that.

Diane cleaned up, despite Kendrick's urging her to leave everything. Her desire to feel needed won out. Once she and the Joneses left, Kendrick found a spot on the couch. The relief he hoped would surface from forking over $2,000,000 of his money never showed up. A lesson was learned during lunch. Money had not brought happiness to either the giver or recipients. There was no peace of mind, and Kendrick doubted there ever would be.

Brenda joined Kendrick on the couch with two glasses of wine. She passed one to him. "Well, that went well, didn't it?"

"I did what you asked me to do. I gave you your press conference. A lot of good that did now that the cops are hot on my ass. And coughing up that sizeable restitution was a complete waste of time. You know why? Because none of us feel any better."

"Whoa, hold on a sec. I offered you a way to keep your ass out of prison. I never promised you'd feel guilt-free."

"I keep asking myself how you as a woman can do this."

"Do what?"

Kendrick waved his hands to underscore what was obvious to him. "You've had three miscarriages. Don't you feel even a little bad that Yvette and Antwon lost their kid?"

Brenda shrugged. "I mean, what do you want me to say? I figure I wasn't meant to have kids. Sure, sometimes I wonder what my life would've been like if I'd carried to full term, but that wasn't in my deck of cards. I'm not going to cry over what could've been because I choose to live in what is."

"And as a woman, you feel not one ounce of pity for Yvette?"

"Sure, I feel for her, but I don't see what the big deal is. She said herself she can't handle the other children she still has."

Kendrick no longer recognized the person sitting with him. "I can't keep this up. I'm done."

Brenda's eyes flickered. "What do you mean you're done?"

"I'm done with this whole thing. I tried it your way and it hasn't made anything better."

"So, what are you saying?"

"I'm saying I'm turning myself in."

The flickering in Brenda's eyes gave way to something dangerous. "You're doing no such thing."

"You're not running things anymore. I said I'm done."

"I'm not sure if you're just playing dumb, or you really don't understand how this works. I told you before that I've invested a lot of money in making you a star, and we're finally starting to see a return on it. You're not going to mess this up for me, Kendrick Black."

"And you can live with knowing we're keeping people from truly finding their peace?"

"You gave them two million dollars' worth of peace. If they can't find peace from that, too damn bad!"

"No. Peace is knowing that the person responsible for their pain is punished."

"You're not turning yourself in. Get that idea out of your head."

"Or what?"

"Don't play with me, little boy."

"Little boy? Are you threatening me?"

Brenda sipped her wine.

"There's nothing you can do that's worse than what I've already done."

"It was really nice meeting your mother today. It would be a shame if something were to happen to her."

"You better not go anywhere near my family!"

"You'll be in jail. What do you think you could possibly do about it from there?"

"I need some air," Kendrick said before leaving the apartment. If he stayed, he knew he would have been forced to do something very bad to Brenda. Fear or no fear, he loved his mother, and did not take Brenda's threat lightly. Later, as he walked the long city blocks of the neighborhood, he pondered Brenda's question.

Brenda called Kendrick as he approached a convenient store to buy gum.

"What the hell is wrong with me?" Brenda said, sounding as if she were regaining consciousness.

"I don't know, but I don't like the direction any of this is going."

Brenda's voice trembled. "I'm so sorry. I don't know what got into me. I didn't mean any of what I said."

"You're beginning to sound like that bitch Sabathany. You two playing on the same team or what?"

"Not at all. I'm just under so much stress. And I know it's nothing compared to what your family is going through. Please believe me, I don't want to add to that. I meant it when I said, I'm here to help any way that I can."

"Tomorrow we're burying my sister. Try not to freak everybody out," Kendrick said before hanging up the phone. With that call ended, a new call came through from a welcomed source.

"Hey there," Kendrick said with a renewed spirit. "I thought you'd forgotten all about me."

FORTY

When Tammy opened the bathroom door, she found Sabathany standing on the other side; an accusatory hostility simmered in her stare. "Who were you talking to?"

Tammy had seconds to eradicate the guilt from her face. "My ole man wanted to know when I was coming home. I think he's missing me."

Sabathany studied Tammy's face, her eyes lowered to a tight squint. "Well, we wouldn't want that now, would we? When are you going back to L.A.?"

"I told him as soon as you get situated."

"That's very loyal of you."

Tammy smiled. "Hey, you know I do what I can," she said, heading to her bags. She dug through, pulling out a pair of cut-off jean shorts and an orange and white tie-dyed t-shirt that reminded Sabathany of a melted creamsicle. "Thought I'd take advantage of that pool. I can't use the pool at the apartment. Not after some kid took a crap in it."

A laugh pushed through Sabathany's distrust. "Are you serious?"

"Swear to God. Saw a turd float right past me."

Sabathany's laugh splintered into a maniacal cackle. Tammy laughed, too, happy to have extinguished the awkwardness. "I was thinking, instead of going somewhere for dinner, why don't we grab something at the hotel restaurant. It looked nice. My treat."

Sabathany did a double take. She knew Tammy rarely had two nickels to rub together; every paycheck spent before she got her hands on it. "Isn't that a little expensive for you?" she asked.

"All the times you've treated me to nice meals I think I can afford to splurge this once," Tammy said.

Sabathany looked down at what Tammy planned to wear to the pool. "You know, since you're in a spending money mood, they sell really nice bathing suits at the boutique downstairs.

Tammy thought of the loose cellulite at her midsection. "Nah, this'll work out just fine."

"Suit yourself. When did you want to go down for dinner?"

"I don't care. Whenever you want."

"Fine. I'm going to go take a nap." Sabathany left Tammy to change into her swimming outfit. She retreated to the bedroom and lay down, waiting until she heard the click of the closing door. Sabathany got up and went to the door, opened it a sliver to hear the ding of the elevator down the hall. Once she heard the sound she listened for, she poked her head out just in time to see the last of Tammy disappear inside the elevator.

"Good, she's gone," Sabathany said to herself, tiptoeing to Tammy's purse as though Tammy were still in the room. She eyed the not very good Michael Kors knock-off, determined to find something that would give reason to the uneasy feeling she had. She carefully picked through the purse. It did not take her long to find what she was looking for, and she smiled when she found it.

That night's dinner was expectedly delicious. Both Sabathany and Tammy awaited their chocolate torte desserts. After four martinis, Tammy failed to realize that Sabathany had stopped at two. Sabathany let Tammy have her fun. After all, the good times would soon come to an end.

When the server delivered the desserts, Sabathany waited until Tammy had enjoyed two bites before she made her move.

"So, who were you *really* talking to on the phone earlier?"

Tammy paused, the third bite had just gone into her mouth, her lips closed around the fork. The clump of chocolate dessert slid down her throat. "I told you . . . my ole man."

Tammy watched the quick dissolve of Sabathany's cordiality as hate filled her eyes.

"You're sticking to that story, huh?"

Putting her fork down, she looked at Sabathany stupidly, looking guiltier than she intended to. To avoid Sabathany's hardened eyes, she looked at the partially eaten dessert, which suddenly had become unappetizing. She wished she had just dropped Sabathany off out front of the hotel. She now regretted the food, the road trip and the $20,000 Kendrick Black had given her, especially when Sabathany slid the phone number in front of her. Swallowing audibly, she said, "I know what it looks like."

"So do I. But I'm not one to jump to conclusions. Why don't you explain it to me?"

Tammy looked up, trying to dial back her resentment. "He just wants to keep an eye on you. I don't know what the hell you said or did to that man, but he doesn't trust you."

"How many times have you been in contact with Kendrick?"

Tammy averted her eyes again. "I haven't."

Sabathany kicked Tammy under the table, causing the table to shake. Tammy lurched forward, surprised and embarrassed as her right shin throbbed in pain.

"Hurts, doesn't it?"

Tammy nodded. Tears spilled from her eyes; the throbbing became a burning pain.

"If you don't tell me what I want to know I'll do it again, and I don't care who sees it."

Tammy's face crinkled like a child fearing an impending ass whipping.

"How many times have you been in contact with him?"

"Twice. Once just before we left Wyoming. He wanted my banking info to transfer some money."

"Really? Well, for my own information, how much is your betrayal worth exactly?"

Tammy shook her head.

"How much?"

"$20,000."

"That much, huh? You're an expensive traitor."

"Sabath—"

"When was the last time you spoke to him?"

"Today."

"When you were in the bathroom?"

Tammy choked back tears. It hurt to talk. She nodded.

"Does he know where we are?"

Tammy nodded again, feeling Sabathany's heeled foot landing on her left shin to complete the torture. She felt something both wet and warm trickling down her leg.

Sabathany shook her head, genuinely disappointed. "How could you do this to me? You know I have trust issues."

"He told me you were talking shit about me."

"Aw, bitch, please. That's no excuse! You know, I was *really* hoping I'd be able to make it to Mexico without any more drama. Looks like you brought the drama right to San Diego."

"What are you going to do?" Tammy cried.

"Well, now that you've got him after my ass, I'm gonna have to get out of dodge pretty fast."

"I meant to me," Tammy said meekly.

"Come on, you know perfectly well what I'm going to do to you."

Tammy erupted into loud sobbing.

"Don't bother crying the blues. That doesn't work with me." She slid the remainder of Tammy's dessert toward her. "Here, you may as well finish it. And don't worry about dinner. I got it. It's the least I can do."

FORTY-ONE

The eulogy for Paris Black was held the next day in the church she grew up in, a dilapidated structure, made of white stucco and brown wood. The church brought back memories for Kendrick—first Sunday potlucks, guest preachers, baptisms and weddings.

For two hours, family and friends packed the main chapel. It warmed Diane's heart to know her daughter lived in a space of immense love, with the hundreds of people decked out in colorful and unusual outfits in celebration of Paris's colorful life.

Several people got up to offer their accounts of the woman whose life was taken tragically. The pastor finished with a prayer, then motioned to the small choir. They sang one of Paris's favorite hymns, "Just a Closer Walk with Thee." The family walked out, followed by the pallbearers holding up the casket to load into the hearse.

Only immediate family and friends went to the cemetery. As the group stood near the six feet of partially frozen burial ground, watching Paris's casket being lowered into the earth, Brenda held Kendrick's hand. He went along with it, inwardly wanting to flick her hand away. Kendrick kept his eyes focused on the burial, while in his periphery Brenda focused on him.

When the group dispersed, Kendrick felt his phone vibrate. A text message appeared on the screen. *"Deals off. Say goodbye to freedom!"*

Kendrick looked up from the text into the starkness of everything around him. The white, sunless skies and the snow bleached everything out. His crestfallen face changed to fear. Brenda noticed the switch.

"What's wrong?" she asked. Her gaze fell to the phone, then back to Kendrick.

Kendrick handed the phone to Brenda. Tension edged the outlines of his face.

Brenda read the text. "Who sent this?"

"Sabathany."

The two moved away from the gravesite.

"What does it mean?" Brenda asked.

"After I told her I knew she had her mother killed, we agreed she wouldn't say anything about Kayla. She must've found out that I was keeping tabs on her."

"Sounds like a threat."

"It is a threat."

"But, is she just blowing smoke, or is this something we need to be concerned about?"

Kendrick did not say anything.

"Kenny?"

"I don't know."

"That's not an answer. If she's going to tell on you then we have to deal with the situation head on."

"I'm already up to my eyeballs in trouble. I don't need anything else to have the cops coming after me for."

"Where is she now?"

"The Rising Sun Hotel and Spa in La Jolla. But her friend said she's going to be making a move across the border soon."

"Yeah, especially now that she knows you've been spying on her."

"I only did it because I didn't trust her."

"Okay, we've got to get back to L.A. right away. I'll charter a plane and we'll leave tonight."

"No, I can't leave my family like this."

Brenda sighed. "You don't know what Sabathany's told the cops. They could be looking for you as we speak."

"I don't care. I need to be here for my family. I'm going to head back to their house. Take the key and go back to my apartment."

Brenda sighed a second time, more forcefully, pushing her swirling breath into the cold air. "Don't you want me to come with you?"

Without answering, Kendrick headed back to the remaining family standing at the grave.

"Will I see you tonight?"

There was still no answer.

FORTY-TWO

Lenox sat across from Detectives VanDrunen and Ramirez, noting the conspiratorial smirks on their lips.

"Did you get some rest?" VanDrunen asked.

"Not even a little bit," Lenox said.

"We paid your wife a visit this morning. How do you think that went?" VanDrunen asked.

Lenox shrugged.

"We figured she might be a character witness on your behalf."

"For real?"

"Yep. She was very gracious. Offered us coffee."

Lenox smiled, recognizing the trait of generosity in his wife.

"I asked her about the day Paris came by the house."

"What did she say?"

"Just that Paris was very confrontational. I asked her if she thought you killed Paris."

Lenox squinted. There was something in VanDrunen's tone, and it matched the *I know something you don't* expression on his face. "I know she didn't say yeah."

VanDrunen shrugged. "She didn't have to say anything. We found your DNA all over the apartment."

Ramirez said, "But, your wife did say you were in a rage after Paris left."

Lenox sat up in his chair. "That's because she came to my house starting all kinds of static. You'd be in a rage, too!"

"Did you kill Paris?"

"I already told you no. And, I already told you who to look for. Sabathany killed her. Why else was she so hot to get outta town after I asked her about going to Paris's place?"

VanDrunen cleared his throat and said, "I guess we'll never know. But I can tell you that your wife was full of surprises."

Lenox rolled his eyes. "Man, just say what you gotta say, and quit playing games!"

VanDrunen smiled. "You know what? I'm back in my wife's good graces, which means I'm in a really good mood. So much so, that I'm not going to take issue with your tone. After all, you seem to have forgotten that you're addressing an officer of the law," he said, the smile fading to dead seriousness.

Ramirez took over. "Mr. Hunter, your wife killed Paris."

"What?"

Ramirez nodded. "She went over to Paris's apartment in the middle of the night while your children slept, and she stabbed Paris forty-one times. Then, she severed Paris's male genitalia. Now, your wife may have you snowed with the whole innocent routine, but today when we were at your house, your little boy came running from another room swinging a plastic grocery bag in his hand. When he tripped, and fell, a carving knife fell out of the bag and spun across the floor with enough DNA on it to match Paris's."

"And she confessed?"

"Yes."

Lenox sank to his knees and clasped his hands together. He looked thankful.

VanDrunen tapped his pen against the edge of the interrogation table. "You don't seem too broken up by it, or Paris's death."

"As far as Paris's concerned, I cried all the tears I'm gonna. Yes, there was a time when I loved her, but she showed me what kind of a person she was when she couldn't get her way. She didn't deserve what Ashley did to her. My wife is clearly sick for doing what she did. But, I ain't gonna lie, I'm glad you know that I'm no murderer."

Ramirez said," I think that officially clears you from this case."

Lenox stood up excitedly. "That's what I'm talkin' about! Guess that means I get to go home to my kids now."

"I'm afraid we're not quite done yet."

Lenox looked perplexed. "We're not?"

"Not by a longshot," VanDrunen said, staring coldly.

Lenox lowered himself back into his seat. "Then what else is there?"

"I'm glad you asked. You know about the little girl who was run down by the car?"

"I heard about it."

"Then, I imagine you'd like to see whoever was responsible brought to justice, right?"

Lenox just stared.

"Fortunately, when you've been doing this job for as long as we have, you get really good at what you do. See, we know what vehicle was involved in running down Kayla Jones, and we know the name to whom it was registered. Any idea who that could be?"

Lenox continued to stare, but said nothing.

"Not one guess? All right, it was your buddy, Kendrick Black. Now, I bet you're thinking, 'So what? There's a whole bunch of people who own a 2013 black Escalade.' And you'd be right. The thing is, there's only one that was reported stolen on October 13th, the day Kayla was killed."

Lenox began to squirm. A flush of heat overwhelmed his face.

VanDrunen rose from his chair, his eyes twinkled. "Oh, but it gets better. We were able to check the 911 and cell phone records. Both show the call originated from your cell phone."

"Who stole the car, Lenox?" Ramirez asked.

Lenox dropped his face into his hands. He could smell the trouble he was in. He thought about the $50,000 he took from Kendrick sitting in his account, and how he intended to keep it.

"Look, you already know who killed that little girl," he said.

The two detectives smiled at one another before Ramirez said, "Yes, but we don't have proof. You want us to believe the car was supposedly stolen? All right. How do we know you weren't the one who stole it and hit Kayla?"

"You know that's not how it went."

"Okay, tell us how it went. Give us the proof we need."

Lenox swallowed hard. "If I talk, what do I get in return?"

VanDrunen smiled. "We'll get to that, but first you gotta give us what we want."

FORTY-THREE

Kendrick felt the comforter slide creepily away from his body. He opened his eyes to find Kayla standing at the foot of the bed, her eyes glimmering like a feline at night.

"What do you want?" Kendrick asked.

"I'm disappointed in you, Mister. You should've turned yourself in."

Kendrick was struck with how different Kayla's voice sounded. It was like a grown woman's, only her body was still that of a young girl. "You know that's not possible. Why do you think I gave your parents $2,000,000 of my money?"

Kayla's eyes hardened. "You know what? I think I'm going to enjoy making your life a living hell."

"Didn't you hear what I said? I gave your parents money! I understand the money can never replace you, but it's a start!"

"If you know what's good for you, you'll turn yourself in."

"I can't! What don't you understand about that?"

Kayla shrugged her soiled pink shoulders. "Okay, have it your way. Just remember this, you're gonna get what's coming to you . . . and it's coming soon!" Kayla stepped back into the dark of the room as Kendrick's cell phone rang. The ringing was distant at first, becoming louder and louder . . .

Kendrick's cell phone woke him from the dream. He found himself in his old bedroom at his parents' house. "I'm leaving now," he answered, knowing who it was.

"Why didn't you come home last night?" Brenda sounded restless.

"We drank all night, and I decided to stay put."

"Yeah, but you could've called to let me know."

"You're right. I'm sorry. Let me say my goodbyes."

"Good. I'll send the car for you."

"Okay."

"It should be there within the hour."

"Fine."

"And just so you know, Kendrick Black, there's going to be some changes when we get back to L.A."

"Okay, whatever *that* means."

Kendrick got up and put on his clothes. The smell of fresh coffee enticed him downstairs. As he descended the stairs, the toasty warmth of the house reminded him of winters from his childhood.

He found his mother in the kitchen, humming along to Ella Fitzgerald singing "Something's Gotta Give." The moment she laid eyes on him, she smiled the smile of a proud mother. Kendrick had never seen her look at any of her other children the same way, and he knew at least a few of his siblings resented him for it.

"That Brenda woman is nice. Too bad she couldn't come by the house to visit for a bit," Diane said.

"She's okay."

"Uh oh."

"What, uh oh? We're taking things slow," Kendrick said.

"She's better than that girl you brought a couple of months ago."

Not really, Kendrick thought.

Diane put down her coffee mug and moved closer to her son. "You make me so proud. I know I ain't supposed to say this, but I will. You're my favorite."

"Mama!"

"What, you think your daddy is the only one who can have a favorite?"

"You mean Alvin?"

Diane nodded. "Both of you had a dream, but you were the one that got the hell outta here to go claim it. And, while it made me sad to see you go, you've done well for yourself. How can I not be proud of that?" Her eyes rippled like an otherwise still lake.

Kendrick took his mother's hands. "Mama, sometimes I wish you wouldn't carry on like you do. The other kids hate me for it."

"Honey, I love every one of my children. But, you're special, and you made something good out of what God gave you. I admire that. I wish I had followed my dreams, but then if I had, I wouldn't have had my wonderful family. I wouldn't change that for nothin'!" Tears fell from her morning eyes. "And, for the record, you're not my only favorite, you know? I have a lot of respect for Paris being who she felt she was meant to be. A lot of people don't understand that sort of thing. But she had her family's support . . . well, except from your father."

Kendrick stared at his mother. He wondered if she would still love him if she knew what he did. He uttered *I killed Kayla Jones* in his mind, hearing the words hover above him in an echo. He envisioned the morphing of his mother's face from brief incredulity to rage. And he could almost feel the thud of her balled fists against his chest as though they were meat tenderizing mallets.

"That was really nice what you did for that poor couple. I know they had to be out of their minds," Diane said, breaking Kendrick's internal story. "And I hope whoever did this rots in hell. I can't believe a person like that can lay their head down at night."

"It was an accident," Kendrick said absently.

"If it was an accident then they should've taken their ass to the police."

"You're right, Mama," he said, extinguishing the beginnings to an argument. "You're right."

Kendrick pulled at the gooey cinnamon roll his mother placed before him, drifting into silence. He already said too much.

Diane spoke about the relationship problems Alex was having with his wife. Kendrick listened, but offered no opinion. As he finished the last morsel of the roll, the theme to *The A-Team* sounded from his phone.

"Yeah?" he answered, wiping away the stickiness from his fingers.

"Mr. Black, I'm outside when you're ready, sir," the driver said.

"Okay. Be out in a sec."

Kendrick ended the call and turned to his mother. He could tell from the sadness on her face that she knew it was time for him to go.

"You be safe. Call me first thing when you get back to California, ya hear?" Diane said, helping him fasten his coat.

"I think I can handle my coat."

"I know it. You're thirty-years-old, but sometimes I still see you as a little boy. Ain't that nothin'?"

Kendrick smiled. "Yeah, and you loved me even when I was bad, right?"

"What kind of question is that? Of course, I did."

"That's good to know. Try and remember that when my name is all over the tabloids one of these days," he said.

Diane looked mildly concerned. "Why, what happened?"

"Nothing. Just saying."

FORTY-FOUR

When Kendrick returned to the penthouse, he found Brenda in the bathroom, putting cosmetics into a transparent case. He stood in the doorway, expecting the silent treatment as punishment for staying out all night, but she had a piece of news for him.

"Just got off the phone with the studio. They're greenlighting a project where you'll play opposite Kevin Hart as his younger brother. His character needs a kidney transplant, and yours is a match, but there's bad blood between you. They said they'll give you ten to do it!"

Kendrick grinned. "Don't play. Ten million dollars?"

"Yep. Now, bear in mind, it's not what Kevin is probably gonna get, but now you can only go up from here. No more six-figure deals."

Kendrick's smile dimmed. "You don't think they'll renege, do you?"

"Nope. Kevin's movies usually do well at the box office, so they aren't taking a huge risk. Trust me, they'll make their money back. And then, I'll get my return from my investment."

Kendrick dropped to his knees, clasping his hands together. All the hard work had finally paid off. He was now playing in the big leagues.

"And you thought I wouldn't deliver."

"There was never a doubt in my mind. I knew you'd work your magic." He rose from the floor and pulled Brenda close.

He kissed her tenderly. "How are we doing with time?" he asked.

Brenda looked at her watch. "We're good. Why?"

"Because I was thinking about taking you in the bedroom and putting it on you. When's the flight?"

"At one. By the way, I got some good news for myself. I finally was able to schedule a meeting with a potential new client I've been after."

"Who is it?"

"Devon Thomas. Know him?"

"Doesn't ring a bell."

"I'm meeting with him tonight."

"Cool."

"I'll be in there in a minute," she said, finishing the packing of her makeup.

Kendrick went over to plug in his phone to the charger, passing a mirror. He froze, not recognizing the man staring back at him. He was just about to sleep with the woman who had threatened to do harm to his mother.

She said she didn't mean it, he thought as he pulled the black cashmere turtleneck over his head. He caught his reflection again. *How can I sex her when earlier I wanted to break her damn neck?* Kendrick closed his eyes, and imagined signing contracts, and the number of zeros added to his bank account. "Guess I got more Hollywood in me than I thought," he muttered.

The intercom erupted with loud incessant chirps. Kendrick put his shirt back on and ran to answer before the intercom chirped again.

"Yes?" he said.

"Mr. Black, there's a couple of detectives on the way up to speak to you," the doorman said.

A pounding in his chest was instantaneous. He walked toward the elevator doors as though he were being led to the gallows.

When the doors opened, Detectives VanDrunen and Ramirez emerged. Like every other time Kendrick saw them, both wore serious expressions.

"Mr. Black?" Ramirez said.

"Yes?"

"We'd like you to know that we found the person responsible for the death of your sister. It was Ashley Hunter."

Kendrick's face relaxed. "Are you serious?"

"Yes. We have a full confession."

"Revenge?"

"More or less," VanDrunen said, noticing the luggage propped against the wall. "Someone going somewhere?"

"Yes, we're heading back to California this afternoon," Brenda said, entering the room.

"I'm afraid Mr. Black won't be going anywhere with you."

"I beg your pardon," Kendrick said.

"Sir, we're going to need you to come down to the station with us," Ramirez said.

"For what?"

"We'd like to ask you some questions regarding your involvement in the vehicular homicide of Kayla Jones."

"This is outrageous! The only involvement my client has with Kayla Jones is forking over $2,000,000 to the family so they can get on with their lives the best way they can," Brenda said.

VanDrunen turned to Brenda. "Are you his attorney?"

"No, his publicist and agent."

"Then, Miss . . ."

"Vaughn."

"Miss Vaughn, if you have no legal reason to speak on his behalf, I suggest you stay out of this."

"Absolutely not! My client will not be speaking with you until he's conferred with an attorney first."

Both detectives looked at Kendrick, who averted his eyes.

"You saying he's guilty?" Ramirez asked.

Choosing her words carefully, Brenda said, "Uh, no. I'm just thinking about the optics of the situation. We wouldn't want tabloids running stories that aren't based in fact. How do I know someone down at your precinct won't leak lies to the press?"

"With all due respect, Miss Vaughn, if he was so concerned with his image, he should've went to the police immediately following the accident. Look, we have it on good authority that he was involved. In fact, the informant was more than happy to blow the whistle on him."

"It would be nice if everyone stopped talking about me as though I ain't even here!" Kendrick said.

"You don't have to say anything to them," Brenda said.

Kendrick turned to face Brenda. He saw fear in her eyes. "I'm going to go with them. I'll get back to L.A. on my own."

He tried putting forth a calm demeanor in hopes that she would not find the likelihood of that to be nonexistent.

"Okay, fine. I'm still going to contact your lawyer."

There was a peace that settled on Kendrick's face that she took as him accepting his fate. The last thing she saw him do was put on his heavy coat before following the detectives into the waiting elevator. His back remained to her as the doors closed.

The tears were immediate, though Brenda had no idea what she was crying for. Was it the loss of her investment? Or was it that this delectable man had made her feel beautiful again, if only fleetingly? She doubted she would get another chance at happiness with such a premium specimen.

Brenda called her driver to tell him to come earlier. No sense in waiting around a place that now felt as though she were trespassing. As she went throughout the apartment to make sure she had everything, she heard the distant ringing of a phone coming from where Kendrick had plugged it to charge it. Its screen was lit up, showing the number of the incoming call. She pulled the phone from its charger and answered it.

"This is Kendrick Black's phone."

There was a long pause, with activity going on in the background.

"Hello?" she said.

"May I please speak to Kenny?" a panicked voice asked.

"Who the hell is this?" Brenda asked. Insecurities of not being good enough resurfaced.

"This is Tammy. *And who is this?*"

"This is Mr. Black's publicist. What do you need, Tammy?"

"I need to talk to Kenny."

"Kendrick is unavailable right now."

"Well, can you please tell him to call me back? I need help." The woman's fear seemed genuine.

"Is there something I can help you with?"

"I'm in trouble."

"What kind of trouble?"

"I think Sabathany is gonna try to kill me."

"Are you two still in San Diego?"

"How do you know about that?"

"I just know. Are you?"

The line went dead.

Brenda stared into the phone after the call ended.

"I see the bitch made good on her threat," she said to herself. "This is all Sabathany's fault. Now I'm out a whole lotta money thanks to her!"

Taking Kendrick's phone with her, she went back to the living room and put the phone in her purse. She reached in further and pulled out her own phone. Scrolling her contacts, she came to the number she was looking for, and dialed.

"Hey, Blu! Been a long time, Baby. Say, is that friend of yours still out in San Diego? He is? Good. I've got a little situation."

FORTY-FIVE

From the moment Kendrick left his apartment with the detectives, he had every intention of coming clean. The Jones family came to mind, and how relieved they would be to know he was in custody. He hoped they would receive solace from that. He would finally enjoy sleep uninterrupted by a decomposing phantom-child. However, by the time he arrived at the police station, something changed. He remembered the great news Brenda had shared, and all that awaited him in L.A.

When he was brought into the interrogation room, he decided to stand mute. The detectives were tickled.

"Do you know what I like most about my job?" VanDrunen asked.

Kendrick sat across from his captors, arms folded.

"I like that sometimes, not often, a miracle happens where I get to kill two birds with one stone. Basically, solve two disparate cases at once."

VanDrunen searched Kendrick's otherwise expressionless face for any sign of emotion. His experience told him it was there, but he would need to dig a little deeper for it. He gave Ramirez a look, prompting her to slide a manila folder in front of Kendrick.

"Open it," she said.

Kendrick looked down at it, but was otherwise still.

She flipped open the folder, and took out four large photographs taken at the accident site. Each photo was of Kayla's corpse. She laid them out, side by side. "Look at them," she demanded.

Kendrick peered at the photos. Kayla looked unlike what he thought she would. She was lying on her back, head turned to the side. There was no twisted, bloodied heap of flesh lying in the street. There was blood and a vacant stare, the only two things that resembled what appeared in his mind's eye. He took comfort that her body had not been broken horribly, considering the damage to the front of the Escalade.

"Everyone in this room knows you did this," Ramirez said, pulling the reports from the folder. "We know, because Lenox was willing to give you up to save himself."

Kendrick's face showed mild surprise. "Wow," he said.

"See, he begged us to cut him a deal, especially now that he's all his kids have now. Funny how he didn't give a shit about this kid right here," VanDrunen said, tapping the photo closest to himself. "Minimally he's looking at possible obstruction with aiding and abetting, so he was more than willing to throw you under the bus. Little does he know there's not gonna be any deal. For him . . . or you."

Kendrick began to breathe hard. His eyes became moist.

"We know Lenox Hunter was the first person you contacted after the accident. We know you ultimately gave him the okay to junk the vehicle for $10,000," Ramirez said.

"Yeah, but the funny thing is," VanDrunen said with a chuckle. "You wasted your money. *They never junked it!*"

"What do you mean they never junked it?"

"Just what I said. In fact, they fixed the Escalade and had plans to illegally sell it. So not only did they pocket your ten grand, but had we not gotten to them first, they stood to gain a profit from an illegal sale of a vehicle that was used during the commission of a crime. You really shouldn't feel bad," VanDrunen said with a cool smirk, "You're not the only one getting nailed for this."

Kendrick again looked at the photos, finding it easier to look at the deceased than at the detectives who were taking pleasure in bringing him down.

The thought of his two homes sitting uninhabited materialized in his mind. He also envisioned the contract to star in a Kevin Hart film going up in flames. But he was okay with it. He had to be. He thought of Yvette, who looked so emaciated and detached. He thought of his sister, and how he still thought her murder was God's punishment stretched over an entire family. Tears fell onto one of the photos.

"I wanted to come forward so many times, but people kept telling me the money would cover everything. After a while, I started to believe them."

Ramirez frowned. "Nobody here feels bad for you. The only reason you're crying is because you got caught. Pure and simple. How do you even sleep at night knowing what you did?"

Kendrick glared at her, taking the detective by surprise. "How in the hell do you know I sleep at all? This isn't who I am. I wanted out of that Hollywood life where everybody is in it for themselves. I kept telling myself that somehow I wasn't like those people, when all along I was just as bad. Right before you guys came to get me, I was about to make love to a woman who the day before had threatened to bring harm to my mother." Kendrick shook his head. "I ain't no better than any of them."

"What woman?"

Brenda's face came to Kendrick's mind. He imagined her chartered jet ascending into the skies as he sat in the police station. "Nobody important."

As Det. VanDrunen read him his rights, Kendrick barely heard a word said to him. Closing his eyes, he could hear Kayla's effervescent laughter. Although he never did as she had asked him by turning himself in, the police got him anyway.

He wondered whether she forgave him despite that. Then, he doubted it.

FORTY-SIX

It was late afternoon. Sabathany spent much of the day by the hotel pool, sipping La Jolla Breezes, wondering what to do about a situation named Tammy?

She watched Tammy sit at the outdoor bar, inebriated, and making ugly, drunk faces. Sabathany knew Tammy well. The only times she had seen Tammy drink to this extent was when she was bothered about something. In this case, it was the guilt she felt for double-crossing her friend.

After dinner the previous evening, Tammy spent all night trying to make amends for what she did. It was guilt keeping her in San Diego long after she knew she had served her usefulness. However, despite Sabathany's sudden change of heart, she still did not trust Sabathany's intentions, fearing there would be a hit out on her once she returned to Los Angeles. After an unsuccessful call to Kendrick for help, Tammy thought it safer to stick close to Sabathany's side until she knew how safe she was.

Sabathany continued sipping her drink, observing Tammy's pitiful attempts at flirtation with three men at the bar. One of the men made it clear from his brooding and constant watch checking that he was not interested. Unfazed, Tammy set her sights on the two men sitting to her right. They were businessmen using their last day in San Diego to catch sun and sex. The men had enough booze floating in their systems to be open to any sexual adventure presented.

Sabathany continued watching what she viewed as Tammy's buffoonery. It was a shame they had arrived at this place of distrust. Tammy had always been such a loyal, hardworking underling of a friend. However, those qualities went out the window when she aligned herself with Kendrick, purporting to be on Sabathany's side. Not to mention the moment in South Dakota that changed everything—receiving confirmation that Sabathany brought about her own mother's demise. That confession could go no further. As Sabathany watched a woman who had no idea this day was to be her last, one question orbited her brain. How was she going to kill Tammy? Her attention shifted toward the height of the hotel just beyond the verdant trees and brush. That's when the possibility dawned on her of an intoxicated Tammy having an accident over the ledge of the hotel room balcony.

"Girl, what do you think you're doing?" Sabathany said, approaching Tammy. She made sure to speak loud enough for the businessmen to hear.

"I'm trying to enjoy myself. Why? What are you doing?" Tammy responded in the same insolent tone that had been like nails down a chalk board to Sabathany.

"I think you'd better slow down. You're getting sloppy. You could hurt yourself."

"And I think you'd better stop killing my action with these sexy men!"

Sabathany glared. She would enjoy watching Tammy's body plummet to the ground, hearing it splatter like ground meat upon the pavement.

Tammy caught something in Sabathany's visage that said she crossed the line. Her own sloppy hostility turned into contrition as quickly as a once crying baby began to laugh. She sat back in her stool, her body seemed to deflate. Tammy squinted to pull her double vision into a singular image. Bad news for her in that it meant she would soon be sick.

"Let me stop. I'm sorry," she said, fighting with her tongue to formulate words without slurring them.

Sabathany noticed the standoffish man at the end of the bar was watching them, paying closest attention to her. He looked suddenly captivated. She relaxed her face and calmed her tone. "You know what? You'll have plenty of time to sleep that off. Stay awhile and have your fun."

"Nah, I need to go upstairs," Tammy said, almost losing her footing as she stood up. With a determined look on her face, she turned to face the path which led back to the hotel.

"Aren't you going to help her?" one of the businessmen asked.

"I know, right? Some friend," the other cracked.

"Listen, don't let her appearance fool you. She's tough," Sabathany said, not really caring what those fools thought. She was buying herself a little time. Better to have witnesses confirm that Tammy had been inebriated and had wandered off alone. These same witnesses could also vouch for the fact that she remained at the bar, and later she would be sure to pop her head inside the gift shop. It was a perfect timeline to forge an alibi.

"She's only going upstairs. She'll be fine." Sabathany said assuredly, finishing the last of her drink. "Bartender, may I have another, please?" After she received her drink, she turned seductively in the direction of the handsome man who caught her eye, but he was gone.

The moment Tammy set foot back inside the hotel, she knew she would not make it upstairs to the room. She made a dash into the public toilet, falling into an open stall. When she opened her mouth, a stream of chunky vomit splashed into the toilet. She hugged the toilet, for odd comfort, unconcerned how dirty it was. Her eyes watered from the sudden lurch forward; her stomach tightened. She wiped the tears with the back of her hand and looked directly at the motion sensor on the toilet. She could see with some clarity, though the sickened feeling remained close.

"You okay in there?" a woman called to Tammy from outside the stall. "Want me to call somebody?"

"I'll be fine. Thank you." Tammy heard the restroom door swing open and hit the wall, followed by heavy footsteps.

"Uh, yeah. I'll be going," the woman said before scampering off.

The toilet flushed as soon as Tammy stood up. She tucked her shirt into her pants, then opened the stall door. A man stood on the other side, glaring and waiting. She recognized him as the one from the bar, sitting off by himself. His massive hand found its place around her neck, stifling her ability to cry out. He pushed her back into the stall and slammed shut the door. With a broad sweeping motion, he swung her around, backing her against the door. Tammy caught the gleam of a knife through her peripheral view.

The stranger took his hand from her throat and forced it over her mouth. With the other hand, he gently pushed the blade's tip into the side of her neck. Tammy's body trembled with fear.

Although she tried willing herself to do so, she could not speak. Dry air chapped the back of her throat.

The man twisted the blade point until a thin line of blood ran down the length of her neck. Tammy wished she could scream through his cupped hand.

The man saw a sufficiently terrified woman before him, causing his manhood to rise inside his pants. He wanted to put an end to her writhing. All it took was a final push of the blade through her neck. It would require so little pressure. Watching her lifeless body fall to the floor would have been glorious enough to put him over the edge. He could have busted a load in his pants just from that alone. However, sadly, she was not his target.

"Please don't kill me," Tammy managed to say once his hand lifted from her mouth.

She was making it difficult for him to control the impulse to kill her. She was the perfect victim—ripe with helplessness. He found it euphoric, needing to take a moment to collect himself.

Tammy found his unresponsiveness frightening. She peered into his eyes, desperate to find reassurance that he would not harm her. She clutched her stomach; the two of them heard a loud gurgling emanate from her insides as her bowels moved down the backs of her legs and piss trickled down the front. Terror deprived her of the luxury to feel embarrassment.

The man finally smiled with his eyes. "Look, I'm not gonna hurt you. Just give me her room number."

"Whose?"

The man's eyes turned cold. Malice flashed through them. "Don't play with me, bitch!" he seethed. "Who the hell do you think I'm talkin' about?"

Think, dummy! Don't give him an excuse to kill you! Tammy thought.

"The chick you were talking to down at in the bar!" he barked.

"We're sharing a room."

A smirk interrupted his menacing scowl. "Then you're gonna take me up to your room," he said, allowing her blood to catch on the tip of his index finger. He retraced the blood back to the superficial wound, then licked the blood dipped finger. "Then, you're gonna get whatever you need and get the hell outta dodge. See what happens when you're a good girl and give me what I want?"

Tammy wanted to offer at least a nod of gratitude, but remained stupefied.

The man moved her from the door and opened it, pushing her out. When the man stepped out of the stall he was met by an elderly female patron, glaring at them.

The man smiled impishly, taking Tammy by the hand. "Come on, Baby, let's finish what we started up in our room," he said.

The woman said nothing, though her eyes followed them until they were out of sight.

Tammy let the man into the room. He found a seat in a chair facing the door. Tammy went about the room throwing all her belongings into her bag. She found his watchful eyes to be unnerving and left quickly, grateful to still be alive. The man turned off the lights throughout the double suite and returned to his seat. He was calm and patient. To rush was to invite mistakes. He was given a specific job to do. There was no room for improvisation. He was especially proud of himself for not claiming Tammy as collateral damage. Pity, because there was something in her energy that would have made killing her extraordinary. No one would mourn her passing for very long, he guessed. He imagined a few sad faces at best, but most would have forgotten her by suppertime.

The man rose from the chair with a new strategy. He would hide in wait until Sabathany was vulnerable, and less likely to run. After thirty minutes passed, the suite door finally opened.

"Tammy? Are you awake, you ole drunk bitch?" Sabathany called into the darkness. Her voice was spirited and laced with contempt. She turned on the lights. "Didn't anyone tell you the best way to get rid of a hangover is to get as much fresh air as possible? Get your ass up and come talk to me on the balcony."

Sabathany went into Tammy's room, pausing in the stillness. The room looked vacated. She went into the en suite bathroom which looked as though it too had been cleared out. When she stepped back into the bedroom, she saw the man who had been sitting alone at the bar, standing in the doorway, leering at her.

"You're from downstairs. What are you . . ." her words dried out.

The man stepped into the room, fixing his eyes on her as he closed the door.

Sabathany let out a stream of breath, backing into the corner of the room. She hoped to keep her wits about her, as her eyes surveyed the room for objects she could use to defend herself. Fear coursed through her as easily as blood running through her veins. "Listen, whatever Kendrick offered you, I can double it."

The stranger approached her in slow, minacious steps. The look of evil in his eyes caused her heartbeat to quicken.

"I said I can double it," Sabathany shrieked from her corner.

She ran towards the bathroom, but he grabbed her by her hair. Winding its length twice around his wrist, he smashed Sabathany face-first into the wall, stunning her. Then, tilting her head as far back as it would go, he dragged his blade across her throat. He let go of her hair and pushed her head forward, sending her to her knees. She bore a wide-eyed stare of confusion as blood emptied from her throat before she collapsed onto her side.

The man watched her mouth move like a ventriloquist's doll. He listened to her labored gurgling until she passed a final sigh, and the lifelight dimmed in her eyes. He flicked the remaining droplets of blood from the knife onto her caved body, then hid the knife inside his jacket pocket. After checking his gloves for tears, he took out his cell phone and sent a text that read, "*IT'S DONE.*" He stared at the body, mesmerized by its unnatural contortion.

"All in a day's work," he muttered later, driving off into the night. By the time he pulled out of the hotel exit, he had already forgotten about Sabathany Morris and the bloody mess he made.

Los Angeles,

Brenda Vaughn sat down with her prospective client, Devon Thomas. While she was excited with the prospect of working with new talent, she was a little saddened to find herself in this place again. Not that meeting with talent was anything new, after all it was her passion. But to move on without Kendrick Black affected her more than she imagined it would. She not only lost out on her investment, but the chance at a real relationship. The only thing left to do was to dive back into her work. The tasty morsel of a man that sat across from her was as good a place to start as any. The kid had talent. It also helped that he was just as good-looking as Kendrick, though a lot cockier.

"I saw your reel. Impressive," she said, knowing he probably heard that as many times as he heard he was attractive. "Why don't you tell me about yourself?"

Devon shrugged. "Like, what do you wanna know?"

Brenda fought the urge to roll her eyes. *Great, another one that's not too swift,* she thought. "Well, for starters, what brings you to the Living Color Agency?"

"I hear you've got a good reputation for turning out results."

Brenda looked insulted by the understatement. She was also put off by his humdrum demeanor. Most people who came seeking her representation were turned away, and many of them had far more fire than Devon. Some were determined to the point that if asked to, they probably would have donated an organ or offered their first born. A chirp emitted from her phone. She casually glanced down to read the succinct and uppercased text message, *"IT'S DONE."* She smiled. Satisfied with the news, she turned her attention back to Devon, who looked annoyed that she gave the text her attention while he sat there.

"Let's get one thing straight, if I work with you, the only attitude allowed is mine," Brenda said, her smile dissolving.

Devon was stunned by her directness.

"Now, we'll skip the part where I tell you how great you are. Bottom line, do you want to become a star?"

It was Devon's turn to smile. "Hell yeah!"

"Good," Brenda said, musing over his future and how much she was going to enjoy breaking him in. "Then, you've come to the right place!"

EPILOGUE

January 25, 2016

A Minnesota Correctional Facility

"You can't tell me who it is?" Kendrick asked the corrections officer just before being led into a small room with gray cement walls. A circular table and two plastic orange chairs sat in the center of the room. Yvette Jones occupied one of the chairs.

Kendrick sighed with relief. He approached the open chair with a bouncy exuberance, like a child meeting Santa Claus.

"You came!"

Yvette stared at the convict as he took his seat across from her. She often wondered how she would react if she ever met him face to face in this setting. Even during the drive to the prison, she wondered if she could feel empathy, or would her animosity toward him win out? Seeing Kendrick's cheery expression made the latter more likely. Yvette glanced over Kendrick's shoulder at the CO standing watch in the corner of the room. As far as she was concerned, this man who killed her daughter should have felt lucky the officer was there to protect him.

"Thank you for coming all the way out here to see me," Kendrick said.

"I wasn't going to, if I'm being truthful."

"The guys in group told me if I kept sending you letters, and kept the faith, you'd eventually come see me."

"Well, clearly you didn't understand from my lack of response that I don't want anything to do with you. I don't want you writing me letters; I don't want you expecting another visit from me, because today when we're finished here today, and I walk out that door, you're dead to me. I hope the guys in your group told you that."

Cheeriness dissolved from Kendrick's face. "I thought reaching out to you might help ease the guilt."

"You got a measly three years for killing my child. What makes you think you get to live guilt free?"

Kendrick said nothing.

"I keep asking myself, what did I do to deserve any of this. It's bad enough you took Kayla away from me, and I'm still trying to make my peace with that. But you won't let me. It's like you want to keep some place in our lives after you messed them up. It's sick, actually."

The hatred Yvette felt for him was palpable. All Kendrick needed to do was look into her eyes, past the brewing tears, to realize whatever powers to sway women's emotions he thought he had were failing him.

"Like I said, the group said they thought it would help with the . . ." his words fell off.

"Yeah, yeah, you said that already!"

"No, what I meant to say was that ever since the night of the accident, Kayla's been haunting me. I thought maybe if I wrote to you, maybe not today or tomorrow—somewhere at the end of this, I'd find forgiveness."

Yvette laughed. "So that's what this is about? You want forgiveness? You want me to forgive the fact that not only did you kill my child, but you tried to cover it up? That you tried to buy us off?"

"You act like I've been walking around here easy-breezy. My publicist dropped me! My family isn't speaking to me! I have to sleep with one eye open because some of the other inmates think I'm this hardened child killer!"

"I guess you think you got it bad, then, huh?" Yvette asked, leaning in.

"It ain't been easy. I can tell you that much," Kendrick said, shaking his head.

Yvette sent a wad of spit sailing into Kendrick's right eye.

"What the hell?" Kendrick said, wiping the spit from his eye. He looked to the CO, wondering why he had not stepped in, but instead was met with a smirk from the officer.

"Look, I can't imagine what you go through every day. Please don't walk away with the impression that I've shrugged it all off, and in here having the time of my life. It's been rough for me, too."

"Did you ever think that maybe if you'd just come forward in the first place, I might've been able to forgive you at some point? But not now. Not ever. You deserve a whole lot worse than you got. Be glad my husband didn't come with me. He would've been more than happy to serve time for putting his hands on you!"

"I see that this was a bad idea," Kendrick said, rising from the table, signaling the end of the visit.

"Yes, it was. The only reasons I came all the way out to Red Wing to see you, was because I needed to do it so that I can move on, but I also wanted to see for myself if the man who wrote in his last letter that he was thinking about ending it all, had it in him to do it. And you know what? You had no intention of killing yourself. You're too much of a coward to die at your own hand."

"Goodbye, Yvette," Kendrick said over his shoulder as the CO gripped his arm to lead him to the door. "Don't worry, I won't bother you anymore."

"Wait just a second! You don't have the right to move on like nothing happened! You don't get to have closure! I hope you're haunted by what you did for the rest of your pitiful life!"

Kendrick, looking as though he had been beaten, was pulled away by the CO.

Yvette sat alone. Another wave of tears came. All the work she did to move forward, and now, having indulged him, she had taken two steps back. She hoped after the tears settled that she could begin again.

After a time, Yvette returned to her car, thankful for the opportunity to have looked her daughter's killer in the eye. She knew there were so many families who would never have the chance to come face-to-face with those who changed the course of their lives. Yvette knew in her spirit that she was one of the lucky ones. Still, one question followed her into her car. Was Kendrick sorry for what he did, or was he sorry he got caught?

"Guess I'll never know what's in that son of a bitch's heart," Yvette said, starting the ignition. She gave the prison one last glimpse before embarking on the drive home.

CPSIA information can be obtained
at www.ICGtesting.com
Printed in the USA
LVHW090053301118
598738LV00001B/65/P